THE
LAST
TO
SEE
ME

Also by the Author

The Deadwood Beetle
The Floodmakers
The Medusa Tree

THE LAST TO SEE ME

A NOVEL

WITHDRAWN

M DRESSLER

Skyhorse Publishing

First Edition

This is a work of fiction. Names, places, characters, and incidents are either the products of the author's imagination or are used fictitiously.

Skyhorse Publishing books may be purchased in bulk at special discounts for sales promotion, corporate gifts, fund-raising, or educational purposes. Special editions can also be created to specifications. For details, contact the Special Sales Department, Skyhorse Publishing, 307 West 36th Street, 11th Floor, New York, NY 10018 or info@ skyhorsepublishing.com.

Skyhorse® and Skyhorse Publishing® are registered trademarks of Skyhorse Publishing, Inc.®, a Delaware corporation.

Visit our website at www.skyhorsepublishing.com.

10 9 8 7 6 5 4 3 2

Library of Congress Cataloging-in-Publication Data is available on file.

Cover design by Erin Seaward-Hiatt

Print ISBN: 978-1-5107-2067-1
Ebook ISBN: 978-1-5107-2068-8

Printed in the United States of America.

For the spirits at my side,
Alison and Chelsey

Never make peace with the thing that's trying to kill you.

1

He's come to clean me out.

It's as simple as that.

He's come to scrape me clean, like a strand of meat clinging to a mussel's shell.

He wants to put me down in Evergreen, in the tangled graveyard set aside for lost souls. This hunter, he hopes to put me down there with the poorest of the poor, the forgotten, the graves no one tends to, their crooked stones leaning aft, as if taken aback by how far injustice can go, even after death. In that cemetery, hard by St. Clements Church, the animals pile insult on injury. They burrow down toward the collapsing coffins, our boxes softened underground, and bring up bits of bone and tats of lace. And the dead can do nothing about it, their hands and feet tied.

But what ghost has ever asked to be gnawed and stripped? Who wants to lie down in a cold bed she didn't choose or make? Who wants their bones rolled into a hole, like dice weighted to land on only one number, and always the worst?

Now, let's say you want to change the odds. Let's say you refuse to be put down in a pauper's grave. What do you do?

You fight.

It helps to be trouble. Troublesome. Irish stubborn. A mighty *will*—that's the ticket. It takes will not to be what everyone expects you to be. It takes heart not to go where they tell you to go. Especially here, along the rugged north coast, in this place where the tides would as soon see you dragged under as drawing breath.

In the seaweed that washes up on my village's cove, you'll find all sorts of things the tide has dragged along with it: bobbing globes of buoys, ruined fishing line, plastic grocery bags choked with sand. Things that can't fight back. Look up from the beach, craning your neck toward the top of our crumbling cliffs, and you'll see the village of Benito itself, ignoring the flotsam below, dressed in its Sunday best, even on the blackest days. For we do have black days here, even in this most beautiful part of California.

In winter, our sky grows so heavy it's like a box lined with padded silk closing down on you. The fog stifles. The foghorns moan. The waves turn to claws on the black rocks, and the air smells of cold, wet lead.

In summertime, it's better. That's when the tourists come up in their bright, sparkling cars and their smart summer clothes, and they marvel at the view from our peninsula, and lick at expensive toffees and taffies, and don't even guess that what they might be tasting, on their tongues, in the air, isn't only summer's seasoning but the ashes of all the brave women and men who once lived here, as I did, before each life turned to salt.

It's funny, isn't it, how the people who eat up the most in this world often don't taste what it is they've dined on? How those who have the means to eat whatever they like are always hungry for more, always more, while the truly famished among us sweep the floors and scrub the dishes and leave the village at night to sleep in places where the rooms are smaller, away from the water and the views, in the woods, in simple beds behind doors as thin as paper, the best wood having been cut for somebody else—for Augustus Lambry, and his like.

When the loggers first came here, a hundred and fifty years ago and more, they were poor—but their will was mighty. They might have worked for men like Lambry who slept in clean, white sheets, but the trees those lumbermen felled were their own business, their own life and death at the edge of the void, and they cut only the biggest, loftiest trunks and shoved and dynamited them downriver, toward the mills and the sea. In those days, Benito's cove was a half-moon's sweep of deep water, deeper than it is now, with cypress trees perched thick as crows on the cliffs, except for where a track was cleared to make way for the Lambry logging chutes. Even after the boardinghouses and saloons started going up—once there were so many loggers, a town had to be built to manage them—those trees, and the mounds of salt grass covering the headlands, stayed free and wild. Then, in time, the Main Street Hotel sprang to life, where maids who washed and ironed and cooked could hope to stay clear of grabby sailors; and the peak-roofed storefronts all along Albion Street; and St. Clements Church, its white steeple driving away the last of the Indians; and finally the temple the Chinamen built, with its roofs curled like red shoes left out in the sun. And closer in, on the first hill after the fine houses of the merchants, Evergreen Cemetery was laid out. Evergreen, where even now my poor family rests, broken footstones all in a row.

Above the marble monuments of the wealthy, the gulls rooked and called, and the white-waisted clouds floated, while down in the cove the doghole schooners bobbed at anchor, creaking, and over at the Point, the lighthouse swung its jeweled lamp in a wide circle, warning of hidden dangers.

Just because you can't see a thing doesn't mean she isn't there.

The hunter has parked his bright car at the foot of Evergreen Hill and is coming, now, from the direction of the cemetery toward me. I know what he is. I've seen and heard a hunter's boots before. They make a sound like a sawblade scraping on sand. This one, he's tall and bulky and box-jawed. He squints at the house, his cheeks taking up the slack skin under his beard. I'm standing in the rose garden in my white dress with my red ribbon twining though my hair, and a little shiver runs through me, a piece of my own will. I hold steady, the way you do when you know a wave is coming, and you lock your knees to meet it. The sandy street leads him to the wrought iron gate at the edge of the garden. He opens it, then turns around to make sure he's latched the groaning lock securely behind him, but maybe also to be certain he's alone. So this is a hunter, I think, who watches his back. He looks up and sees the black-railed tower of the house, the steeple meant to rival the church's with its white shingles layered like gulls' feathers, though here the paint is starting to flake off and show the older white underneath, the ghost of its old self. He narrows his eyes again, and I see that his skin is rough—a working man's face—and that his clothes are black and simple—a working man's clothes—and that although he is, to be sure, one of the living, he's one of the dying, too, because there is gray at his temples and gray blurring his whiskers, his own flake showing.

He turns his peppered cheek to his left, then to his right, and sees, not me, but the great bundle of life beside him: one of our famed Lambry rose bushes. He reaches his hand out, entranced, cupping one perfect, yellow bud. A breeze coming from far out at sea stirs its petals and my dress. And it's this flutter of wind, he might decide, and be wrong, that pushes the black thorn deep into his skin, under his sleeve, at the wrist.

The name the living give to such blows is "accident."

I watch him lick the blood from the root of his palm. I see the flash of silver inside his sleeve. It's that metal band these hunters all wear. The thing that marks them.

Then, with a motion as calm as when he opened the gate, he takes the yellow Lambry bud and lifts it gently back into its place in the overgrown, latticed arbor, as though putting a child back in its high chair, and he turns away to move farther along the garden. As though I hadn't just warned him not to.

I'll need to adjust my thinking, then. His is the strut of a man who takes the first cut lightly. Or maybe he's like me. Emma Rose Finnis. Irish born. Irish stubborn. Raised to be staunch in the face of wounds. The bells of St. Clements are ringing, and the sun can't make up its mind about where it wants to burn, dancing in and out of the mists over the cove. But I've made up my mind already. I'll keep this man close.

2

It's ten in the morning by the church bells, and in the cove the seals are moaning and sliding off their barnacled black rocks in search of some breakfast. My hearing is so much finer than when I walked alive and with a heartbeat. It's something I've had a century to ponder: how much does the beating heart of one creature drown out the heart of another?

My senses are my pride and joy now. I can feel, twisting toward the smell of the headlands, each wildflower rubbing up against the other. That ticking sound—it's a poppy opening up to the June sun. That whisper—it's the mustard seed losing its buttery fluff and color. I sense, too, the dirty bits of a tern's nest loose in the wind and the stench of a single starfish dying on the rocks, having aimed too high.

I can smell the mossy rankness that clings to our village's old-fashioned water towers, loitering like headless windmills behind the houses. On some, the rotten wooden tanks have fallen away or been pulled clean down, and shingled rooms built in between the struts, bed-and-breakfast nooks for the tourists. These visitors are the ones I can hear stretching and yawning in the distant yards, as they open their heather-wreathed doors, hungry.

I cross the lawn ahead of the hunter, moving along the flagstone path and onto the curved porch, drawing aside as he comes close. He's done nothing dangerous yet, as he nears the steps, only wiping his hand along the smooth white railing as he climbs, lifting his fingertips and rubbing the grit between them. He squints again and turns and looks back across the lawn as though gauging the distance between gate and arbor and house. He listens and glances down at his coat pocket before taking out his black device. Someone is calling for Mr. Philip Pratt. I know his name, because I've heard the real estate agent (the little one who always comes to the house now) say it. He taps the device and puts it away and looks off in the direction of Evergreen, the cemetery. He might look and look and look, I think, and yet he'll still know nothing of all the poor souls who sleep there. The loggers and the millers, the sailors and the boardinghouse keepers, the maids, and the dead washerwomen like my mother. I can feel myself beginning to grow angry, upset, which isn't wise with a hunter near—giving way to anger gives up the ghost, as they say. I know I must calm myself and leave the porch and rise up toward the strengthening sun, whose light keeps me safe. I sit on the steeple and wait. Like all of his kind, this Mr. Pratt won't be able to see me unless I'm foolish enough to let anger paint my face, my jaw, my father's cleft chin, and my wide Finnis forehead, stark white.

Any ghost who hopes to hold her own against a hunter has to know how to still the rage inside her and blend with the weather of every moment. And so I do. I still myself. The sun is cheerful, bright enough to screen me. How odd it is that most of the living think we spirits live in shadows. Why, when we are always trying to hold back the darkness?

Pratt will be waiting now for the young real estate agent, Miss Ellen DeWight. I've been watching her all these weeks. She's a small, sweet thing, trying hard to make her way in a world that will tell you when you're small, you're nothing at all. I remember how she went around the property talking to herself that first day she came to the Lambry House. Bucking herself up, reminding herself not to be nervous that she'd landed such a prize but to stay sharp and not be flustered by the new people about to come calling. She'd stood on the fine, wide porch that noonday with me beside her and waited, sweating, her little suit buckling at the ankles and shoulders, her face like a folded dinner napkin, white and fresh but with lines on either side of her mouth, as though her lips had been pressed for a long time into a single, careful shape.

Her telephone device had rung, and she'd pulled it from her leather satchel and answered the woman on the other end.

". . . No. No. I won't overdo it, don't worry. I have a good feeling about this. I really do. They said they've been waiting for a property exactly like this one. I will. You can count on me. I'll be sure to call you right after. Okay. The office is fine. Everything's fine. Have fun in LA."

She put the thing away and looked at her watch, puckering her small mouth, but also keeping it steady. It's her littleness, maybe, that makes me feel so free and easy around her. I haven't minded her the way I've minded so many others who've come through the house over the years.

We waited together, at the front, until the great black Rover came up the street, sleek as a hearse with its dark windows. It parked by the house, its wheels slowing to a stop, big silver platters rolling on their sides. Ellen DeWight lifted her head and set her small chin, all business.

The door opened. Out of the black metal slipped a shining blond head, a pair of golden sunglasses, and a soft blouse tucked into a belt stitched with many tiny beads. Another door opened, and a balding man came out. Their skins were a golden orange, as though the sun followed them everywhere they went. Mr. and Mrs. Dane.

Ellen hurried down from the porch, over the stone path, and through the arbor, between the bobbing roses.

"Mr. Dane. Charles?"

The man stared blankly at her, pulling off his sunglasses. "You're the broker?"

"The agent. Ellen DeWight. I represent the heirs of Alice Lambry, the late owner. My broker is on business down in LA, so I'll be taking care of you today. It's wonderful to meet you. Welcome to the Lambry House!"

"Oh—Charlie, look!" the woman next to him fawned. "It's just like I pictured it! So stately but lush."

"Welcome to you, too, Mrs. Dane." Ellen held out her hand, but the woman didn't take it, and Ellen pulled it back. "Those are yellow heirloom roses. And a full acre of gardens. Very rare on a narrow peninsula like this."

"I *so* get that. So different from Napa. Fabulous."

"Let's wait for the mouth-feel before we get ahead of ourselves," Mr. Dane said, putting his sunglasses back on. "That's been the deal breaker for us on these old houses so far."

"Of course, of course, absolutely. Right this way."

"Charlie, I do love all the gables, though." Mrs. Dane leaned into his silken shirt. "And that steeple. Is that a little iron walk around it? And the weather vane, is it original—Ellen?"

"Yes."

"I love it."

That quickly, Ellen brought them up to the porch. My porch.

"So! We have a pair of fine double front doors, as you can see, finished in etched glass, dating to 1899, when the house was built. They're in mint condition and also all original. Step right into the foyer."

She let them into my house. The Lambry House. Still fitted with the finest of carved English furniture, still gleaming with scrolled wooden paneling, glowing warm and rich as it did when I saw it being carried in by bent-backed Lambry workers a hundred years ago, when I was just a lumberjack's little girl. The floors still thick with carpets dressed with fringe softer than a girl like me could ever expect to wear on her shawl. The rooms deep and full, the hall mirrors and pier glasses so tall, like Augustus Lambry himself. In the corners, around the high ceilings, white plaster and painted wood prettily molded into the shapes of angels and roses and trumpets. And enough paintings in gold frames to have filled another mansion.

I flitted into the light of the chandelier in the foyer, hanging from the plaster rose above Ellen and the Danes. I must be very cold now, and give nothing away of myself, or my feelings.

"And here," Ellen said, "above this incredibly preserved wainscoting, we have some history, as you can see. Photos of the original owners."

"Oh, I don't want to see those." Mrs. Dane wrinkled her nose at all the dead Lambry faces. "To be honest, it makes a house feel, you know, already *used*. These carpets are special, though."

"Turkish. Antique."

"We may bargain for them," Mr. Dane said.

"Why don't we go into the parlor on the west side of the house? Watch your step over this rug, now. Tassels."

"Charlie, these wood floors are a bit too dark for a beach house. They're not *airy* enough."

"I agree," he said. "The whole house is a little choked."

They looked all around. I followed above and after them. They didn't seem to notice Alice Lambry's wild watercolors hanging like open windows on the walls, painted boxes of gray and green and blue-tinted land and sea and storm and sky. The finicky Danes: they brushed their hands over the antique furniture and looked into the tall mirrors and tried to keep their faces closed, as if they weren't pleased enough to smile or disappointed enough to frown.

"Let's take a look at the east side of the house now," Ellen said, smiling.

"Too many rooms on this side, Charlie. There's no feng shui happening at all."

"I agree with you. Everything would have to be blown out here."

"But Mr. Dane, Mrs. Dane, you haven't seen the back of the house yet. It's a modern, open-concept addition. A conservatory. A sunroom. It could be whatever you like! With so much natural light. It's right this way." Ellen pushed aside the great pocket doors, opening the way to the back parlors. Her fingers seemed nervous, but she kept her voice steady.

"Oh! Now that's more like it. That view!"

Mr. Dane put on his glasses again, and whistled. "Wow."

"This is Benito's original harbor," Ellen said and stepped forward, beaming. "Isn't it gorgeous? You can see all the way across our cove from here. And the cove itself is always changing color, light, intensity. Sometimes it's deep blue like this. Sometimes gray. Or green. And what do you think of this *fabulous* conservatory? The glass dome is stunning, isn't it? Please, come in, take a look."

The Glass Room, our newest room, is the finest in the house now. Alice liked to paint here, sometimes, standing in the middle of all the wicker furniture and chintz covers and vases filled with flowers from the garden.

"We've counted all the panes in here," Ellen said, looking out across the water. "There are over three hundred of them. We call it the Glass Room. I think it feels just like dancing inside a dream on a perfect day," she added, trying out one of the little phrases I'd seen her practicing in front of the mirrors.

"Very nice. But please don't tell me that's the kitchen over there?" Mr. Dane pointed back into the house.

"Charlie!" Mrs. Dane pleaded. "Use your imagination!"

"It looks like a relic from the Stone Age."

"We'll just gut what we don't like. Keep the outside only."

"Yes. That could work . . ."

"I am required to tell you, though"—and I could hear, plain as day, Ellen's heart beating, her voice trying to be loud and bright to cover it—"that we do have a few historic guidelines here? Certain building codes. A house can't generally be altered in any way that substantially changes the original structure. It's one of the ways we here in Benito preserve our town's character and charm. You have to go through an approval process to . . . But if I could just show you more of the beautiful, original woodwork upstairs—"

Dane put up his hand. "Stop right there. We hate codes. They're un-American. So given what you've just told us, you'd better give us a minute to think about if we even need to spend any more time with the property. Why don't you just step outside and let us have a look around on our own, all right? Then we can decide if we want to talk to you about options. Or not."

Ellen twisted her hands behind her back, trying, I saw, to keep them under control. "Of course! Of course. I'll just be out on the front porch, and you can call me in if you need anything or have any questions. Make yourself at home. It really is stunning, on every level. You'll see."

"One question." Mr. Dane jerked his chin toward the arched door of the butler's pantry, beside the kitchen. "What does *that* door there lead to?"

"A pantry."

"Not a wine cellar?"

"No. Sorry." Ellen looked back once, worried, and left them.

And then it was just the three of us.

"I think that scared her." Dane took off his glasses and nudged his wife.

"Charlie, come into the pantry. It smells like cinnamon."

They switched on the lights and stepped inside and leaned against the empty, burled shelves, leaving the narrow door open. The Lambry pantry is only big enough for three. The glass-covered shelves stack high and dark, and the wooden counters close in tightly on two sides. I sat on one of the counters, quiet as a pin.

"So, Beth-y? What do you think? Codes?"

"Schmodes. I love it here. The atmosphere. I've been waiting to feel the pull I feel here. That cove. It's just what I wanted. Our very own little Xanadu. I thought we'd never find it."

"But no feng shui." He ran his hand over the dust on the counter where Mrs. Broyle used to polish the silver.

"We could torch the whole inside."

"*Codes*," he whispered again, darkly, his arm circling her waist, just beside me.

"Well. It's probably just like Aspen. Find the right people to pay off. And we bring in all our own crew."

"The Napa contractor?" He stroked her.

"I don't mean just that. I mean, for help. I hate to say it, but you know it's nothing but rubes out here for miles around. I get so tired of the *inexperience*, Charlie. There's probably no help around here that can polish anything without streaking it. And did you see that poor little thing, in her factory seconds? Please. If I were her broker, I'd have to fire her and hire someone less . . . hick."

"Embarrassing. You're so right. But only a bellhop. And only for today."

Coldness in their voices. Coldness, and looking down their noses at someone only wanting to do some work and to try to get ahead, if she could.

Sometimes, when it's a case like this, the anger comes to me and I don't stop it. Some people don't deserve my quiet and my patience. There are some who believe this earth was made for them and them alone. There are some who believe theirs are the only hearts, the only drums of blood that count. And so, when they hear the wooden floor of an old house creaking, giving underneath them, they can't imagine it could be anything but their own weight.

I shut the pantry door.

3

W hat the—?"

"Great," Mrs. Dane sighed.

"The door is stuck. The knob's not turning."

I blew the lights out.

"Charlie?"

"Bad wiring. I knew it. These old houses." He tried the switch again.

"Just open the door."

"It still won't turn."

I know how to make a thing hard. Unforgiving. The knob, the more he tried it, stiffened, as though some heavy, cold pressure were fighting against him.

"Okay, Charlie, let's get out of here. It's getting stuffy."

"Give me a second."

"There's got to be another light in here somewhere."

"Then *you* find it."

"I'm trying. I can't feel anything, except—"

"What's that? Is that you?"

A breath. A whisper. A hissing sound at his side. But not his wife. She's backed away, as far as she can in the small room.

"Charlie?"

"Beth-y, is that you?"

"No."

"It sounds like—a leak. Is it a broken pipe?"

"Charlie. Okay. Get us out of here. Please."

"I can't—"

"Just bang on the door. She'll hear us, that silly waif outside."

He banged and cried out: "Hey! Hey! Hey!"

In the dark, he strained to see. He reached out for his wife, his love. But she wasn't there. Because a blackness, a blackness only a ghost can summon, was opening underneath them. His wife was near his feet, being pulled under. Pulling at him.

"Charlie! Help me!"

"Beth! Beth!"

He fell to his knees with her. He felt her wet, sinking cheeks. He reached for her arms. But his hands fluttered, thrashing, in something else. Water, water rising all around them.

He screamed.

When the living are near death I can hear their thoughts. Poor Charles Dane. He'd gotten himself cornered, trapped, tricked, as he'd never been tricked in his whole life. He'd always known there were dangers, deep things in the world, but he'd always imagined he was in charge of them, in charge of the light and the dark. Now he could feel his wife sinking, being sucked away from him, down, down, down into the blackness. The feeling of her slippery, shredding skin under his nails. Was this dying, sliding thing even his wife? What are we, who are we? What's left of us in the end?

Then he felt my hands, groping, coiling around his knees. It was his turn. He kicked and fought. He screamed, *I don't want to go. I don't want to go*, as the water circled around his mouth, all his fear seeking a drain.

And my whispering told him, *go on, give in, give in*.

I kicked them both out, leaving them crumpled on the hallway floor.

Poor Mrs. Dane had wet herself.

I watched them from where I hung, under the winking pantry light. It took Dane a moment and then—I saw it in his bald, blank face—he understood what had just happened to them. Such things were still reported. Even though the hunters had been doing their work for twenty-five years, since the turn of the millennium, not every poor, dead thing in the world had been snuffed out the way some thought ghosts should be. Because there were still some of us left, in spite of all the work the hunters had done, over the years, to put us down. Because in an old house, you might still expect to find one of us, here or there. Even one who was willing to forget herself and what it would mean to show her anger, just for the treat of putting you in your place.

Dane crawled to his feet and staggered and lashed out, waving his arms as though he could see me. "Scum! I know you're there, and I know what you are, and it's not going to stand! I'll buy this son-of-a-bitching house and I will have it sucked clean and dry, you dead, you sick— Nobody gets between me and—I will *destroy* you, I—"

Mrs. Dane wept and begged and said she wanted to go outside, *please, now*.

Ellen said into her phone, afterward: "And then, believe it or not, I made the sale! I know! I told him. I told him the house had already been checked. I told him the whole village was cleaned out, we were certain of it, ages ago. But Mr. Dane insisted. He said he was going to get the best hunter in the business and have the house flushed, like— like a port-o-john . . . No, I don't know if his wife is totally on board. But he certainly is. He told me no lowly scum was going to get the better of them or what they wanted. He told me he was going to buy the house and punish it. Yes. He was dead serious. He said if you give freeloaders an inch they'll take—Right. He overbid. He's already transferred twenty percent. He says we'll get the rest, I mean the heirs will, when the house is certified clean. I think we need to talk to the heirs . . . Okay. I can handle it. Okay."

She stood in the garden that late afternoon, the sea breeze whipping through her soft, bobbed hair, the shingles of the Lambry House behind her turning slate-colored as the afternoon chilled, and she'd squeezed and hugged herself. She looked, from where I stood staring down at her from the tower, amazed and shaky and ready to jump for joy and cry all at the same time.

4

Now, three days later, Philip Pratt watches Ellen's car pull up again to my house. He steps off the porch, in his workman's coat, and licks his lips. A man with a job to do, who's been called the best, it seems.

She hurries up the path toward him. I know her by now. She doesn't like being late. I let her pass by me in the arbor, without a scratch.

"Mr. Pratt, did you get my text? I'm so sorry I'm late, you let yourself in through the gate, I see."

"Ellen?"

"Yes. How are you? How was your trip? Okay?"

"It was. I did let myself in. I hope you don't mind. It's a beautiful garden."

"Yes. Yes." She's breathless. "A full acre. Which is very rare on this peninsula, and—and—"

"A real selling point in a village like this, I imagine. It's all right, catch your breath." He smiles down from his bulk, his height, at her. And I can see the smile makes her happy. Why is that? It needles me when someone small thinks someone large is closer to the sun.

"Thank you. I'm so sorry again." Ellen sets her satchel down at her feet. "It was—It's my cat. I can't find her."

"Sorry to hear that. Pets are so important."

"She's just . . . tricky. I rent a place out in the woods, south of town? It's a little wild out there, and I don't want her to get into any trouble. So I prefer to get her safe in the house before I leave. Especially because she's not a hundred percent well right now."

"I understand completely."

"So I'm a little frazzled. Anyway." She tucks her hair behind her ears and looks around. "So. You can see how the property is situated here. A lot of privacy. Especially with the headland behind it. The Lambry House practically sits on its own. It's an old and unique setting on the coast. Which is one reason I think the Danes are fighting for it. I have the keys. Let's go right in. I can't tell you what a relief it is to have you here."

"I came as fast as the highway could carry me."

"Thanks so much again."

She's still catching her breath. Her walk is an uneven march next to his calm, steady one. But she gets him to the porch. "Okay. Come up and let's let you get going. Have you been filled in on all the details?"

"Mr. Dane gave me some insight."

"I bet."

I linger behind them, on the stone path, in the sun. It's funny how small Ellen and Pratt, from this bit of distance, look on the curved stage of the porch. Like actors in a scene that's too grand for them. It's something the living don't know: how lost and childish they can seem.

Ellen fits the key into the deep brass. "It all happened inside."

"The Danes told me you were present during the event."

"Well, not exactly. I was outside, right here. Texting. Giving them some privacy to discuss things. But I was here, yes, at the house with them, all the time. That's the law."

"Ellen, I need to know if you'll be frightened coming inside with me."

She shakes her head, certain. "I know this might sound strange, but I don't get frightened by incidents that don't happen to me personally. I know that sounds—selfish. I don't mean it to. But I've been in the house alone so often, so . . ." She glances back at him, beckoning him inside with her head. "Getting it ready for sale, to show, there was never any sign of—anyway, it totally surprised me because Benito's already been through some good, solid cleanings, really thorough ones. I just wasn't expecting anything to happen. Or else my broker would never have listed this property as having a clean title."

"But you do understand the supposedly clean title accounts for the Danes' . . . reaction."

"They must have still been pretty angry when you spoke with them?"

"You could say that."

"Once I was able to get to them—I mean, after I heard them scream-ing in the hall—they looked just terrible. Especially poor Mrs. Dane. I thought it was all over for me, honestly. I thought I'd lost my job. Mrs. Dane wanted out but Mr. Dane started shouting that he was going to buy the place lock, stock, and barrel, and flush it, and I should get the contract out. And here we are."

She stands back. He walks around the foyer slowly, like someone who has plenty of time. It's not the normal way, with his kind. Usually, hunters strut in, put their noses in the air, and get out their horrors, their weapons.

At the turn of the millennium, when the hunts began, I was as scared as any ghost could be. But fear, in the end, does a body no good. If you let yourself be afraid of what can kill you, it weakens you. So you can't let yourself be afraid. You have to believe there is something in you that was made to meet the fear. Something that was given to you at birth, your right as a human being. So many of the poor ones I've seen who got sent back down into the ground, it was all because they thought so little of their right, of their own light. I've watched the mirrors empty because the ghosts hiding inside them were so afraid. Worst of all have been the cries of the ghosts of little children, who like to cling and hover longingly around candles—birthday candles especially. And then they shriek and are, themselves, blown out.

"So nothing about being inside this house frightens you."

"Not unless you tell me it should, Mr. Pratt. I've been in and out three times since the Danes left and nothing's happened. I'm not saying I don't believe them, but . . ."

"You don't. This is a beautiful entry. The height of it."

"That's the original chandelier. The whole house is just a jewel. The last owner took wonderful care of everything."

"Alice Marie Lambry?"

"Yes. Let me turn on a few lights. It's getting overcast."

The brightness makes it easier for me to move around, too. Thank you, helpful Ellen.

She stashes her satchel next to the stairway's carved newel post and straightens in her suit. "So, what I can tell you is Alice Lambry died—let's see, a few months ago now. She died in one of the bedrooms, upstairs."

"So I've been given to understand. And also, to be clear, she never reported any trouble with the house."

"No, not that the constable knows of. I wanted to do my own research, so I checked with him. But he said no member of the Lambry family has ever reported any trouble here."

"The Lambrys were always a wealthy family, I assume. People of means." He gestures with his heavy arm all around, at the paneling, at the art, at the angels in the corners. He looks as wrong as a bull in a china cabinet.

"Obviously." Ellen nods. "If they'd had any trouble, they could have paid whatever they needed to get it put down, especially around the time the whole village was being cleaned."

"Except that now it seems the whole village wasn't cleaned."

"Unless you think it's possible the Dunes could have gotten them selves jammed in the pantry and—just—panicked?"

"You really don't believe them, do you?"

"I'm just hoping they're wrong—and you'll tell me so."

"I'm curious." He leans against the banister and folds his arms. "How old are you, Ellen?"

She blinks. "Excuse me?"

"I just like to know the age of anyone helping me out."

"I'm helping out? Twenty-six. You look older than your website. Does being around dead people"—she puts her chin up—"do that to you?"

"No, it's more being on the road all the time. And yes, you're helping, thank you. Who do we have in the photos, here?"

"The original owners. The timber family."

"Serious and healthy-looking."

Yes. Mr. and Mrs. Augustus Lambry, sitting in their great peacocked wicker chairs, a century and more ago. Standing behind them, stiff in their collars, their handsome sons and their dutiful daughters. All of them posing in the rolling garden, bare of arbors and rose bushes then because the roses hadn't been planted yet. And off in the distance the smoke rising from the family's mills. But no pictures of the workers inside them. Just smoke dancing in the air over their heads, as if the white puffs came out of the Lambrys' imaginations and nothing more.

"Would you like to go right to the pantry, Mr. Pratt? Or up to see where Alice died? I thought maybe she would be, you know, the best candidate?"

"She would be. But was she the only person to meet her end in this house?"

"I honestly don't know the answer to that. I ought to tell you I'm still a little new to this area. So I don't always know the things the old-timers do. But I can find out anything you need."

"Then let's find out. Do you mind making a note?"

She takes out her device.

"Find out," he says, peering over her shoulder, "who else might have died at this address. At any point before, during, or after the house was built. The constable can help with that, or county records. And let's start by you showing me the house exactly the way you showed it to the Danes. In this direction?" He walks through the carved archway, brushing it with his bull's shoulder, into the west parlor, the Red Parlor. "Very nice. Who did all the watercolors?"

"Alice did. She loved to paint, they say."

"Did she sell to anyone?"

"She didn't need to. She had the Lambry money. Or what was left of it. And she liked keeping to herself. She liked going down to the beach to paint. She took care of the roses. She spent a lot of time in the garden. They say."

Pratt has stopped to study one of Alice's seagulls flying through a storm. Wings slicing through the air, its shape like a heart cut in two.

Ellen opens the parlor's heavy drapes. "Some of what I know about this property my broker told me. She has a string of offices along the coast. Very successful. But I'm the lead on this house. I know all the stops and views."

"What did you tell the Danes here?"

"Well, I said, from this room, you get this wonderful northern exposure and the best views of the garden, all the roses, camellias, rhododendron, poppies. When I was readying the listing, I spoke with Mrs. Fanoli, who docents at our Botanical Garden, to be sure I was getting all the details right. She said some of the rose vines are exceptionally old—you can tell by the way they've twisted and thickened around the arbor. Now, if you look this way," she says, moving over to the next window, "you can see all the way up the hill, toward St. Clements Church. There, past your car. That's Evergreen, our cemetery."

"Yes. I took a quick peek in before I came." But Pratt goes on staring at the garden. "Those yellow roses. I'm curious about them. One nicked me as I came in."

He remembers. Good. I'm glad.

"They've gotten a little wild. Sorry. I should have noticed. Alice had a man who used to help her tend the garden, Manoel. But things have gone a little south since she died. I'll call him and have him tie back the creepers."

"I'd like to know what kind of roses those are. See if you can find out from your contact at the Botanical Garden."

"Are you thinking they're somehow important?"

He rubs his thick wrist near the silver band, his weapon, his protection, my enemy. "We'll see. Keep going."

I follow, keeping close. Studying, reading them to find signs of things they can't read themselves. It's my own work, in a way. To see what the living can't see. Notice what they can't notice but is being written across the envelopes of their skins. Ellen, for instance: she clenches her jaw when she's nervous but pretending not to be and twitches ever so slightly just below her right eyelid. Pratt strokes his sideburns and wipes his stubbled chin and doesn't know that the base of his neck is damp enough that I can taste it, like the fog before it sweeps in. Yet he's not really sweating; he isn't nervous at all, I think, but curious and alert, and that dampness is part of him. It's the kind of stickiness a fly might have on the tip of its tongue.

Ellen is telling him, rightly, that the Lambry Timber Company was one of the greatest in the North till the mills closed down, one by one, done in by wars and progress. What riches were left trickled their way down to Alice, the last Lambry in the village, who at least had enough to live on and be the hermit she was, shut up for the most part with her paintings and shells and bits of sea glass. And Manoel.

"And her heirs have no interest in keeping up the place," Pratt says matter-of-factly, pushing open the great pocket doors between the parlor and the dining room.

"They live in the city. They don't care for it up here. Too isolated for them."

"It would take a hardy breed to live here year-round."

"I like to think we're hardy, sure. But we're a good place for vacationers, too. For weekends. For pretending life is quiet and refined, the way it used to be."

"I believe that's a big part of the attraction for the Danes. Do you think they'll be good keepers of the Lambry legacy?" He curls his hand around the back of one of my Chippendale chairs.

"No, to be honest. They basically want to blow everything inside up. I mean, in addition to blowing up the ghost that might live here. I mean *resettling* the ghost."

I don't like it, her using that lying word.

"I know that's the correct term, these days," she says. "Isn't it?"

"I prefer to think of cleaning as organizing. Everything into its place."

"So . . . I know there are really only a few of you cleaners who are actually top-notch." She steps in front of a mirror and rubs a little dust from her suit sleeve. "I googled you. They say you're one of the best in the state. I'm glad Mr. Dane got a hold of you."

"Thank you."

"But I also read that you've all been so successful at what you do that the ghost population is getting a bit . . . thin? That there just aren't as many hauntings as reported before?"

"And yet, there always seems to be just one more. Well now. Look at this."

He's come to the Glass Room. The shimmering dome of air and light that Alice had made because I told her to.

"The conservatory. And over here is the kitchen. The Danes want to blow it out, too. The pantry is this way."

"We'll get to that in just a minute."

"But don't you think we could get on with . . . it?"

Pratt doesn't seem to hear the impatience in her voice. He walks forward instead, into the light and sheen, facing the sweep of the cove.

He says, without looking back at Ellen, "I wonder: do you have a listing that's more beautiful—valuable—than this one?"

"Not right now. Not even close."

He gazes through the prisms and panes, the ocean broken up into a hundred, smaller oceans. I often stop to stare at this view, too.

"Amazing," he says.

"Shouldn't we keep going? Get to the pantry?"

"Impatience is the enemy. You said the village had cleaners in before."

"You think they didn't take enough time to do the job right?"

"I'm certain of it."

"All right." She breathes and seems to relax.

"Next we'll take the charge in the pantry."

"I don't know what that means."

"It means I need to see what kind of anger has been here, what kind of impulse."

"You mean—how mad the Danes were?"

"No." He shakes his head and looks down at the cove. "Not living anger. Not the kind of anger you or I would feel. At least—" But he doesn't finish his sentence. "Imagine," he shifts, still gazing at the spray bursting against the rocks, "a wave that has no outlet. Like those waves out there hitting on the beach. Again and again and again. Unsettled souls are like that. Trapped. They don't release emotion the way that we do. If they did, we'd have to say they were still living. We can try to imagine what they're feeling, but we can't really do it. Because they are what they are, and we are what we are. The charge isn't life. The charge is all that's left."

This is the terrible part.

The terrible, terrible test.

I have to keep still. Around talk like this. Unmoved. Stay cold and unfeeling behind the mask, the veil of light, under the three hundred broken suns of the Glass Room. I have to be careful not to be angry or allow myself to feel any emotion at all, feel the very thing he says I cannot feel, because if I do, if I show for one minute that I'm human, then in the next moment I won't be allowed to be.

The charge is what they call our lasting. That's all they think we are. A bit of static left in the linen. A spark when you rub your gloves together in the cold.

So I make myself go as cold as ice. I turn myself into the nothing he believes I am. I push all my anger and love and hate and hope deep, deep down inside me, and only when I've done it do I glide and stand even closer to both of them, right by their sides, but closest of all to Ellen DeWight, to her ear, so close that any heat, any hint of feeling that might escape my soul he'll mistake for hers. Oh, how I've learned how to manage such moments as this. Haven't I? *Still. Dead. Be still.* I've learned things that you, Mr. Pratt, and Ellen, would never dream of. But also things the living know very well how to do. How to act as though you don't care about the life you live. How to lie and seem to be one thing while being another. I've gone to school all these years, all this long century, on you, the living. On the young and old and everything in between. I've sat in your classrooms and studied your books and I've touched your slates and screens and glowing tablets and I've listened at your keyholes and to your telephones and I've learned more than any living soul will ever know, because I've learned the one thing that people give away when you think no one is there, when you think no one is watching: that you're frightened beyond belief of that place you happily send others to.

Ellen touches her shoulder where I've rested on it and shivers.

"Over here—more Chippendale," she says and turns toward the breakfast table. "These are called hairy-clawed chairs. See, the feet are like lion's claws? I've always thought they were a little frightening. I don't know why."

"Even though nothing scares you in this house."

"It generally doesn't. I've been in the pantry several times, already. Like I said."

"You're braver than most civilians."

"No." She twitches. "It's my job. The heirs liked me when they interviewed agents because I'm young and in touch—that's how they put it—and that's what an old house needs. New blood."

"All of this architecture at the back of the house was a later addition, I take it?"

"About twenty years ago. Some members of the historical commission didn't think a domed conservatory was in keeping with the original structure—but Alice got her way. Apparently the Lambrys pretty much got whatever they wanted. Always. And being in timber, they loved to build things. The steeple, I'll show you later, and the widow's walk. But the butler's pantry, it's this way . . ."

"Before we inspect it, I need to ask you, Ellen: have *you* ever been angry in this house?"

She seems surprised. "If I'm being honest? Absolutely. When the Danes started screaming at me right after I came back into the house. When the whole thing wasn't *my* fault; they *wanted* to be alone. But they tried to blame me for it. I felt they were just trying to set me up, telling lies about a ghost so they could low-ball the price on me. On the heirs. Things like that happen all the time, Mr. Pratt. And I hate to say it, but in my experience people with money are the worst when it comes to money. But then I saw how scared they were and I calmed down and got them away from this part of the house, back out to the porch. Here's the pantry door." She presses it with the flat of her hand. "I've been keeping it closed. Should I open it? Or do you need to?"

"Go right ahead."

She turns the tight brass knob. The door opens inward with a little breath.

"And the lights?"

"Please."

She tucks her hand into the dark.

Electricity. A little miracle. Nobody thinks of it that way anymore. Once, light was hard work for us, for maids like me and Frances, who had to lug oil, every day, to fill the lamps; to say nothing of the toil at Lighthouse Point, where a single beam had to be turned by a chain and fed hour after hour, night after night.

I stay perched on Ellen's shoulder while Pratt slips into the mote-filled room. He finds, of course, nothing there. Nothing but the blank, dusty shelves and counters, no life left, though Lambry servants once ducked inside to rest and whisper where no one could hear them, and children snuck in to pinch a stick of cinnamon, and Mrs. Lambry, after her family were all dead and gone, would sweep in and close the door behind her and stand in the darkness, managing her breath, trying to get her life to slide in and out without getting it caught between her ribs.

Pratt is moving his bulk around, now and again lifting a hand to touch a surface or stroke his chest, as though he's trying to manage his breathing, too. That's an odd thing. Each time he touches his chest, I see the hunter's band at his wrist more clearly. The gouged black markings striped into the silver. The thickness of it, like a cuff a man in chains might wear. Any ghost worth her salt knows what such a band is, the watch with no face, the clock that keeps no time. If only such things didn't exist, our village would still house spirits by the score, and the mirrors would be full and dancing, and the cemetery empty. If only the hunters lacked their tools.

But Pratt is going about his evil in a way I don't follow. He's brought no other devices with him, nothing other than the band. He keeps tapping and stroking his chest, as though the only meter he needed were inside him.

"Mr. Pratt?" Ellen blinks.

He closes his eyes and again he lifts his fingers to his chest. "Yes. Something was here."

Ellen backs away from the door. "You feel it right . . . right now?"

He opens his eyes, excited. "Something flared and then was controlled. A residue's all that's left now. But something. Enough. To begin."

"Is that good?"

"It's excellent."

"But I don't get it—what do you do next? Don't you have to—get it, before it gets away?"

"It's already gotten away. It's probably found a safe hollow, somewhere. An empty space that it can fill. An unsettled space or room. Or the image or feeling of a room. They don't like tightness. Claustrophobia. Feeling trapped."

"But this village is full of rooms. How do you find the right one?"

He closes the pantry door carefully behind him. "Patience. Care. Gentleness. Attention. Slowness. Then more patience, if necessary."

"And how long will we—I mean how long do the Danes, and the heirs, have to be patient *for*?"

"For as long as it takes me to crack its shell. A haunt is like a hermit crab on the move"—he points Ellen toward the grand staircase—"always stealing what doesn't belong to it. It has no real home. So it can be forced out into the open. Forced to act. We'll want to catch it moving, unsteady. That's when it's at its most vulnerable. When it's exposed for what it is, a migrant with no country."

But don't the living need to move to survive, too? As the Irish did when they came across the ocean, and a continent? And would that be stealing, too? From logging camp to logging camp my father and mother trudged, trying to make their way in this new world, this grand America they hoped would be better than the old country. Up and down the coast they moved, until my mother started having babies, one after another, with me the last one, the one that sent her to her final home. And then it was me always on the move. From cot to cot I was carried, by my Da, until I could walk on my own and started to work bringing lunch pails to my father and the other men at the mills. And then, when my father died, I moved again, to the boardinghouse on Albion Street. I did the laundry, and cooked, and swept, and everything else, because what choice does a soul have but to keep moving if she wants to get by? Yet a soul can crave rest, too, just like any tern on the cliffs. Only a soul that's finished doesn't flutter and fight. Only a soul that's dead takes no flight. Can't you see, Mr. Pratt? Why would you fault the will to move?

5

Upstairs now," he announces.

On the first landing I let them pass in a row underneath me.

"Beautiful staircase. And rosette around the chandelier," Pratt says.

Ellen takes him to the north bedrooms first, where the Lambry daughters used to brush their long hair with ivory combs, then across to the boys' rooms, their paper kites and nautical telescopes and boxes of games long gone. And then to the room poor Alice died in.

Pratt touches her satin-covered bed, looks under the old-fashioned canopy.

"The heirs left all her things in the house," he notices. "Why?"

"They haven't gotten around to doing anything about them yet. I don't think they knew Alice or cared much about this place, anymore. We offered to empty the house and stage it, but they said to leave everything because it added character. And in case buyers wanted any of it."

He brushes his fingers across her marble-topped nightstands, then touches his chest again.

Ellen watches. "Anything?"

"Anger here. Although nothing unusual. People suddenly passing out of life generally don't go without some pain or anguish. She died right here." He points to the floor next to the bed.

He's right. How did he know that?

"How did you know that?" Ellen asks.

He doesn't answer. "Is this Alice? On the nightstand?"

A photo of her when she was young, with a fan in her hand and her long, thin hair streaming at her side.

"I think so."

"Is it very like her?"

"I don't know. We never met. She looks like a character, doesn't she?"

It was one of Alice's favorite games, all her life, to dress up in Chinese robes with coiling dragons all over them and walk around the house in embroidered slippers and pretend she was someone else.

"She spent a lot of time in her studio." Ellen leads Pratt on. "It's the next room, here."

Her work tables and easels stand under the high gable. All of it bare now, though she used to spread out her sheets of watercolor paper everywhere and shuffle through her bottles and tins and poke a long brush into an oval of paint like an eye she was gouging out.

Ellen stops at the windowsill. "You can see she got good light in here. And also that she liked to collect dead things. Sand dollars and starfish and sea glass. Do they mean anything, you think?"

"Maybe, if there were some charge around them. But there isn't any."

They pass through what was once the governess's alcove, then reach the small, brass-hinged door that leads to the spiral staircase and up to the timbered tower that old Mrs. Lambry had blacksmithed and fitted with the widow's walk. She wanted it, she told the workmen, to be higher than St. Clements Church, and as lofty as her grief. And the steps, those had to be metal, iron and hollow. When she stepped on each one, it must ring like a bell.

Pratt and Ellen rise, going round and round, their shoes pounding and ringing with each step, until they find the smaller door at the top and open it and come out into the air and sun and the fog burning away and a view of the village in all directions.

Pratt steps out and grips the iron railing. He stares down to the back lawn, where Mrs. Broyle used to have the rugs brought out for beating. And then, at the edge of Lambry's Acre, where the lawn meets the headland before it tumbles down to the sea, he sees the house's sagging water tower.

"That's original, too," Ellen tells him, holding the railing with both hands. "It's in bad shape and needs to be torn down or re-purposed. Thing is, to take anything down in Benito you have to go through code reviews and inspections, and Alice didn't want to do that, and now the heirs don't want to do that, so it's just sitting there, basically an eyesore. The tank is empty. Everyone's on town water now."

"If the tank is empty, I'll want to get in it."

"No, I don't think so, Mr. Pratt. It's in terrible shape. See where some of the planks are falling off? Most of the ladder steps are gone, too."

"Then make another note, please. I'll need a ladder."

"But—"

"It's a space." He points to it. "It's a shell. I told you. I'll need to check it out. I'm not feeling much more around the house. Is there an attic?" He moves around the walk and scans the gabled roof.

"So you might find this interesting. This house doesn't have one, technically. The Lambrys were ultra-modern. For their time. Those gables distract from what's really a low peak, there"—she points between the brick chimneys—"and underneath the sub-roof every corner used to be stuffed with wool batten to keep the cold and wet out.

Now it's all high-tech fiberfill, of course. But you still can't squeeze even a hand in. Cutting edge at the turn of the century."

"And what about that oddity?" He looks down at the small, wooden-railed balcony off the second-floor gallery where more of Alice's paintings hang.

"That's an old balcony that got left in place during the remodel twenty years ago. It's older than the Glass Room. It used to be the main viewpoint toward the cove, before this widow's walk and the Glass Room were built. Alice loved to add things, but she didn't or wouldn't tear anything off."

Because I told her not to. *Let the balcony float*, I whispered to her. *It can float above the glass without falling in.*

Pratt leans over. "So that's why it's stuck there over the dome."

"What did you mean by you're not feeling much around the house? Are you disappointed, Mr. Pratt?"

"Why don't we make it Philip, Ellen. I have the feeling we're going to be working together on this for a while. No, I'm not disappointed. I would say I'm . . . puzzled. There isn't much to go on, yet."

"I'm actually kind of glad. I didn't want the house to be infested."

"It isn't."

"You *do* sound disappointed," she says, wonderingly.

"Because it's my job to find what frightens people and lay it to rest."

She leans her elbow on the railing. "I don't know. It's hard for me to wrap my mind around what you do, Philip." She looks out, and her bobbed hair blows toward the cliffs. "It must be a strange feeling. I mean, not just for you, but for the person you're looking for, too. I try to imagine going along, you're living, and then suddenly you're dead, and then suddenly you find out, oh-oh, I'm *not* dead, but I'm not alive, either. And then you find out someone is trying to kill you all over again. I hope it never happens to me."

I hope not either, truly, little Ellen. It's not for the faint of heart.

"Then try hard not to become a ghost, Ellen."

"Okay, but how do I do that?"

"Try to live a happy life."

"Or else live forever?"

"No. Not that. Trust me. Forever's a terrible, lonely place. You see it in their eyes."

"Maybe that's because you're the one making it lonely for them. Killing all their company."

He straightens in his coat at that jab, almost stiffening. *Good on you,* I nod at her, though she can't see me. Not so faint of heart, after all.

"What I do," Pratt insists, "is bring peace to the living as well as to the dead."

It's what they all say. It's what they all tell themselves.

"But what if the dead don't want your peace?"

"They do. Even if they don't always know it."

"But how can you *know*?"

I've wrapped myself, coldly, around the peak of the steeple, where I can't feel them or what they are saying so much, resting my cheek against the point of the weathervane, turning it.

"Because being a ghost is pure torture."

"You're absolutely sure about that."

"I can make it clearer. If you really want me to."

In the shadow of the vane, his back to the cove, Pratt stretches his neck out, loosening it in the way I used to see the priest at St. Clements do when he was about to read the catechism.

There was a time, Pratt tells Ellen, when he wasn't considered one of the very best. In the years when he was a young practitioner and had to pick up work wherever he could, he agreed to do nearly any job. His assignments included dirty missions in settings older hunters didn't stoop to, hauntings that were messy and tricky.

In one case he took on, Pratt agreed to settle a haunt out in the gold country. The abandoned mine had been sitting empty for decades, but flush with cash the new owners had high hopes of sending down engineers with plans to go deeper and lay tunnels for fresh metals. But whenever the digging crews went below a thousand feet, the lights went out. Each time the engineers went down to take a look, they found the sheathing ripped away from the electrical lines. Gnawed. Shredded to pieces.

Animals were considered as a possibility. Or local activists who didn't approve of the mining company. Security around the perimeter was strengthened. And then the lights failed completely. The engineers went down and discovered what they thought were ruddy streaks of iron dripping from the walls. When they realized it wasn't iron, they surfaced and refused to go back. There was only one specter that could survive at such depths.

Pratt took the job when no one else on the list of licensed hunters would. He made his way to the site and spent days studying his surroundings—the old cave openings, the ruins of the cabins that had housed the mine families, the bits of rusted and cast-off machinery. He spoke to the security chief and insisted he be allowed to go down into the shaft alone. Too many anxious, breathing bodies, Pratt explained, too much pulsing life in such close quarters, would make it harder to pinpoint the solution. He was given a hardhat with a headlamp and two sticks of phosphorescent light. Down the elevator he plummeted, down, down, and down, until he felt the pressure in his ears shifting. The creaking metal cage stopped at a thousand feet, and the door opened. He took a last gulp of air that still tasted of life above ground and waved one of his wands of light out in front of him, into the darkness.

The floor slanted, pitted under his feet. To his left, he heard the sound of dripping water, or something else bleeding, and a rumbling in the earth, a tensing sound, like the moaning of something too heavy for whatever held it in place. The ceiling hung low. The smell of ancient creosote floated down, along with a cleaner, drier odor. Calcium.

In the dark, he pointed his headlamp to the floor and saw his own reflection in a wide, standing puddle. Then he saw something else in it. Refracted. Upside down. The face behind him and to one side. He turned and shone all of his light on the waiting child, suspended like a knob from the glistening rock.

"Do you want me to go on, Ellen?"

No. Tell him no, Ellen.

"I don't know. Do I?"

"Do you still want to know what it's like to be alone forever?"

A boy. It was impossible to tell with certainty, but it was probably a boy. Its body was black as tar. Its sinews smelled of earth, woven with rags. It looked more like the matted root of a living thing than a thing that had lived itself.

Pratt had done his homework, of course. He'd read about life in the shanties where the mining families had once lived, and how young boys, in the latter part of a cruel century, had been sent down into the mines and crouched in niches in the walls so they could grease the wheels of the ore-cars as they passed. Untold numbers of children had died in such holes when tunnels collapsed and the air stopped flowing and they couldn't be reached.

This rotting child, if it was one of those, went on swinging upside down, its eyes lightless.

It was always a grim, difficult matter, putting down children. They hadn't lived long enough to become finished human beings. So they hadn't lived long enough to become finished ghosts, either. They fell to pieces if you went at them too quickly; they disappeared. Then, too, a child was often difficult to pin with its own anger, because when you tapped into its rage it was often only a fit, a confused tantrum, aiming at everything and nothing. What was left was guesswork.

A shot in the dark: Pratt asked the ghost if it wanted a bit of fun. If that was why all the lights were out.

Its torn mouth spread into a smile that broke its jaw loose from its skull. Poor creature. Pratt understood the trick. The child was trying hard to be terrifying. Like all children, living and dead, it confused the horrible and the fearful. But the smile was also a hint. Like all ghosts, the boy offered clues without meaning to. That's what lonely ghosts in eternity do.

No. That's what Pratt *thinks* a lonely ghost does.

He asked it to play a question-and-answer game.

Are you here all alone?

Yes.

Were you left here by others?

Yes.

Was it an accident?

The jaw swung. The skeleton of an arm pointed.

Something hit you? In the face? Something crushed you?

The hollow eyes turned gold.

And now Pratt had to do the thing that no one wants to do to a child. Be cruel to it. He had to, because he needed to get it to hold its blazing anger still, all while reminding himself that this boy in front of him wasn't a child at all, not any human thing, only a vessel for rage. Only an empty space filled with howling.

That is what Pratt believes our lasting is.

But you know, Pratt said to it, *it was all your fault.*

The ghost froze.

You must have been a very bad boy. Children who are bad, who are wicked, get exactly what they deserve.

The ghost contracted and let out a scream that filled the tunnel, shaking it, and pounded its head on a boulder, until Pratt could come so close to it he could see the tattered knit cap woven into the boy's skull. And now his job was to change his tune and act as though he was sorry, he was very, very sorry, and croon as though he cared, as though he brought kindness with him as well as punishment. Pratt opened his mouth to say the words, *It's all right, son*, and at that moment he felt a shock, and every light on his body went out.

"I can stop now if you want, Ellen."

No, I think and hold to the weathervane. Go on. I dare you.

"No." Ellen swallows. "You can't leave it like that. You said you give them peace."

I cling to the vane like a mast in a storm while Pratt looks up at the scudding clouds in the blue sky. *Hold fast, Emma Rose Finnis*, I will myself. *Keep close, and learn all that you can about this man, and how he does it, and why.*

In the blackness, he fumbled for the radio he'd been given, but it was dead. He reached blindly in the direction of the elevator, only to hear it close and ascend with a long shriek. Children. Always the cleverest with machines and devices.

He said to the boy in the dark, *I'm glad you closed the door. Because I'm never going to leave you, now.*

A soft, answering whimper.

That's right. We'll stay down here together, forever now. You and me. Just the two of us. What's your name, little man?

A whimpering answer. Then sharp fingers, stroking Pratt's hair. He felt but couldn't see. He sensed rather than knew where the edge of the boy was, and the edge of his own body—it was as if he had become a ghost too and couldn't distinguish between where he ended and the other began. *So this is what it's like to be nothing*, he whispered to it. The darkness bristled with a tiny tremor of hope.

No, I've changed my mind, Arthur. He had learned, with practice, that this was the best way to arouse their anger: to say the name, softly. And then betray that softness. Swiftly and unexpectedly. *You are nothing to me. Arthur, listen to me. I'm leaving you.*

The ghost roared. He turned pure white. His rage flared like a torch in the dark. He showed himself. A boy in corduroy.

"And then you gave it peace?"

"I did."

"Did it . . . hurt?"

"Of course not. You can't think of it that way." Pratt looks away from the sky. "It isn't fleshly pain."

"I have absolutely no idea what that means. But I see what you mean about forever being a lonely place." She wipes her hands as if they've suddenly gotten dirty. "Can we go down now? We can see about the water tower."

"If that's what you really want."

"Yes."

"Are you all right, Ellen?"

"I'm fine. I think I understand you better now. I guess a few loose boards aren't going to spook you, not if you're used to offing kids." She turns.

He stares, his jaw a little open as she passes him. Another fine jab of truth, that was. And all at once, I'm feeling safer. Lighter. Pratt hangs back before following her down.

I'm really beginning to like little Ellen, I think. I'm beginning to like her company very much.

I float off and watch them from high above as they wander over the back lawn. If only I could have been there in that mine with that boy. I could have protected him, hovered over him just as I'm hovering over Ellen now. *Little boy*, I would have told him, *be careful, don't gnaw at the metal, the wires, so often. Only enough to make them wonder and keep back. But not enough to have them hunt you down.* There's nothing wrong with our little pastimes and habits—forever is a long time, and we have to do something to keep our heads steady—but there are other ways to make the pain go away, get the aching to stop. And never say your name. Never, never let them get close to you, that way.

I watch Pratt as he stares up at the great barrel of the wooden water tank, the cask that once held so much—and I think he looks a little less certain, glancing over at Ellen beside him. He can't climb the legs of the tower, not today. I wonder if it's making him feel, as Ellen leads him back to the front gate, a bit helpless. That's a feeling that perhaps every creature on Earth should experience, not just some—though the high and mighty never do, not without a little help.

6

That's it then, Ellen, for today."

She's plainly surprised. "Really? Now what?"

"Now I go to my hotel. And rest. And have a good meal."

"I hope you'll like it. I've booked you the Main Street Hotel, the best we have. But—you really mean there isn't anything more we're doing today?"

"I have a few things I need to mull over, first. Besides, don't you have other things to tend to? Don't you need to get home to your cat?"

"I'd like to."

"So. We'll go our separate ways for a little while." He holds out his meaty hand, all business now, friendly and smiling, and she takes it. "But you'll remember about the ladder for tomorrow morning."

"I'll call Manoel Cristo, Alice's handyman. If there's anything else"— she pauses outside the groaning garden gate—"you have my number?"

"And you have mine."

"And you can't give me any sense of how long all this is going to take."

"Step by step, Ellen. Patience and care. Slowness."

Once Pratt has driven away, her shoulders sag a little in her rumpled suit. She drops into the driver's seat of her own car, looking into the space he's left behind. After a moment she stretches her mouth wide, as if she's been carrying something heavy inside her jaw all day long, and needs to let it out. Her little skull makes a popping sound. She rubs her chin. Then she sighs and turns her key.

I like riding in cars. I ride with her around the edge of the cove. It's a twisting gray ribbon, Benito's sea-road, threading above the cliffs and beside the great red trunks of the trees.

We cross the river that feeds its heart into the cove. I can see the deeper color where the captains used to anchor their doghole schooners, called that because they could turn tail in a narrow circle and survive the shoals. Where the docks once stood, there's nothing now but stumps of blackened wood jutting up from the sand, like trees that haven't given up hope of the sun.

From here, the far side of the bay, Benito's painted houses and curio shops appear small and sparkling, like lumps of sugar. My home, my home. It's a sweet place. And I mean to keep it that way. It's sweeter, too, knowing that Pratt had no luck today and has gone off to rest his empty hands, as other hunters have before him, on the bar at the Main Street Hotel. Alone. Alone. And why shouldn't he be?

Ellen guides her wheel and turns away from the cove and into the woods. Such deep shade here, and bracken, away from the road. The air turns thick and misty. We pass the small cabins and trailers filled with those who work in the village but sleep among these planted pines. The strong, virgin woods are long gone.

It's nice to go off with Ellen, like this. It's brought back to me how I miss old Alice's company. She was quiet, too, when she drove. And also didn't know I was beside her, helping her, as much as I could. *Slow down, now, watch out for that limb.* Like Ellen, she listened to me without knowing, which always gave me a warm feeling—as getting a Lambry to do your bidding would make anyone in Benito feel. In fairness, I did try to make her happy in return. I'd nudge her gaze toward a perfect white shell lying on the beach. Or help her catch one of her jars of wet brushes before it shattered on the floor. I kept young and then old Alice company while she painted in the fog and wind, while she called out, lonely, to the lowing seals, creatures she always believed were answering her because she didn't know they're really tough, territory-minded things, and bark not in friendship but in warning. How nice it was, at the end of a day, for us to tramp back together, Alice and me, through the sand and wind up the headland, toward the house, side by side. For fifty years, just the two of us—at least until Manoel came along.

Ellen's gone deeper into the piney lanes, passing the old huts where the opium-smokers used to live. She brings her little car to a stop in front of a house sitting alone. It's shaped like the letter *A*, its roof sliding all the way down to touch the ground. A painted FOR RENT sign still leans against its moss-covered flank.

She gets out, taking her satchel with her but leaving behind her keys, in the way of someone who thinks no harm can come to her in an out-of-the-way place like this. *Careful*, I whisper. *Careful*. She reaches back in to get them. A good thing, too, because even a ghost can't always know when an intruder might be nearby.

I follow Ellen up the steps to her door. She smiles, glad it seems with what she's accomplished today. She hums to herself as she goes in. How sweet. The living wear their hearts on their sleeves when they think no one is looking. Though sometimes they try to hide what they're up to, even from themselves—I've seen it with Manoel. But even then, it doesn't take much to see right through them, any more than it does to peer through a pair of boardinghouse curtains. I warned Alice about her handyman. *Well, if you're going to keep him around, then at least let him be useful. Tell him to build something. Keep him busy. Tell him you want to see the water and the sky all the way around. Tell him to leave the little balcony upstairs above the dome, floating, floating.*

At the very end, when Alice and Manoel had their terrible argument, and she'd fallen to the floor of her bedroom, I'd been there, too, to tell her what to feel. I'd heard her thoughts and her question, and told her that it was all right. *It's only where others have gone before you.* She'd lain very still, her eyes wide open and finally seeing me, as they all do at the end, and I'd gone to close the curtains so the sun wouldn't make her cry, and moved the pillow that had fallen to the floor. To make her more comfortable.

A piece of fear twisted her mouth when I stroked her gray hair. *What are you going to do to me?* I heard her think.

Yet all we can ever really do for each other, as my Da used to say, is what we hope will be the best.

Inside, Ellen is turning on all her lights. She shivers a little, rubbing her hands together. There are just four little rooms in this pointed house. Downstairs is the kitchen and living room with bright new things placed against the dark walls and floor: a vase here, a comfortable chair there. On the fireplace mantel she's put a single photograph of a man holding a baby up in his arms. Otherwise, there are no pictures, nothing private at all. A bookshelf full of business books. A door to a small bathroom. Upstairs, a loft with a neatly made bed. Above the bed, the roof is pointed and pitched, like the hull of a ship turned upside down. Everything is tidy. No dirt on the braided rug. Even the empty dish on the floor beside the back door is shining and clean. For her cat, that must be.

I like seeing how Ellen lives and where she sleeps. I wonder what it must be like to live here with her. To be the secret pet who depends on her for comfort and company.

She opens the back door and calls through the screen for her kitten. But no answer comes, no rustle from between the trees. She sighs and pushes the screen door out and together we walk through the light turning gray and cold, to a neglected garden. A plant cage has tumbled, and crumpled leaves litter the ground. She tramps over the earth in her good business shoes and turns this way and that, calling for Kittums, Kittums, and only turns back, sighing again, when she hears the sound of the phone she's left near the door.

What a ghostly thing it is, a telephone, that with only a sound it can make the living jump. So amazed we all were, as children, when the first line in the village was strung and went, of course, straight to the Lambrys' post—the Lambrys always the first in line to get anything new and exciting. We stood hushed outside the iron gate that kept us from their garden, and strained to hear the telephone bell ring. Now my hearing stretches so far I don't need to be near Ellen and can linger in the woods and trail my skirt through the leaves.

"Philip."

"Calling to thank you again for all your help today."

"No, thank you. I hope I helped. Especially since I don't have much background in—what you do."

"It's not something they spend much time on in real estate classes?"

"A little. Not much."

I can hear a soft tapping sound. Pratt touching at something.

"I've been going over a few details here, Ellen. The Lambrys have always been very orderly about their estates and their money. Alice's will, for example"—I hear more tapping—"is very specific and directed the house to be sold to the highest bidder and the proceeds disbursed to her relations. So that would seem to argue against a dead Lambry being angry at the sale of her property and—"

"—taking it out on the Danes?"

"Exactly."

"Well, can't ghosts change their minds?"

"They don't have minds to change. Their desires are fixed at death, like compasses. Also, I went ahead and checked on any deaths in the house."

"I was going to do that for you. I thought you said, 'patience.'"

A fine piece of silence on the other end. I come a little closer to Ellen.

"I just didn't want to overwhelm you with chores, right off the bat. Luckily, your public records people here are wonderfully cooperative. What I'm seeing here"—more taps and clicks—"is comfort and peace. Lambrys who lived to ripe old ages and died in their beds with their affairs in good order. Which, again, argues against any upset about wills and inheritances."

"I guess I didn't know ghosts could be so touchy about money."

"I stopped counting, a while back, how many of my cases were about who took Aunt Imelda's pearls." I hear him laugh and take a drink of something and the clatter of silverware against china.

"Are you having dinner?"

"I am. You?"

"Just out looking for my cat."

"No luck?"

"She gets into all sorts of places when she's feeling sketchy. It's all right."

"I do have one new request for you, Ellen. Can you get me a list of all the currently empty or abandoned buildings, properties, and structures in the village?"

"I can—but there won't be many. Space is at such a premium here. There's not even much that's for rent or sale. We're just too small a market."

"Do your best. And another question: are the Lambry heirs likely to come up from San Francisco anytime soon?"

"I don't think they're even planning on coming at all. Like I told you—they don't want anything to do with the bother of all this. I think they just want the money in their hands and to be done with the last bit of Lambry property. In the village, I mean. Apart from—from the graves."

"You sound a little tired over there."

"I am. I feel worn down."

"Take a shower. You'll feel better. Get the dirt and dust of the dead off of you. I should have told you. It sticks to you. Deadness. It weighs."

Another part of what they all say, another lie they tell about us. But no, it isn't the dead that stick and soil. It's only the dust of the past that weighs and dirties, and the grime of the hunt itself. It's not me. I'm not dirt.

Stay calm now, Emma.

"You could have told me that sooner. Creepy as it is."

"Clean up and rest and have a good evening. And I'll see you tomorrow. And thanks for arranging the handyman."

"I'll call and make sure he'll be there in the morning. I have another appointment but I'll try to be there with you both as soon as I can."

"Excellent. Good night then."

The light's fading fast. And Ellen, inside the house, is pulling off her jacket and blouse and going into the bathroom.

Dirt. Dirt. Dirty. Why that word? Why, when all we're trying to do is survive? *You just watch,* the village gossips used to say about me, *now her father's dead and she's in the boardinghouse, she'll fall into dirty ways with that pretty face of hers. She will, she'll get herself into trouble, turn herself into a slatternly thing, slopping around with mill hands and who knows what.* When all I ever wanted was to take a long hot bath, too, after a day of cleaning and cooking and filling the plates of men who stank, handing me their laundry, their drawers stained with ash and pitch, in those days when the smoke from the mills hung over the village, clinging to your neck, to everyone and everything, rolling in billows through the doors.

I sweated, so of course I stank at the end of a day—just like the loggers who came from ferreting out the trees with sticks of dynamite, sweating and grinding them downriver toward the mills and the men who took what had been living and whole and turned it into one dead thing only, and that the same thing over and over again. The same plank of wood, the one grand lush thing turned into a thousand dead, dull things. That's how the living think of *us*. That we're all the same.

But I wasn't any *thing*. My black hair was long and shining. My back was sturdy, my hands and nails clean and clipped. My face, shaped like a heart, mirrored my father's chin, with his cleft in it.

I run away from Ellen, leaving her to her bath, and wind through the dead rows of the forest, dragging dirt with the edge of my skirt. The earth might touch me, but it doesn't stain me. I spy the skeleton of an old, cracked greenhouse, tucked in its shadowy dell, a place once used by the sellers of smoking pipes and forgetfulness in these woods. Now its door hangs from one loose hinge. I go inside, rest in its room of empty clay pots. But only for an instant. I don't, won't linger in such places. I can't. Nothing lasts, nothing can live in a hollow place. Only loneliness. And it's loneliness that makes a soul easier to snuff out.

Like that poor boy in the mine.

And yet this is where Pratt thinks he'll find me—like any other ghost, hiding in a ruin, in an empty building, in a deserted hut, along a wall of mirrors, in a buried shaft. I look around at the abandoned shell of the greenhouse. But what—*for I do have a mind, Mr. Pratt*—what if a hunter could be tricked into thinking he'd found the very thing he thought he was looking for, in the very place where he thought he might find it?

What then?

For it's sure, my Da used to say to me, that there's nothing simpler than to give a man what he wants.

So. Give it.

7

I walk in darkness under the sparkling drops of the chandelier.

I pass like foam over the deep Turkish carpets and glide along the smooth paneling, my sleeve brushing it.

I pass in front of the fine mirrors and the carefully framed watercolors.

It's night again. And this is my place, now. My home. Lambry House.

I always dreamed I'd live in a fine house, someday. When I was young, not yet nineteen, I'd walk back from Evergreen Hill with a basket on my arm, after tending to the graves of my family, and I'd glance up and see the elegant globes of light in the Lambry parlors. I'd think: how wonderful it must be to live in such brightness. I'd stop in front of the closed garden gate, its metal glistening with dew, and study how grandly the white pillars held the porch roof up, like a kind of throne, with fine copper gutters trimmed all around it, and I'd wonder what it must be like to be someone whose rainwater passed through money.

A servant would move into the light. Mrs. Broyle, the housekeeper, or the girl who served the meals, who was Irish, like me. Sometimes, I saw the Chinaman who took the ashes out. Sometimes, the lace curtains in the Red Parlor would be pulled back, and I could see deep inside, into the dining room, where the men lounged in their smoking jackets and the Lambry girls, in gowns as pale as honey, stood by the mirrors and seemed to chatter with their own faces.

One more look—all I'd allow myself—and then I made my feet walk on. A Finnis might long for fine linen and silver, but gawking at it did no more good than asking for a plate of full moon when only the new one was being served. I hurried back to Mrs. Strype's boardinghouse so I wouldn't lose the roof over my own head. I had no time to think about gowns like honey or hair ribbons streaming down straight, ironed hair. Girls like me and Frances wore our curls pinned up tight and our shirtsleeves rolled up to keep them clear of the steam off the washtubs.

In that summer, 1914, when I wasn't yet nineteen, a boy, Tommy Allston, came one day from the Lambry House to Mrs. Strype's to ask for a girl to come and do some extra work that needed tending to. The girl who was asked for that day was me.

There was nothing surprising about this. Those of us who worked in the village, women and men both, could be called up to one of the big houses at any time, to help with the glazing of a window or to re-shingle a water tank or to carry the heavy rugs into the backyard so they could be beaten with a mallet. Sometimes, if the Lambrys had a shipful of guests, the laundry alone overmatched the staff, especially all the shirts and collars that needed turning out and starching and pressing, to say nothing of the coats that needed buttons and brushing, and the gowns that needed their torn hems fixed, and the men's cuffs that needed extra scrubbing—for the Lambry sons, Quint and Albert, were known to dress as fancily as their sisters. I'd seen that up close.

A girl like me wouldn't usually get close to the Lambry children except during some hubbub holiday where the whole village rubbed elbows—like the Fourth of July, when we crowded together on the cliffs to see the fireworks splash in the cove. Quint Lambry had stood near me at the edge, trying to get as close as he could, like me, to the boom and the cannons. When we both let out a whoop at one loud, bright burst, he turned to me like a gull surprised to see another flying at the same height. Another time, I'd caught him eyeing me as I swept off the porch at Mrs. Strype's—though when he saw I'd spotted him, he'd dropped his head in a short, funny nod, like something inside him had snapped and broken. Everyone in the village knew the Lambry children had been told not to act too proudly as they walked down the street or looked in at a shop window. Mrs. Strype had snorted through her flat nose at me, *And why do they teach them that? Because there's no good fortune in being rich if people think so poorly of you they want to kill you in your bed.*

Still, I was surprised to be called to the Lambry House on that Monday, which was washing-day at all the boardinghouses, not a day that girls like me were usually called away. My shirtwaist stuck to me, damp as a sail, and I looked a mess when Tommy peered over the fence. He grinned and whistled.

"Stop your flirting, Tommy Allston," I jeered back at him. "Go back to the telegraph office and get your messages."

"You're wanted at the Lambrys. Right now."

"Why?"

"Dunno. Find out yourself." He let go of the fence and put his cap back on, whistling.

I stepped away from the tub and took off my apron and wrung it out and flopped it on the clothes line. Promptness was expected and paid well. I called up to Mrs. Strype that I was needed by the Lambrys. Mrs. Strype was a fussy, sour woman. She stuck her head out of one of the second-story bedrooms and called, "Have a Chinaman gardener and a

54

steamship that brings them silk on a Sunday, but they don't think to ask if I can spare you. Lovely."

"I'm going," I said, glad to be away from her moods. I passed through the boardinghouse hall and tucked my hair in at the spotty mirror and then strolled out onto Albion Street, where I kept my head down and my arms folded across my wet chest, the best way to keep out of trouble with the sailors. Before I turned toward the Lambry House I looked up the hill at Evergreen and kissed my hands in honor of my family there. It's a pity, Da used to say, that the best piece of land most men will ever own will be the one they get to enjoy the least.

At Lambry House, I opened the gate and closed it behind me. Mrs. Broyle was already standing on the wide porch, in front of the frosted, scrolled doors, her hands folded over her apron.

"Come up, please, now, Emma Finnis," she said.

She turned her back on me, and I followed her into the entry with its ferns standing up in their china pots as big as soda barrels. I remembered to wipe my hands clean on my sleeves and look capable. To my right, through the high arch, was the red-papered front parlor I'd passed by before on my way to help with the laundry or the rug-beating. To my left was a matching arch that led to the White Parlor, with its marble side tables resting on tasseled carpets. And in front of me was the grand Lambry staircase with its crystal chandelier. The walnut steps came down through two landings and ended in a carved newel post, thick as a confessional.

Over my head, some stirring, and now Mrs. Lambry was sweeping down, reaching the second landing, reaching the first, coming toward me between the banisters. She wore a blouse so finely laced it hurt to look at it. Its neck was so long it made her head look like it was sitting on top of a ship, her black hair like a sail. Her skirt was gray and trailed behind her, old-fashioned, its embroidery spread out. I stared. And to think that some girl had to bend over all those tiny stitches for hours on end, yet Mrs. Lambry, with all those flounces at her back, didn't even see or notice what trailed behind her. What was all that work for, then?

"Emma Rose, how are you today?" she asked politely.

I said I was doing very well, thank you. No one will ever say Finnis manners are bad. Her hand rested for a moment on the newel post. How often she must touch that, I thought. Such a beautiful thing.

"You can go now, Mrs. Broyle," she said. "Emma and I have everything in hand."

Mrs. Broyle went down the hall.

"It was good of Mrs. Strype to let you come." Mrs. Lambry's voice was low and soft, like a cushion. "I hope she could spare you without any trouble?"

"Yes ma'am."

"Would you like to come into the parlor with me and sit down?"

I didn't know what to say. It wasn't at all the normal thing to be called to the Lambry House only to sit down. I followed her pointed, ringed finger; it stretched toward the Red Parlor. I understood and went obediently in ahead. That plush room . . . it was like walking into a heartbeat. I looked around for a proper seat to take. I spotted a small one, fitted with old velvet that I thought wouldn't mind the dust from my skirt. I brushed off my backside and sat.

Mrs. Lambry's head made a funny, catching motion, like a clock stopping its time.

"You're sitting in one of my son's favorite chairs."

"Oh," I said, not knowing what else to say.

"My eldest son. Quint. I think you might know him?" She sat down in a tall chair across from me, pulling her skirt along beside her.

"Not to speak to, no." Though everyone in town knew Quint Lambry, a head taller than his look-alike younger brother.

"That's the chair we liked to prop him up in when he was just a baby," she said dreamily and sat back and folded her hands. "It made him look like a little king."

I couldn't think of a thing to answer to that, either.

She stayed quiet for a time, looking at me. Just looking. Was she thinking, maybe, that I would get up from the chair and choose another? If so, I knew I certainly wouldn't. Because it wouldn't be right. She'd asked me to sit down. She hadn't said *where*. I'd made my choice, and if a person is given a choice, and is polite and well-behaved about it, too, and brushes off her backside, then there's no reason to make her feel clumsy and wrong. Aren't there some things—I felt my chin going up—every person is entitled to, no matter how thick her stockings?

"My son has always been a generous boy," she said.

"Yes ma'am."

"And sweet. And charming. You may have seen him, calling on people on Albion Street. While you looked out your window?"

"What window would that be, ma'am?"

"Mrs. Strype's dining room. While you're waiting on table?"

"I wouldn't notice; my hands are so full then."

I put my chin up a little higher. I couldn't say why, but I didn't like the prying tone in her voice and I wanted her to see it. *Maybe now you're the one sitting somewhere you shouldn't be?* I stared at her.

"Do you know, Emma"—she smiled and changed her tone, going kind—"that I once knew your mother, Mrs. Finnis?"

I wanted to say something kind in return. But what did I have to offer?

"No ma'am."

"But I did. I was a younger wife then. New to this piece of lonely coast. Anxious and new and a little afraid. And your mother, like you, was one of those who came to help us from time to time, when we needed more hands. I remember she had hands as steady as my own mother's. And I so appreciated that, in those days."

"Was—was I born yet?"

"I don't think so. I remember only a little boy. At least . . . I think it was a boy . . ." She frowned and looked down.

One of my older brothers, whom I never met. Just one of the Finnis babies sleeping in Evergreen, diapered in dirt.

"I do remember the child was a small, quiet thing." Her eyes cleared and her brow turned smooth again. "And that your mother loved him so much. It can't be helped, can it? A son is a special thing to a mother. As are *all* children, of course. And we women should always do all that we can for our children, isn't that right?"

I stared at her without speaking. My poor mother didn't live long enough to do anything for me but bring me into the world.

"Yes ma'am."

"I'm glad to hear you say so. It will help you to better understand what I'm about to share with you." She unclasped her hands and rested her wrists comfortably on the chair's arms. "Because it is about a mother's love that I want to talk to you today. As a mother, if I may. As a kind of parent to you, in fact. Because I know you've lost not only your mother but your fine father as well. How long has it been, now, since the sad event?"

Only two years since he'd died in the apron chute accident—and doing Lambry work, too. And yet she acted as though she couldn't remember it.

"Two years."

"And how old are you now, Emma?"

58

"Old enough to manage without my mother or father."

"No, no, I disagree! I think we never outgrow our need to be cared for by someone else, someone older. I think about how Mr. Lambry cares for me, as both my husband and my guide . . . I think about how I care for our children . . . The older must always guide the younger, I believe, if they can. As must anyone who stands, in some way, *in loco parentis* to another. Employers, for instance. We feel that way about our workers and their children. And that's why I've called you here today, dear child. Because I do care. And because I want to share with you some wonderful, wonderful news, and guide you in a helpful direction."

If she'd meant to help me after I was orphaned, then why, I thought, was I only hearing about it now, two years after the loading chute broke away from the ship and cut my father's head clean from his neck?

"You're thinking about what I said about needing a guide? You agree? I'm so delighted! I was so hoping you would see what I mean. But what am I doing?" She let out a happy laugh. "I shouldn't be keeping you in any more suspense. Such a lucky thing! Such happy timing. We've just recently welcomed a new assistant lightkeeper to the Point, and his family. Did you hear? And the good fortune is, they'll be needing a housekeeper at their residence. Augustus, my husband, has agreed to recommend you to the post. You're such a fine worker, Emma—the whole village knows that. And to have the chance to work at Lighthouse Point . . . such a quiet, happy place . . . so delightfully fresh and wild and open . . . Well, I'm sure you'll agree it's just the kind of chance any young girl would jump at. And you'll grow so fond of the Folde family, I'm sure. They have small children, and I hear they're quite lovely and lively. And such a happiness it is for me, I can tell you, to be able to sit in this place, where your mother herself might have sat, and share with you such an opening"—she leaned forward, watching me closely—"as can only help you along in this world and in this life."

59

I sat, trying to imagine my dying mother in a red-cushioned Lambry chair, recommending me to the post of housekeeper at Lighthouse Point, and I wanted to ask: in what world would such a thing have happened?

"You have nothing to say, my dear? You're startled? But I haven't even told you the salary!" she went on. "Five dollars a week. Five whole dollars. Only think what good use you could make of such a boon! And the Point is so remote and self-sufficient you'll hardly ever need to spend . . . And in any case, it can be no good thing for a girl of your age to be at the beck and call of every rough customer at Mrs. Strype's. Can it? When the Point is so genteel. So peaceful. I've always taken note of that, whenever I've been there. It's like they're all one happy little family. Not like all the comings and goings we have here, the riffraff with its bad habits, although the Ladies' Committee and I have been doing our best to make things more civilized for all of us, with the Music Hall, and the new Lending Library, and . . ." Her voice trailed off, distracted.

I waited. Not yet understanding.

"And Mrs. Strype will be made to understand the situation. We'll help her make other arrangements for assistance. But you haven't said anything about what *you* need, Emma." She went on leaning forward in her fine, laced blouse but seemed nervous now, uneasy. "Do you like the idea? Of caring only for one family? And with two whole hours off every afternoon, or so I've been told? And you should know the housekeeper's quarters are so very charming. I've been told it's a little cottage or anyway a room, all by itself, right behind the assistant lightkeeper's house. You could make something wonderful and pleasant out of such a place, I'm sure of it."

Something strange had happened. Was still happening. The Lambrys had suddenly decided they wanted to help me, to help me get away from Benito. But why? Two years after my father's death they had found me a good position but not, it seemed, with their own family. They wanted to put me into someone else's family.

And then, sitting in their son's chair, I understood.

"Only five dollars a week, Mrs. Lambry?"

"Plus your room and board."

"It's awfully lonely at the Point though, I hear. And difficult to get into town, if you need to."

"Six dollars then. I'm sure Augustus could arrange it with the head lightkeeper. And we'll find a way for conveying you there as well. In one of our own wagons."

"I know seven is a lucky number. So the signs outside the Chinese temple say."

"That's true enough. Seven dollars. I think it can be done. And the wagon. One way."

One way, north. To a ragged spit of rock jutting out into the sea. Far enough out to warn a ship before it drew too close to a false cove. Far enough away to keep out of sight a girl, a Finnis, that a mother didn't want her son to look at.

"Seven dollars, Mrs. Lambry."

"You'll take it then?" She sat back, relieved. "Very good! Then let me return you to Mrs. Strype. Just until we can get everything settled, of course."

I didn't move. "And how long will that be, Mrs. Lambry?"

"I'm sure it will be no more than a few days. Come now." She stood and swept her skirt aside and made a sign for me to rise. "Impatience to be free is no sin." She smiled.

Sometimes, at least according to the priest, it was.

I stood slowly. Mrs. Lambry pointed toward the door, her long neck reaching up again, quivering, like a pine that knows it's just missed being cut.

8

But now Mrs. Augustus Lambry is dead. And her girls in their honey-colored dresses, too. And her two boys. And Mrs. Broyle. And Mrs. Strype. And Tommy Allston from the telegraph office, who went off to fight in the war in France because he thought the girls would be nicer there. And all the men from the boardinghouse, not riffraff but honest lumberjacks. And everyone in the village then. There's only me now. The last.

Me going out of the house. Me floating over the garden gate. Me not bought by anyone, not anymore. Going because I choose to go. Because I have my plans, too.

I find Pratt just finishing his breakfast at the Main Street Hotel. He's standing over his table by the window, dropping the waiter's tip beside his empty plate. He takes his black coat from the hotel's brass hook. He steps out of sight and then appears again, passing through the salt-coated doors. He has a paper map rolled up in his hands, the one all the tourists pick up that shows which buildings are historic and when the restaurants and the museums are open, and who lies sleeping in Evergreen that's important enough to visit. The hunter turns his collar up at the curb. His automobile is a fine thing—a two-seater, full of style—though bought and ridden, never forget it, over the backs of luckless human souls.

Pratt drives as if he knows exactly which cemetery gate he seeks. I remember he told Ellen he'd already stopped in at Evergreen once. So now he's going back, I suppose, to give us dead a better look. Evergreen has not one but three graveyards, the oldest from the days when the first settlers put their heels and axes to the trees; then the Catholics crowding together, including my family (even though my Da was never much one for priests and prayers); and then the war dead, the white markers for Tommy and all the others who never came home again. Pratt pulls his car in at the first stony gate and leaves it there. He stands under our fine gray-shingled church, its stained glass windows filled with chariots of yellow fire and white doves flashing over a blue sea, and two logs lashed together with rope, the Holy Cross.

He takes a minute to read over the stones of the dead priests lying in their little nest of fenced grass by themselves, apart from us townsfolk. Then he looks at his map again. His shoes grow damp as he plods over the wet grass. The paths are narrow at Evergreen, and moss and turf grow over the lanes, bare ground showing only where some recent grave has been dug, a fresh body laid in, or where the animals have been busy tunneling and trafficking between the coffins and the junipers.

He approaches the Lambry monument. It stands as big and solitary as a steeple cut from a church. The air is very quiet. The obelisk looms over him, a pointed finger made of marble. Its base is a cold, chiseled pedestal with four sides and graves all around it. A Lambry ghost must be considered, if the Lambry House is haunted. Any hunter would come to the same conclusion. Pratt studies the map and raises his eyes to the gouged lettering:

DEDICATED TO THE EVERLASTING MEMORY OF
LAMBRY
FIRST CITIZENS OF THIS VILLAGE
WHO PLANTED THE SEEDS OF A
GREAT PROSPERITY
TRANSFORMED WILDERNESS INTO A
SEAT OF DELIGHT
AND GAVE GENEROUSLY TO THE WORLD
AND TO GOD'S HOLY MISSION

The marble hasn't been scrubbed since long before Alice died, and the lichen has started to bloom in orange posies near the grass. All the Lambrys who died in this village lie in a circle here, packed in earth like herring stacked in salt. Above them their spire reaches high as the tallest cypress trees, with a good view at the top, for me, of the village and the headland and the rocks where the seals lie patting their stomachs.

I wait, patiently. It takes a while for Pratt to walk the circle and read each headstone. At last he comes to Alice's grave. He sees two footprints left in the damp soil. A workman's boots. Manoel's, though he can't know that. The handyman's last words to Alice, after they had fought all over the house like a broom and a cat, were that he didn't need to take any more of her orders, listen to any more of her guff. The words on Alice's headstone, which Pratt looks over now, are the ones her will ordered the mason to chisel into the marble: THE LAST TO SEE ME BE THE FIRST TO REJOICE.

Pratt's hand creeps to his chest in the way I'm beginning to grow accustomed to it doing. He waits, pressed to himself, and doesn't move. I still don't understand him—this hunter who doesn't shoot often and quickly, the way the others do—so I move safely into the trees as he stares for a while longer at Alice's tomb before letting his hand fall and lifting his nose to the breeze. He seems to shrug something from his back and turn and leave the Lumbryo to their sleep. He walks down to the rows of the Children's Garden and pauses over each grief. SCARLET FEVER TOOK OUR DEAREST. OUR LIGHT THAT WAS, IS GONE FOREVER. BUDDED ON EARTH, BLOOMING IN HEAVEN. ALL BOYS, OBEY YOUR PARENTS.

He's at the row where my older brothers rest under tiny footstones. John and Michael. A little farther down, two more, PRECIOUS BOY and PRECIOUS BABY, who never made it to church, sliding nameless under their bibs of grass.

My Da told me that my mother became fearful of baptism, and before she died begged him not to take me to St. Clements too soon but to let my heart grow strong, first. I didn't visit a priest until I was nearly four years old, my father judging it safe for me by then. He tugged me along, both of us reluctant, toward the font, where the priest dribbled water on my forehead as I looked up at the great colored windows, at the dove, and the cross, and the fire, and the blue and white glass that stood in for the sea. I didn't feel God in the room, truthfully, but I felt the tide somehow, and it seemed to me that it was much stronger than any invisible host, and more certain, too.

I love my dead family. Though I never knew most of them. I love them now, so much it hurts. I love them stupidly and blindly, the way you love a sad tune that was written before you were born but doesn't feel as though it could have been, the words are so fresh. PRECIOUS BOY. I love them even though there is nothing I can do for them as Pratt passes by.

Pratt doesn't stop at my father's grave or my mother's, either. Because there's no map that tells of my parents' lives. Only their names are left behind. JEAN ANNE FINNIS, 1896 and JOHN FINNIS, 1912. Pratt is bigger than my Da, who was lean for a timberman and fit easily into his coffin, with his cut head set to one side. My mother was slim-boned, Da said, like me.

I keep to the trees, my sorrow bottled. It's been a long while since I've gone down to visit my parents by traveling the tunnels left by the mice and the ground squirrels, only to find their bones yellow as wax. I don't know why they didn't become ghosts, as I have; why their wills didn't live past the hours of their deaths. Unless it was that they never thought they belonged, really, to this place.

Pratt sits on a stone so weathered it has no face, and talks into his device. "Ellen. Hope you're well this morning. Good. And your cat? Excellent. About the ladder . . . Yes, I got your message. For insurance reasons, I understand, but it's generally better if I go up and check on things first, not a layperson. I'll talk it over with Manoel Cristo. And what about that list of abandoned spaces? Thank you. A question or two. Tell me more about Mr. Cristo, please. I see he has relatives in this cemetery . . . I see. An old family. I see. He found Alice? No. She's stone cold. Yes, it's surprising. The newly dead usually leave some residue. No, it's more like she was dead before she was dead . . . The stroke. Yes. Possibly. Listen, do me a favor. Call up Manoel again and tell him to wait outside the house for me. Don't let him go inside or have him go around back yet. Have him wait for me out front. Excellent. Hope your other appointments go well today. I've heard from Dane . . . Impatient. I'll be in touch."

He stretches his neck and seems to uncoil. I wonder why. Maybe it's done him good to make contact with the living. I don't know. And I don't care. We have nothing in common. We're both cleaners, but I was paid by Mrs. Lambry only to make myself go away. Philip Pratt is paid to make others vanish from the sight of the sun itself.

He stands again and buttons his coat and walks at a faster clip through the rest of this yard, stretching his bare hands out beside him, his fingers rippling on either side, as though he's running his fingers quickly over piano keys. I can hear him whispering "Sweet chariot, sweet chariot," though no ghost rises, foolishly, to his bait.

When he reaches the boundary of Evergreen, he drops his arms and wanders comfortably between the oldest, unmarked graves, those empty plots set aside, in memory, for the bodies washed out to sea or in from it; for the logger whose pieces couldn't be gathered after he fell across his own dynamite; for the sailor who hit a sou'sou'easter and was washed overboard, never to be seen again. Some call this the Garden of the Lost and Unknown. In its center a white angel bows, her drooping wings nearly touching the clover. Some of the graves here have no etching on them and house unnamed bones. Others are marked but lie hollow. Pratt slows. He's come to the plainest stone in the yard, a stone old and familiar to me but that has no meaning left to it, or feeling. Pratt stops, all at once. It's as though a wall has come and hit him square in his black chest. He lifts his hand and begins beating his heart, like a drum.

"Yes. Yes. Yes. Yes."

What can it mean?

I wait until he's run back to his car so that I can come down and stand right where he stood—but I feel nothing at all facing this marker I've known for a hundred years. What did he feel hovering over it? I look toward him, scanning the green slope, and see his bright automobile pulling away. It's safe for me to be angry and worried now—but nothing comes. I wander to the edge of the cemetery where the turf is blank and unused. If I were below ground, sleeping with my family, maybe I wouldn't feel this nothingness. *But you don't have to be lonely, you don't, you don't,* I remind myself. *You only need to find some new company, Emma Rose, now that Alice is gone. But it might be best if it were company that wasn't so very dangerous.*

9

Pratt holds out his hand. "Call me Philip."

The Portuguese handyman takes it. "Manoel. Cristo."

Here's what's certain about Manoel Cristo: he's one of the uneasy living. He doesn't know if he's a lucky man or isn't. He doesn't know if he's living the best life he can manage or the worst. He doesn't know that just to be living is the luckiest thing in the world. He's foolish, in a way.

He's a skilled, hard worker. But he's a man who's always afraid he's being cheated. He's thin and strong with the face of a pug dog. He can be generous and selfish and hungry. He often hides his hands in his pockets but he lifts his shoulders up at the same time, as if he's going in two directions at once.

But Alice loved him. He was the young man who, for many years, tended her old woman's garden. He built her things. He came when she called. He was never sure that he liked doing it. But now it's too late. Now he's growing older, and Alice isn't.

"Ms. DeWight said for me to wait out here? Oh, and to give you this key." He digs his hand out of his pocket and hands the key over to Pratt with the slightest bow. It's the Portuguese in him. Like us Irish, they came to this coast looking for work (after the Spanish, but before the potatoes all rotted). They built ships and docks and apron chutes so strong they were supposed to last a hundred years. It was only after my Da was struck in the head while stacking an order of planks that they admitted their chutes were too fast-moving and stopped using them to lurch the lumber down to the ships, and built winches instead, so the cut wood could be lifted and set in place rather than flung at the loaders like an ax.

I know the Portuguese. They were never the bosses of Benito. Like us, they only did what they were told. So I've held no grudge against Manoel's blood. When the picture of my Da with his head cut haunts me, I've thought up penances for Manoel instead. *Alice, tell him the porch needs sanding again. Alice, tell him all the roses need dusting for black spot. Every one.*

"Thanks." Pratt takes the key. He pockets it and turns the bulk of his black coat toward Manoel's white truck, loaded with tool boxes and scrap metal. "Nice wheels. Your sign says Fort Kane?"

"Live up there now. Work there too now, mostly."

"I thought maybe you were from the village."

"Born and bred. My family goes way back here. But we don't live in town anymore."

"Why is that?"

Manoel starts to move around to the side of the truck where the ladder hangs strapped. I sit on the roof of the cab, my white skirt spread in a circle all around me.

"Made more sense to sell the old place," Manoel says at my feet. "We made a bundle handing it over to some Silicon Valley-type. And things are cheaper up north. Cuts down on the overhead."

"But you still work here."

"People who can afford to live here can afford to pay."

"Like Alice."

69

"Where do you want this?" He's businesslike and just wants to get on with his job.

Pratt comes alongside him. "Do you mind just setting it inside the fence? I have a few things I need to go over with you before we go in."

Manoel nods and heaves the ladder by himself—he doesn't like help, I know, except when he asks for it—and carries it and lifts it over. He's strong for his size. He loosens his shoulder with a twist and hooks his hands into his pockets again, tucking his thumbs away. Pratt mimics him, as if he's trying to be a handyman, too.

"So I guess you know what's been going on in this house," Pratt says.

"I do."

"Are you still okay with working around here?"

"I'm fine with it. I've dealt with some old houses that needed cleaning out before. Comes with the job."

"But you never had any problems here."

"Not of that kind. Not once."

"And you worked for Alice Lambry for a number of years."

"I did. Cigarette?"

"No, thanks." Pratt taps his chest and smiles. "Part of the job."

"Mind if I?"

"Go right ahead."

"I've been around this place"—Manoel bends and lights—"for about fifteen years."

"Good work?"

"Enough. Sometimes a bit much. Alice—I mean, Ms. Lambry—she needed help, but she didn't like people around her very much. So, when she hired me, she sort of latched on. Had me doing everything you can think of. Carpentry, errands, yard work. About the only thing she kept an eye on herself was trimming these roses. All the women in her family did that. Big on roses, all the Lambrys. But the rest was up to me.

Dusting. Weeding. Kitchen. Electric. Painting. Roof. Sometimes she'd ask for work that, in my opinion, shouldn't be done. I've always thought the Lambrys were over-doers. All that added fussery." He points his lighter at the widow's walk. "Steeple and balconies and whatnot. But anyway, a man needs work, so I pretty much always said yes. Even if I thought it was getting a little freakish. Like that conservatory. I told her we'll be cleaning salt off the glass the whole time. And I still am, for Ms. DeWight. Ask me, an addition like that is just a burden. But Alice threw a fit when I tried to stop her, and then the permit office. She might have been old but she was determined. So that's how it was. Twenty years. Nice lady. Not saying she wasn't. But demanding."

"You were the one who found her body. Upstairs." Pratt points to the gable over Alice's window.

"Not a good day. Some things you never want to see."

"I'm sorry."

"I was supposed to come in a little earlier, but . . ." Manoel blows his smoke and looks uncertain.

He should. He should forever wonder if the fight they had that afternoon brought on Alice's stroke. He's never said anything about the fight to anyone. Only I know what he did and said, and what she did and said, in her bedroom.

"I came in to do some work in her studio. I guess you've seen all her paintings? She was obsessed. They're all over the house, framed in gold and all that. I never really got if they were any good, but she was proud of them. Anyway, she didn't like anything interfering with her painting or her work, and there was, I remember, some little something wrong with one of the shutters in the studio and the way they hung. Nothing, really. Anyway, I told her I would take care of it. And I went off to the mercantile to buy some screws, and when I came back, that was that. She was looking up at the ceiling. Just—gone."

He looks down. He isn't going to tell Pratt what really happened. How he'd shouted at her that she was always making him do these nothing-jobs just to make him feel like nothing, like less than she was. How she shouted back at him that he was a high-school dropout who didn't know a thing about light and shade. How he said she was senile, of course he knew about light and shade, he wasn't stupid. How she said *Then do what I tell you to and what I pay you for and give me all the light I want.*

Pratt studies the ground with him. "You were sure about her being gone."

"I touched her." He shuffles his work boots. "She was cold. I couldn't find a pulse. I put the call in. They said later, stroke."

"Did anything about her surroundings look . . . disturbed?"

"No, not that I noticed."

"Would you say the expression on her face was . . . peaceful?"

"How do you mean?"

"I know it might be hard to judge." The hunter rests his hand for a moment on the handyman's shoulder, as if they've become friends. "But this is important. Did she seem surprised? Terrified? Or at rest?"

Manoel shakes his head. "I honestly don't know how to answer that, Phil. The stroke didn't make her face look *natural*. She looked . . . shriveled, I guess. Shrunken inside her clothes. She liked to wear these fancy robes, these long, Oriental things. So she had on all this color but she just looked . . . white. Dull. And so small. Not bad, really. Not like she'd been struggling, or anything. Like it dropped her like a hammer."

"I see. And there was no other sign of injury that you could see."

"Nope. She was old but she was still pretty fit, till then. She could manage a paintbrush and rose trimmers. I'm not sure she needed me as much as she claimed she did. My wife would get on me about it all the time, how I was spending too much time at the Lambry House. But, like I say. A man's got to make a living."

He isn't telling Pratt about all the other fights, either, and how at times they threw themselves at each other so hard they ended up in bed, wrestling and squealing like two weasels trying to escape the same trap. And when they started to moan, I went away, confused. It's funny how, when it comes to love, you can't hear the music others hear.

"I guess we should be getting after the water tower now?" Manoel asks, trying to change the subject, moving away from Pratt and dropping and stomping out his butt. "I have some other responsibilities today. My wife . . ."

"Of course. I don't want to take up your whole morning. Please, lead the way."

"Just so you know," Manoel says, opening the gate, "I'm not here just for you this morning. The historical commission has an interest in all this. They want to know if the tank shouldn't be rehabbed or torn down. Alice—I mean Ms. Lambry—could never make up her mind about it, even though it hasn't been functional since I don't know when. I might get her close to agreeing it was a waste of space and then she'd change her mind and end up going on and on about how you need to leave the past rotting right in front of you where you can see it so you can have a sense of how long it takes. Artsy stuff like that. Anyway, in this village, you have to show something is unsalvageable before you can have it removed. But if it's unsalvageable, then you *have* to remove it. That's why so many people have turned the structures into guest houses, instead. Because they don't want to lose the history, but history has to pay, so to speak."

"I understand. One more—Need help with that ladder? No? Then one more thing. When you found Alice—Ms. Lambry—did you in any way—ah—rejoice?"

The ladder dips suddenly in Manoel's hands and brushes the rhododendrons in the side yard. "Excuse me?"

"I guess I'm asking"—Pratt helps him guide the back of the ladder around the branches— "did you stand in any way to benefit from her dying?"

Manoel's pug face closes, and he says nothing, lugging the metal rungs, carrying the ladder himself all the way around the house, and still nothing as he plants the ladder's feet in the heather at the base of the water tower. He pulls the rope that snakes and clanks the highest rungs into place. The flashy, expensive watch Alice gave him peeks out from his work sleeve. Then, with everything ready, he grunts, "No, I didn't, as Jesus is my savior. I never expected anything out of this job except decent pay. Besides, anyone's dying in this town means less work for a man like me, not more. And I know as well as anybody Alice left everything to her family. And that's exactly where it should go. So let me help you move things along so that can happen."

He's almost upset. If only Pratt knew; he's seeing the same Manoel who stormed out of the house that day, cursing the woman who gave him his orders.

"Manoel." I can see by Pratt's face he wants to slow the handyman down, but is trying not to show it. "Let me ask you. Do you think Alice Lambry is the ghost who's troubling this house?"

"What do I know? But if she is, it doesn't make any sense to me. She liked people who helped her get her ideas done. She wouldn't want to stop anyone from selling this house if that was her idea. She wants people to do what she wants—even if there aren't very many of us patient enough to do it. Now. I guess I'll be going up there to check things out. Ms. DeWight was supposed to tell you I need to go up first."

"She did tell me. But I'm not in favor of it, insurance or no insurance. I've got my eye on that tank because it's a possible refuge. You understand what that means?"

"I've worked with cleaners before. I won't go in. All I'm checking is the bolts and the struts and the soundness of the platform. That's it. Up, down, that's what's required. I told Ms. DeWight. She understands the situation."

"With all due respect, I think I understand it better."

"Maybe when it comes to your line of work, okay, but not ours, Benito's way of doing business. Ms. DeWight is new but she seems to get the right way to do things. Just brace the bottom for me, that's all you have to do. Because there are no ifs or buts about this. I'm going up first. You let me know if you notice anything other than structural." He starts up.

A flash of impatience crosses Pratt's face, but he holds the ladder and braces its feet with his, calling up to Manoel as he climbs, "Once you give me the go-ahead, I'm coming up."

"Let's see how stable she is first." Manoel looks up at the screwed boards under the tank. "Once I'm all the way up, you stand aside from this ladder, just to be safe."

In the old days, the Lambrys' Chinese gardener used to climb the wooden grapplings. It was part of his job to make sure there was nothing dead and floating in the water. But also, I learned later from watching him, he needed a moment to look out across the ocean, as if toward his own country, far away.

Manoel makes a clicking noise with his tongue as he nears the top and my boots, dangling over the edge.

Pratt steps back, as he's been told to do, his hands loose at his sides. "All right up there?"

"So far so good. I'm feeling a slight vibration. Not too bad."

"Come down if you have to."

The tower shivers underneath us. Manoel stops and waits and whistles, then nods.

Pratt's face, down below us, is small and worried. It's the first time I've seen him anxious for someone else. I wonder if he has a wife, too, or any family.

I slip to the side of the tank where some planks are missing and into the opening I glide and hide. It's shaded and nice here, bedded with dry needles and leaves mixed in with squirrel droppings and downy bird feathers. A fine, fine nest for a ghost. I can see why Pratt would think to find what he's looking for here. And I'll be happy to let him think he's found it.

Little shafts of light quiver through the missing slats and fall on my black shoes. The top of the tower is wobbling now, as Manoel walks around it. "This side seems okay enough," he calls down. "But let me make sure the rest of the platform is secure."

"Easy now!"

Be careful, I whisper and hear his work boots stop.

"What was that?"

"Everything okay?" Pratt calls.

"Dunno. Feels a little wobbly again."

I see his hand fumble at a broken slat as he tries to catch his balance. He can't see it, but as his hand reaches inside the tank, the expensive watch Alice gave him hooks on a nail that has been worming its way through a cracked hole. The clasp catches. The name the living give to such a thing is *accident*. The gold tumbles inside with me, and Manoel lets out a little curse. He tries reaching for it, but his arm is too short. He'll have to come in with me, now.

"Everything still okay up there?" Pratt shouts.

"I need to get inside the tank."

"No, Manoel! Come on down. I'll do that."

"It'll only take a sec," he calls out impatiently. And then, under his breath, "You might be getting paid a fortune today, but not me, pardner. I need my Rolex."

He finds the gap and squeezes in through the wood, though his shoulders have a hard time. Now we're together in the shadows. His gift rests where it fell, in the dust beside my skirt. I'll let him take it, and go back down, and tell Pratt the inside of the tank is safe for him to crawl up and into; and then Pratt will come and feel something of my "charge" here, and think he's found the spot he needs to stay close to and guard with his weapon, though I'll be safe, watching from a distance, planning from a better bed.

"Shit. It better not be broken." Manoel ducks and stretches his arm out to reach the watch. "All I got to show for fifteen years of misery with that old cunt."

Hot. Quick. Anger. I can feel it. What Alice might have felt, what I am sure she would feel were she here to hear such filth and foulness. What I might feel too, hot, blazing, if I were the one who'd given my lonely heart to a dog-faced man who spat on me when my back, my life, was turned. How dare you. How dare you. How dare you.

With another oath Manoel pulls himself backward out of the tank, as a long creak sings through the wood underneath us. The tower leans and lets out a groan.

"Manoel? Manoel! Get off of there *now*! I think she's going!"

I fly free and am out of the cask in time to see the tower begin to twist and coil like a living thing uprooted, a vine twisting and trying to hold itself high in the sun but with nothing to hold onto. Manoel crouches on the platform, gripping its curling edge.

"Do it, get down!"

The tower's rotten legs are buckling underneath him.

"Jump for it!"

Manoel can't move. He's frozen. He's terrified.

"Get clear right now!"

I see the white in his eyes, the blood running backward inside him. I whisper to him: *You can move or you can die.*

He shouts and falls away from me, pulled as we all are by the earth, and the tower chases after him, catching up to his body and driving him into the ground.

Pratt lies motionless on his side, covering his head.

I fly down to Manoel.

Poor man, only his head left untangled, free. He can see me. In the same way everyone who has died in this house has always seen me, in the end.

It'll be over soon, I whisper to him. *You'll rest now.*

He can't nod. His lips move. I hear him.

Is that what you really want?

His eyes blink.

All right then.

I go and find the watch winking in the splintered wreckage, beside the growing pool of blood, and turn its face over. I carry it to him and hold it up so he can see the inscription Alice made for him: *The heart goes all day long.*

He blinks.

I know. You didn't mean what you said. You're sorry for it now, aren't you?

He blinks again.

It's yours, I whisper, and place the metal carefully on his cheek, as gently as I placed the pillow over Alice.

Too late, I know I've done wrong.

Pratt is standing again.

He's seen the gold move through the air, all by itself.
He's seen.

When I've flown, afraid, far enough away across the headland, out to the ledge, the very edge of the cliffs and the cove, I look back and see Pratt, small, raging at the boundary of the property, his chest heaving, his face torn and white. I can see him angry, straining, afraid, too, because he has a terrible choice to make: he can follow where my racing has flattened the tall grasses or he can sit with a dying man while that man draws his last breaths. I see him ball his fists helplessly and then turn and run back toward the piece of empty sky where the water tower once stood. The sun, having hidden behind a cloud, comes out again, its face as bright as Alice's China-yellow robes, as the gift of a gold watch, as the mustard seed waving, as a great globe of electric light and the glow on Quint's face, in the summer of 1914. For it was June then, too, and I went hurrying, like this, through the waving cliff grasses, through the wind, to escape, escape.

10

The Music Hall. Then, in the summer, it still stood. Then, it was a deep forest-green hexagon planted like a carousel in the grass, with wide-sashed windows all around and a striped green-and-white awning out in front. Inside, a beamed ceiling rose to a point, like the center of a circus tent, decorated with striped bunting. At one end was the musicians' wooden stage, in a half-circle, and at the other a banquet table set up with refreshments, punch cups hovered over by the women from the Temperance League, who made faces whenever a sunburned lumberjack came in wearing his Sunday best but looking as if he'd already had a nip of something hard. Still, all the men, and we girls, too, had to be allowed to come, because the Ladies' Committee had decided it would be much better for us all to gather where at least we could be seen and watched, and where our steam could be let off without burning. Dances were allowed only two nights out of the month, and since the Lambrys had put up the money for the Hall, the music was Scots-descended. But the Lambrys rarely set foot inside and their sons and daughters never came, and that was all right by us.

On the night after Mrs. Lambry and I bargained over my seven-dollar wages for going to the Point, I told Mrs. Strype, after dinner, that I would be leaving soon. She'd cursed me for being an ungrateful hussy and for being dim enough to think that lightkeepers would be easier than jacks. I ignored her and hurried under the streetlamps toward the hall, hungry for escape, for a waltz, or a reel.

Frances was already in the doorway, waiting for me. Franny, my dearest friend in all the world.

"Well you're a fast one," she whispered in my ear, "in your short skirt."

I laughed. I'd only shortened it because one row of old ruffles had ripped as I'd pulled it over my boot. Franny looked so fine that night in her brass buttons and sailor-blue frock that I hugged her. The freckles stood out on her cheeks like copper flakes.

The fiddlers struck up and she grabbed my arm and we promenaded around the room, elbows linked, in the thickening smoke and sweat. Her beau hadn't shown in the doorway yet, so we circled again until we came to the punch bowl and took our cups and sipped and watched over their white rims.

"I'm sure he'll come," I said.

"I know he will. I just don't want every calf-eyed saw-boy thinking he has a chance with me when he doesn't. But *you* should look around and make your pick, before Lighthouse Point snatches you away."

"You mean old lady Lambry. Lucky me."

"I call it luck. Seven dollars a week."

"I'm not saying it isn't. And all for keeping Quint Lambry from trailing after me."

"Then who's that standing like a lost sheep in the door?"

"It can't be."

"It is."

The swirling smoke from the men's cigars and the girls twirling their skirts getting ready to reel made it hard to be sure, at first. But then, there he was. His collar high and white, his cheeks shaved, his shirt starched, and his coat cut finer than any man's in the hall.

I turned my back, heart pounding. "I can't let him see me. He'll gum up the works."

"Just keep thinking seven dollars a week and your afternoons free," Franny said, gaping at him.

"Has he seen me?"

"He sure is looking around. Maybe he followed you?"

"He's been doing that." I kept my chin down, behind my cup. "Watching me at Mrs. Strype's."

"Look, the Temperance League biddies are about to faint! A Lambry coming into the Lambry Music Hall? What on earth is the world coming to?"

"Pipe down, Franny. He'll hear."

"Oh-oh, one of the company managers has spotted him."

I peeked that way. The poor, gushing man was waving his cigar and bowing under the flag-draped entry, holding out his free palm.

"And now," Frances giggled, "you'll see glad-handing like it's Easter Sunday and smiles as if the Pope himself had stopped by. And all just for pretty-boy Quint."

It was true a girl couldn't help but like what she saw. The pale skin. The rosy cheeks. The way he ducked his whiskered chin as another manager approached him, like a swan trying not to show its long neck.

"Of course, haven't you heard?" Franny raised her cup. "He's the new village hero."

"Why's that?" I stared.

"Why, he shot a panther that pounced on the trestle over at River Camp today. And I'll bet doing it made him feel just like one of the jacks. Bet that's why he's here. So he can feel like he belongs to us."

"I thought you said he was here to see me." I watched the way his blue eyes darted around the room, searching.

"Well look who's pretty sure of herself now!"

"Look, all the men are going over to him. He's the one being pounced on now."

"No," Franny marveled, "he's breaking off. He's coming this way. He's wants some *refreshment!*"

"Don't you move one muscle, Franny."

"That's a boy who wants his punch."

"I've changed my mind. Go away right now."

"I'm going." She took my cup with her.

Quint Lambry stood right in front of me. I felt my face flush the way it did when the laundry tub was hot and fresh. His cheeks turned red as Christmas. He bowed, awkwardly.

"Excuse me, Miss Finnis?"

"Mr. Lambry?"

"I hope you're well this evening?"

"Very well, thank you. And you?"

"I'm well."

"I'm glad to hear it."

"It's a fine night."

"It is."

"Though it's a little—warm—tonight?"

"It is."

"It must be the damp from the high tide."

"It's always damp in Benito, though, isn't it?"

He blushed even more deeply, and hesitated.

I had to feel sorry for him. It must be hard, carrying the Lambry flag everywhere you went. "It might," I said to help him out, "just be that there are so many people here."

"Yes." He nodded gratefully. "So many. And I don't like—Do you like crowds, Miss Finnis?"

Seven dollars a week, seven dollars a week.

But not until next week. And who said a girl needed to be haughty in the meantime?

"I don't mind the crowd here." I turned to face the dancers. "A lot of us don't have anything else to do in the evenings for excitement. It's dull in Benito for all us jacks and jills."

He came alongside me, rubbing his tucked chin. "I think you're absolutely right. There's never enough to do in this camp and—" He stopped himself. "Do you know what I feel? That too much time isn't good for the modern soul."

"The modern soul."

"I mean . . . the soul that isn't tied down to old ways. To old ideas and forms of thinking. The modern soul needs action and . . . to break out of stagnation."

"Like Quint Lambry talking to Emma Finnis?"

He beamed at my honesty, relieved. His cheeks went less pink, and his shining hair looked less boyish. "My parents are full of such stale notions, Miss Finnis. I'm sorry. It's . . . burdensome. It's terrible."

"I don't know. I think it must be nice—having parents who mind where you go and care what you do."

"I'm sorry. That was stupid of me to say. With your father—"

"I don't talk about it."

"Of course. I'm sorry. It's just I see the world a bit differently than my mother and father do. I want you to know that." He leaned toward me, meaningfully.

Those blue eyes. Enough to turn a girl's head like a flag in a gale.

"Would you like to dance?" he asked. And then he was holding his hand out toward me, and I was taking it, while Franny lay her hand on her cheek and made a face full of fun at me, right under the eyes of the Temperance League gossips, who couldn't believe—I saw it written all over their amazed faces—that Quint of the fortunate Lambrys was about to lead Emma of the unlucky Finnises out onto the floor.

He said as we waltzed, the web of his hand low on my back, "I like this."

"Me too."

"*They* don't." He smiled. "Look at them. So Victorian."

"Is that why you're dancing with me?"

"Why?"

"To spite them?"

"*No.*" His mouth bent close to my ear. "It's only because, Emma Rose, you're so very fine, and no one else sees it. You're so pretty, you could put the lights out."

I felt both of our hearts beating close in our pressed chests, leaping ahead of the music.

"What if I told you," I said, pulling away, "that *I* was doing this out of spite."

"I wouldn't believe you."

"Why not?"

"Because you're feeling the same thing I'm feeling. That's how it works, I think."

The waltz ended. Applause for the fiddlers, who put away their bows. A quartet of young clerks from the mercantile came up to the stage, Tommy Allston among them. They put their heads together and opened their mouths and sang:

Candle lights gleaming on the silent shore;
Lonely nights, dreaming till we meet once more.
Far apart, her heart is yearning,
With a sigh for my returning,
With the light of love still burning,
As in days of yore.

Neither Quint nor I moved. I finally asked, "What did it feel like to shoot the panther?"

"You heard about today."

"Yes."

"I don't know. I just reacted." He shrugged and looked at the pegged slats of the floor.

"Did it . . . die right away?"

He shook his head. "Not right away. It was still breathing."

"And you weren't afraid?"

"There was nothing to be afraid of. There was blood. It was finished."

"How old are you, Quint?"

He straightened. "Eighteen."

"Me too. My father said, on the day I was born, there was a storm and a flood and the seawater pushed so far upriver the current ran backward. You should know that about me, Quint Lambry."

"All right, Emma Finnis. Are you thirsty?"

"Yes."

"Can I bring you a cup?"

"Please."

"And after we drink, maybe we could take a little stroll outside, away from all this?"

"Yes."

My business was all my own, I decided, until the Lambrys started to pay me. Let the biddies stare and the managers step aside, amazed. Let Mr. and Mrs. Lambry hear and know why it was seven whole dollars a week they were paying. Tonight and for a few nights more, I told myself as Quint Lambry took my arm, I was still my own keeper. I would take a chance at dizziness and daring, while I could.

Later, at the cliffs, I learned that a dark edge feels safer when two pairs of feet walk beside it. And that a tongue is made not just for bargaining your wages but for happiness, too. For kissing. And I learned that you can still feel a mouth, long after, even when it's no longer pressed against your lips. For how long can you feel it? For how long can you carry it?

Ask me, ghost hunter. Ask me for how long.

11

Ellen stares past the constable's deputies.

The ambulance stands in the street with its two doors flung open. The drivers in their blue jackets are lifting Manoel from the grass. His body is hidden by a sheet; a clear plastic cup cradles his gray face and feeds him air. They push the rolling bed of the gurney under the yellow tape and toward the flashing lights. The deputies are studying the spars and spears of wood that were once the Lambry water tower. The townspeople and tourists have been pushed back and are coughing, holding their throats in the still-floating dust.

Pratt says numbly, at Ellen's side, "I did this. I let him go up first."

She doesn't seem to understand. "He's going to be all right?"

Pratt closes his eyes. I think he must be playing the collapse over again in his mind. He thinks it was me, my doing. Because he saw me lift the timepiece. Because I was there, with Manoel. But how can he, how can anyone know what the heart might do, or where it might lead you, to what edge? A tower. A cliff. It can all seem so solid. You think you know your own heart and the heart of the one standing, breathing right beside you. But do you?

Ellen's eyes are widening, beginning to see. "I was the one who called him to come."

"Don't do that."

"Why did he go up if it wasn't—"

"He was fine." Pratt squats at the curb and finally sits down on it. "I saw him. He knew what he was doing. This isn't what it appears to be. Trust me." He lifts his hand as though it could explain something to Ellen. Then drops it. "This was no accident. Something brought that tower down on Manoel. Something unfeeling."

Isn't gravity the most unfeeling thing of all, Mr. Pratt?

"You don't mean the ghost." Ellen reaches for the curb beside him and sits down, too, crookedly.

"I saw it. I saw the struts get jerked out from under it. And there's more."

He tells her about my kindness, my gentleness to Manoel with the watch. But he doesn't make it sound kind at all.

"It's called *extensis*. The ability to extend movement outside, beyond. This wasn't your fault, Ellen. We couldn't have stopped this. This was a clear message. Manoel was the message. It put the watch right under his nose. To show him time was running out. It was clear and vicious."

But I only gave Manoel what he wanted. What he asked for.

Pratt looks at the ambulance. I stand cold beside it, people rushing past me. I have to stay unfeeling. I can't let him see what more I can do, can feel. Not now.

Ellen presses her hands to her eyes. "What am I going to say to Manoel's family? How do I explain this, that a ghost could do this?"

"Not all of them could. Or would. But now we know what we're dealing with. Which means we have to be very, very careful. I want you to step away from all this, please. I don't want you coming to this house anymore."

"No." She pushes away from the curb and stands. "This is my property. My client. My responsibility. I have to think about all this. I have people to call. I just need to think about what I have to do." Her small shoulders set. "Are you all right?"

"I'm fine. I jumped clear."

"We should have you checked out. By the medics. Right now."

"No, I have to think, same as you. I have to think about where it went. The way the grasses bent, blew—it was flying. Toward the cliffs." He stands too and stares. "In that direction. It was racing. As if it knew where it wanted to go. I asked you for a list of abandoned spaces . . . It followed a path of some kind. Where could it have been going? Can you think of anything that wasn't on the list?"

And now, Ellen, little Ellen, you must do something for me, please, since Manoel can no longer help me with my plan, nor can my plan be as simple as I meant it to be. You must tell him more about Alice. Tell him where Alice painted her watercolors. Tell him about the little hut hidden down on the beach. Remember and tell him, so I can still lead him where I want him to go.

She shakes her head. "Manoel first. The ambulance . . . I should go with it. To the hospital. I need to be there with his family."

"Just think. Are there caves down there on the beach? Grottoes? Help me."

"I need *your* help." She looks up at him, amazed and almost angry. "At the hospital. Help me explain to Manoel's family, first."

"Not possible. The constable wants to see me right away. The police never know what to do in a case like this."

"Tell them to wait. Tell the constable you'll meet with him in an hour. Two at most. We can go to the hospital together and then to the constable's office. That's what we have to do, need to do."

"Fine. Then let's do that. Now."

But why won't Ellen do as *I* want? Why is Pratt keeping her so close, taking her arm? She doesn't belong to him. He doesn't see what I see—the tense little muscles in her jaw.

"We'll take my car," she says as she loosens from him to get her keys. "The hospital is in Fort Kane. I know the way."

I fly after them as far as Evergreen Hill, where they go off to the north, along the highway. I can't, I don't like to go any farther. Benito is my home, as far as the Point. A ghost stays because she chooses to stay. Her *will* chooses it. My will. I'm not like the visitors who come to the cliffs to stare at the horizon, pulling out their cameras and devices to try and capture a moment they're so afraid they'll lose and forget. A ghost never forgets. The vows Quint and I made, as we walked along the cliff's edge . . . The words we shared, words of faith and hope and some kindness . . .

And Pratt calls me vicious. If only I could shout at him: *if the living don't listen to the warnings of the dead, how are we to blame?* I hover near the spot where once Quint and I waltzed under a broken moon. For what is a ghost, what is a ghost, except a voice in your head you should pay attention to, but don't?

Pratt and Ellen come back at last from Fort Kane. She's the one who leads the way into the constable's station. The constable has been waiting for them, too. On a usual day Constable Knightley doesn't have much work to do, other than handing out tickets to tourists who've parked their cars on the wildflowers or let their dogs run across the headland with no leash. I've kept busy studying him through the window blinds. He's a heavy man, his body carved into rolls by his belt and buttons. He's unhappy watching Ellen and Pratt sit down in front of him. He doesn't know what to do. He wants to keep Benito quiet and pleasant. He doesn't want anyone to know there's ever any trouble along this bright, pretty cove. He wants this village to look safe for the tourists, and it's his business to make it so. He doesn't like cleaners, because cleaners mean there is something messy to clean.

"I'll need to see your credentials, please, Pratt."

From the center of his desk, Knightley slides a curved black device forward. Pratt pushes back his black sleeve and holds the metal band at his wrist under its red eye.

"Licensed and bonded." Knightley nods. Then he sighs and doesn't seem to be any happier. "I don't recognize that model. The latest from the valley?"

"Yes."

"Worn at all times on duty?"

"Yes."

"Can I trust you to discharge your weapon only where warranted and at the appropriate target?"

"Absolutely. This one," Pratt pulls down his sleeve and nods at the metal buckled to Knightley's waist, "makes no errors."

"Oh really? You're claiming there have been no mistakes made already today?"

"Constable," Ellen says quickly, "Mr. Pratt is one of the very best in the state. We're lucky to have him here."

Knightley turns and jabs his finger toward the window and me. "That out there doesn't feel anything like luck to me, I'm afraid."

"I understand how you must feel." Pratt stays calm. "But there's no need for panic or recriminations. You've got something aggressive here that has to be dealt with aggressively. And Ellen's right. I'm here to deal with it. And I will."

Knightley seems to sense he's gone off track and begins making notes. "You've reported this as a haunting."

"I have."

"Not a structural collapse."

"No. Demolition. Deliberate and definitive. With extensis. Extensis is—"

The constable holds his hand up. "I know what it is. But we've never had anything like that here, ever."

"It's rare but not unheard of."

It's quiet in the room for a moment. The clock over Knightley's head ticks like a leak. He looks up and eyes both Ellen and Pratt suspiciously, as though they might be against him, somehow.

"You told my deputy Cristo went up without any difficulty, at first."

"That's correct. We were in direct communication as he checked the tower. He said everything was fine. And speaking solely as a handyman, he was being accurate. There was nothing deeply wrong with the structure. His assessment was sound. But I think he may have angered the presence. I don't know how. He went inside the water tank. After I told him not to."

"Then *why* did he go in?"

"I don't know the answer to that. But when he came out the wood splintered underneath him. It simply . . . evaporated."

"Except that it didn't evaporate. It crushed him, is what it did. From the neck down."

"That was not Manoel's fault."

"Wasn't it yours?" Knightley leans forward. "Did it never occur to you, since you were looking for a ghost that had already terrified two of Ms. DeWight's clients, and since you presumably know what these monsters can do, that something like this could happen?"

He's just called me a monster, hasn't he? But some accidents are only accidents—aren't they? I stay as cold and still and calm as Pratt does.

"It's rare, Knightley. I'll forever have to live with—"

"It was the insurance." Ellen leaps to the hunter's rescue. "The historical commission. Everyone told us Manoel had to go up there. Everyone. And the Danes—they were scared, but they weren't hurt. So how could any of us know it was so dangerous?"

"Well, would *you* have gone up on that tower, Ms. DeWight?"

It's Pratt's turn to flare. "This has nothing to do with her, Knightley. This wasn't her fault or Manoel's, or yours, or anyone else's. This can't be about assigning blame. Not to anyone who's breathing—but you know that. I can see it in your face. You *know* this isn't a crime you can cuff a perp for. There's nothing here that can be vindicated in a court of law. Which is why I'm here." He sits back again. "We clean. We are judge and jury and executioner. I'm here for one reason and that's to keep the living on one side and the dead on the other. I'm sorry Benito is having to see the ugliest side of what I do. I know you've had cleaners here before and gotten what you thought were good results. You had every reason to believe your town was taken care of. But it isn't. What is still here, I'm afraid to tell you, is not normal. It is strong, it is angry, and it is, for now, not going anywhere. And that is why I'm here. Because I will sink this thing so something as terrible as today doesn't happen again. But it will happen again, unless I sink it."

But you won't sink me. You won't.

"With your help, Knightley."

The constable leans back, his weight relaxing a bit into his chair. "I could almost feel sorry for it, the way you talk."

"Good. Don't."

"We like things on an even keel here, Pratt. Everything in its place. Everyone *knowing* their place. That's how a town like Benito goes on, out here in the middle of nowhere. Everyone needs to know we're safe. We're a tourist town, these days. We didn't used to be and we've had our share of hard times, but it's important now that no one sees that. We're a kind of show, to call a spade a spade. People with time and money to spare come here, and they want to see and walk around something serene and happy and pleasant. They don't want to think there's anything unhappy between them and their money buying some happiness. You understand? So we need to take care of this quietly and quickly.

"And you." He turns to Ellen. "As for your buyers, you tell them I want not only their inspections and this cleaning finished, *now*, I want the Cristo family justly compensated for this tragedy above and I do mean above and beyond the terms of Mr. Pratt's bond. You can tell them I know all about the building permits they're wanting. There are no secrets in this town. You tell them we expect compensation for damages done."

There are no secrets in this town? I'd laugh, if it wouldn't shake some of my anger loose.

Pratt stands. "I'll be the one to talk to Dane."

Ellen gets up, too, and I can see she's trying to look taller than she is. Braver. "I'll assist Mr. Pratt."

Pratt holds out his hand. "And Knightley, I'm trusting that I can call on your deputies again if the need arises?"

Knightley has stayed in his seat and doesn't move. "To be honest, you might have some trouble getting them out that way again. They aren't paid as well as *you* are, Mr. Pratt. And they certainly aren't paid anything near enough to cross to the *other side*, as you call it. Not our jurisdiction, you know."

Oh, it's almost worth it. It's almost worth it to have had to freeze my heart and listen just so I can see, now, the amazed look on Pratt's face as he learns how weak and cowardly Benito's law officers are and always have been. Afraid to look into dark places and corners they can't name and don't want to see into.

Pratt holds his hand up so Ellen can pass by him and walks out after her.

"We should go back to the hospital now," she says when they're outside on the street, beside the seashell and kite and taffy shops, the tourists milling in the sun around them. "Both of us."

I think she wants to distract Pratt from the constable's crudeness.

"I think you'd better go on by yourself, Ellen. And you'd better keep away from here for a while, as I said."

"But the Lambry House never hurt me." She looks down at the sidewalk, where a dropped and torn map of Benito lies sticky. "Why is that? When I've been involved, all the time. I even started all of this, in a way. What does that mean?"

"All it means is that it hasn't hurt you yet."

"Will it hurt you?"

"It would have to get close to me to do that. And it won't want to."

"I'm sorry about the constable. He's afraid."

"But not you."

"It's not that I'm not." She picks up the map and throws it in the can at the curb, then fumbles in her satchel for her keys. "I think it's that I still remember that boy in the mine. How do you know if what you're doing is right? How do we know when something is horrible and when it's only desperate?" Her hand is shaking suddenly. "I don't even know what I'm saying."

"Ellen, you're not well. Delayed reaction. Don't go back to the hospital right now."

"No." She shrugs his hand from her shoulder. "I can handle myself. You need to do your work. You need to *fix* this. You heard the constable. The tourists might start to leave. Then the whole thing falls to pieces . . . What time is it now?"

There's a bench on the sidewalk where Main Street meets Albion Street. Pratt guides her to sit down. Beside the bench stands a street lamp. Attached to the lamp, like a child's head sticking out from a merry-go-round, is a clock. It was put there years ago by one of the town fathers. I like to sit under it, too, when I need a moment to think and steady myself, and watch its hands move in a circle all by themselves. A clock isn't a living thing, but it seems to live.

I remember when Alice gave Manoel his gold timepiece. It wasn't just because she was in love with him—she wanted him to spend time with her. They were standing very close together in her canopied bedroom, and he was holding her hand and saying he didn't know how he could wear such a fine thing or explain it to his wife. They'd stood so close their lips had touched, and the gold had glistened between them, and Alice had said, what did it matter, really? No one would ever imagine them together. No one would ever think two people so different in age and looks would ever . . . So what harm could there be in just saying it was a gift for taking care of her garden and leaving it at that?

And in this way the old Lambry habit of doing things quietly, underhand, was managed. And the hand keeps going round and round the clock, unless—or until—something stops it.

I go on sitting beside them while Pratt and Ellen argue about what they should do next. I wait. Dull and cold and dead-bored. For time can be killed, as much as anything else can. A passing couple considers taking a picture of the antique clock—but then senses something, cold and invisible, and doesn't.

It's odd that, no matter how hard anyone stares at the clock, you can't see the minute when it was decided: who belongs exactly where. You never see the moment the bags are packed and the address given or the place from where the wagon started. You can only see what happens afterwards.

Ellen and Pratt seem to agree and stand and begin walking down Main Street together.

But where does a thing start; how far back do you have to go to see when the gears were all wound?

"Now, isn't this better, before going back to the hospital? Just a moment for something comfortable?" Pratt says.

"I didn't know how tense I was," Ellen says as she leaves her jacket at the coat check in the Main Street Hotel.

"We'll go back this evening together. You need some food and drink in your stomach right now. That's why you're shaking," Pratt says, handing over his own coat.

"Before, when I saw Manoel's family, I wasn't even sure they wanted me there. They looked . . . so broken."

"I think of ghosts as breaking things. Things that want to break us. But we can't let them. And we have to take care of ourselves. A drink, first? Or straight to the restaurant?"

"The restaurant."

The green wallpaper in the Main Street Hotel is rich and fine. When dusk settles outside the dining room, as it does now, and the lights are lit, the mirrors come to life with their walnut and gilt gleaming. They double how many bright lamps there are at all the tables and double the elbows of the waiters carrying the wine back and forth. It's so stylish, nowadays, when you sit down. Nothing like when I was young and alive and had a heartbeat.

At the table, Pratt pours the wine they've ordered into Ellen's glass and says, "Drink. You'll feel better."

But Ellen doesn't lift it. "Manoel. Out there fighting for his life. And we go on. Like nothing's happening."

"Not like nothing is happening—but we do have to go on."

"I can still see his family's faces. Are you—do you have any family, Philip?"

"I was married. Not anymore." I can't see his face very well from my hiding place inside the mirror. He's turned his cheek to one side, as though dodging the question.

"Children?"

"None. My ex said my work was too . . . dirty. She didn't want to put children next to it."

"So she left?"

"She fled, more like."

"I'm sorry." Ellen twists the stem of her glass in front of her. "So sorry, Philip. I didn't mean to go there. I think I'm just trying to distract myself."

"Hope it's working out." He smiles.

"Not really. Does that"—she leans forward, putting both elbows on the table and pointing to his wrist—"does that protect you, in any way? That armor you wear?"

He holds it up. "I'm not sure what you're asking. There's no armor that protects you from everything in life and death, if that's what you want to know."

"But it stops a ghost before the ghost stops you, right?"

"It will do that." He looks at the wall behind Ellen, into the mirror, but I can tell he's only seeing himself. Not me. And now I know what I need to do next.

"My weapon only makes things plainer. Armor doesn't make any-thing easy, I'd say."

"Maybe we should talk about something else." She pulls her hands back toward her.

"Agreed. Something you're comfortable with. Tell me about Benito real estate. This hotel. It's quite a showplace."

They order and talk and in a moment the waiter comes and sets their salads down and grinds pepper to ash for them. So elegant everything is now. Lettuces curled like lace. The table covered in white cloths. No more chickens in the yard. And the lamps all electric.

"It goes back to timber days, this hotel," Ellen is telling Pratt. "The bustle and boom and the rowdy days."

"It's hard to picture it," Pratt says between bites. "As quaint and tidy as everything is now, and quiet."

"You mean normally."

"It almost seems too quiet for a go-getter like you."

"No. It's peaceful. I like that. People come here to get some rest. Like the constable said. They come to get away. Did you text Mr. Dane?" She points to his device.

"I did, and he's of the opinion the damages should be charged to the Lambry estate but he's willing to discuss it. I don't think he fully understands what's happened yet. All he kept insisting was that he wasn't responsible for any pre-existing circumstances. Don't worry. I'll make him understand. Eat. You're not eating."

"I guess I'm not that hungry." She stares at her plate, then away, at the other tables.

"Don't feel guilty. You can't. Your business is to sell houses, not shoulder them."

"You're right about one thing." She still looks around the crowded room. Her back to me, to my eyes, to my interest in every move she makes. "I am a go-getter. I admit that. I want to do well, here."

"Then what, I'll ask again, are you doing buried in this out-of-the-way corner?"

She turns to Pratt again and pushes her salad around on her plate with her fork. "I'm not buried."

"Then you must have been somewhere pretty deep before."

"I was."

"Prison?"

She laughs. A deep, good laugh. Like Franny's. "No! No, not that, not exactly."

"What, then?"

"If you want to know the honest truth, I've—I've started over, in Benito. Or actually, I've just gotten started. After a not so good start. I actually don't like to talk about this much, but—I lost someone. No one who became a ghost, no. My father. And then I had to take care of my mother, who was sick all the time. She didn't have much of a life. So neither did I. When she passed away, I moved out. Until then, everything was just—in limbo. Waiting to get out of the house and study and get some kind of life. So what seems like being buried, to you, feels like fireworks to me. I'm ambitious because I finally get to be ambitious. And I don't want to mess anything up." She looks straight at him. "So now you know my sad little story. What about you? How did you get to be who you are? Did you wake up one day and decide you were going to . . . give people peace?"

"I didn't decide. I had no choice. I was born for this."

Pratt lifts two fingers. The waiter comes and pours more wine. Someone drops a knife, and Pratt turns and raises his eyebrows at a noisy table where some drunken tourists are hooting and clapping.

"Do you remember," he says, turning back to Ellen, "when you were small, maybe after your father died, maybe before, being afraid of things hiding under your bed?"

"Constantly."

"Even though no one had ever suggested to you that you should be afraid of such things? And yet you were."

That's true. I was afraid of such things, too, when I was living, even though I was never told I should be. Not by my father. I just knew. Even though nothing had ever come up out of the dark place and touched me. I knew, too.

"Somehow you knew," Pratt says to Ellen, "without anyone telling you, that the space under your bed wasn't empty."

"Yes. That's true."

"What you knew"—he pauses and drinks—"what you guessed, was that the empty space, alone, was enough to make the thing possible. In some way, without ever talking to a scientist about it, or a cleaner, you knew, in your child's heart, that space is never empty. That space is, in fact, the most creative thing in creation—because it can be filled by anything. But now you're grown up, and that sensitivity to space is gone from you." He stares into the mirror behind Ellen, at me, though he doesn't know it. "As it is from most of us. It disappears when you get older. You lose the feeling for it.

"But I can tell you that the reason you felt something was hiding under your bed, all those years ago, is precisely because it was. It just knew better than to show itself to you."

Or maybe, Philip Pratt, it had a deeper heart than you can imagine.

"Children frighten so easily. And then they scream and give the ghost away. From the beginning—as a child—I never screamed. I peeked and tried to draw it out. Something has always told me that the easiest way to get rid of a thing that scares you is to bring it close. Then, once you see what it is, you can figure out how to crush it."

I go on listening as my anger starts to rise. Crush it, he says. That's the only thing he can imagine doing to something that makes you feel the dark underneath.

"But you have to bring it into close range, first. When I did, when I was very young, I saw that it wasn't a real thing. It wasn't a human being. It was a shell. The mold of something that once held a human being. But a mold that can only hold so much, bear so much, before it breaks. All my life, I've wanted to smash the unbearable. There's a mirror behind you, Ellen, for example, but please don't turn around and look. Hold very still."

"Why?"

"Because I'm looking at neither your reflection nor mine."

Because now I've let my anger shimmer loose. Because I have no choice. Because I'm real. I'm no mold. I'm more than you say I am, hunter. Much more.

Ellen stops breathing.

"This hotel had quite a few ghosts in the past, I imagine?" Pratt asks quickly.

"But they were all cleaned out years ago."

"Then they should have gotten rid of the mirrors, too."

"They wanted . . . period detail."

"Bad idea."

"What does it look like?"

"Vague. Clever. Concealing itself with the bright lights all around."

"What should we do? Should we sound an alarm?"

"No. I believe that's what it wants. It wants to scare us. It wants to alarm everyone here. That's what most manifestations are after. The urge is to terrorize. Stay where you are. Let's just see where things are taking us."

I can move very, very slowly, when I choose to. Even when I'm letting myself feel all my pain, all my anger, I can move so slowly that when I slip out of the mirror and flatten against the glowing wallpaper, like this, Pratt loses me. I'm as thin and stretched as paper itself, burning in the light. I can rise slowly up, along the wall, climbing to the ceiling, till the room filled with tourists is spread out below me, every table, with no idea of what is hanging over them. I flow on my back, along the ceiling, toward the edge of the room, where the largest of the mirrors hangs.

Pratt is standing up now, worried, wondering where exactly I've gone. And now, if only he will do what I want him to do, if only he'll notice— *Yes, yes!* He's coming closer to the grand mirror now, where it stands like an open door behind the brace of tourists who've had too much to drink. I glide inside it, and one of the drunken men, laughing and leaning into another's shoulders, thinks surely he must be imagining the shape—

"What . . .?"

From the mirror, I reach a white arm out toward him, detached.

"Wait, wa—what is—"

Who's to say, when you look into a mirror, who's the ghost and who is real? Why do the living believe, when they see themselves reflected, that they're the solid ones? What if you are nothing, just the mold of a human being, and the truth, the real thing, is *me*—the bright shadow on the other side?

The man, and everyone at his table, screams.

I'm what they need to see. I'm a dead woman, her face eaten away. I'm a dead, old woman, wearing a floating, billowing Chinese robe, with yellow dragons stitched across it, breathing fire, and along with my dead, reaching arms and my floating gown a white fog comes pouring from the mirror, my white hair following after it, and the smoke, a choking smoke, begins to fill the room, rising around me.

Hold fast. Hold fast, until Pratt's seen what I've made.

He's standing, running, close enough now. I sink into the white smoke pooling under the tables and around the waiter's feet, down into that inch of space close to the ground, that narrow space the living are told to cling to if fire fills a room, that gasping space where you're supposed to drop and try to breathe, because it's the very last space where life can hold on, just an inch above the coffin of the earth. As I glide along the floor I hear the living screaming above me, pitiful, drowning in smoke, trying to escape but finding no door because all they see is fear and blindness and all they feel is a white robe tangling their heels.

By the time the medics arrive to help, I'm folded and resting in the velvet of the curtains. Pratt is helpless, telling everyone there was no fire, only smoke, listening to everyone wailing all at once.

It was a woman! She wore a Japanese-looking costume!

She had a face!

She had no face.

It was bone.

There was a laughing!

I saw hair.

Something floating. Before the smoke, the fog.

She tried to touch me.

She brushed against me. It was like she was tearing the skin from the back of my legs.

Everything was gone.

The poor, poor tourists. Still weeping into their hands and screaming. But in a different way, now. They threaten to sue the hotel, the whole village of Benito. They grow angry because it feels better than being afraid. Because when you're angry, you know that you're still alive.

"Was it Alice?" Ellen whispers to Pratt.

"It appears that way."

Pratt turns to the white-faced waiters. "There's nothing more to be done here. There was no fire. Calm these people down and get them back to their rooms. And have all charges sent to me. I'll see they're taken care of." To Ellen, he says, "It's time to get you out of here."

"What are you going to do?"

"My job. Just go to the hospital."

"I can't. It's too much." She seems frozen.

"Then go home. Right now. Get your coat. I'll walk you to your car."

I pass through the hotel doors with them. Pratt ushers Ellen to her car and watches until her glowing taillights grow smaller and smaller beside the rim of the cove. But I stay near; I cling to the veil of the streetlight in a mist. He doesn't move for a long time, looking after her. Our shared Ellen. Then he goes back inside, passes the restaurant, goes upstairs.

In his room on the second floor, he paces. I see him through the parted curtain. His is the finest suite, with dark velvet curtains, over-looking Main Street and the cliff's edge and the swinging, lighted buoys. He won't look, for some reason, in the direction I want him to look, in the direction my smoke, my mist, has blown and now lingers—over the beach and Alice's hideaway. He keeps his head down and braids his fingers across the back of his neck, stretching, tense.

The waves crash and hiss below. The mist rises and throws itself at him, at his lighted window.

The guests are leaving the hotel with their bags, crying.

And neither you nor I, I think, are going to stop what's been started. Are we, Mr. Pratt? Neither one of us can stop being what we've become. Stopping, what would it do? It would wipe from the mirror everything we know we are.

I won't stop. I won't be crushed by you.

And you won't stop. I'm counting on it.

He comes to the parted curtains at last. In the deepening darkness, I glide away, leaving another trail for him to see. I loosen my white skin and let it shimmer and float behind me like a shawl, dancing, playing in the air. He can't mistake it: Alice's robe again, her Chinese dragons slithering in one direction, down to the surf.

Follow me. Follow me.

On the beach, as I float down, the waves toss and change, turning themselves over and over. I set my white feet to the sand and walk toward the corrugated metal hut Alice had Manoel build against the shadow of the cliff. The place she came to when she wanted to be in the wind and storm and fog, but not get caught by them. When she wanted, with her brush, to be the one doing the catching. I look behind me at the glistening path on the shore I've left for him—but Philip Pratt still hasn't come down.

He's stubborn. I give him that. It takes will not to do as you're told.

Or maybe he's just not as brave as I was when I went walking under the moon with Quint. Maybe he's a coward, hiding behind his silver cuff. He says he was born to his life. But no one is born to his life. You only die with it, then wait to see what happens next.

The night my father died, I hid, crying, under the bed in the empty space with the frightening thing that I had always known lived there. It had a voice, the creature who lived under my bed, though I didn't ask whose it was and I kept my fingers away from its hot breath. In Ireland, my Da had told me, they have a name for certain spirits: the *far darrig*. They can act for good or ill. If you meet one, respect it. Listen to it.

Be still, the voice hissed beside me. *Be still, be calm, be brave, be patient, or trust me, even worse will come.*

I am patient. I wait by the door of Alice's hut, though no one comes down to the beach in moonlight. No man who has the same heart, the same will, I had. Have. While the waves go on crashing on their chins, and the moon rolls its punctured wheel high in the sky.

12

Y ou're going to be lonely out at the Point." Frances tucks my damp curls back into my cap. "That's what you're thinking. That you're going to be all alone."

"You don't always know what I'm thinking, Franny."

"I know enough to know when a girl's not as sure of herself as she's acting."

We were alone. Her beau had gone back to his camp upriver, and we were scrubbing the pine floors of the mercantile on a Sunday. It was her job, but I wanted to help. We didn't have much time left together, now. I squatted down next to her in my wet skirt.

We were silent for a time, and then I said, "I'll be no more lonely there than I've been here in town."

"Maybe that was true before you had Quint in your pocket. But what about now?"

"He's not in my pocket, don't say so."

"He was mooning at Mrs. Strype's window enough that his mama caught wind of it."

"We've only walked together. Twice. Since the dance."

The second time had been on Albion Street, when he'd come up behind me while I was looking into a shop window, dreaming of buying a valise, a real suitcase. I'd turned away and seen him, and we'd walked toward the Chinamen's temple and kissed under its lanterns and set all the gossips' tongues to real wagging.

And he'd made his vow again. *I will come see you. I will.*

"Leave now and you won't get a chance to walk with him again." Franny wiped the bridge of her nose. "Although I suppose that's his mama's idea. But is it going to work?"

"Well, I just couldn't say."

She sat up and swatted me and laughed. "So that's what you're up to. Has he made any promises?"

"Only that we'd see each other again. And be honest with each other. And modern. He says he wants to do things in a more modern way."

"Does that mean he's hot to have you?"

I didn't know what to say to that. At times, Quint Lambry didn't seem to me like a boy who was hot enough to shoot a wild panther in cold blood. At others times he was so warm, taking my hand and talking about the future as though it were the sun, and every step we took brought us closer to living on it.

I took the dirty brush out of Franny's hands.

"He's serious, Franny."

"And now you're going to miss him. You'll be lonely. Seven dollars a week or not."

"No, I won't, because you're going to come and see me."

"I don't see how." She sat back on her heels. "*I* don't get free afternoons. You'd have a better chance walking all six miles back to my boardinghouse. Except I won't be there because I'm going to be married soon and live in a cottage all my own on the Russian River. Don't think you're the only one with big plans!"

I put my head down and scrubbed. I didn't like to think, all at once, about Franny being gone. Or to admit to her all the dreams I had of going. That I wanted a life, too. In modern style. I didn't want to admit to her how lonely the village had become for me, in the years since my Da's accident. How I was afraid I would grow old before my time and become one more Finnis plunked down into one more poor grave. That I wanted so much more.

"I don't know that I even want to come back to town," I said.

"Why not?"

"Because Quint's going to come and see me at the Point."

She pushed her sleeves higher on her freckled arms. "Sure. Like a buck out of the woods he'll come. You better watch out or you'll end up with a fawn! Nothing modern about that. I just wish Jimmy would marry me sooner. It's the best thing to settle down as soon as you can with someone you know you can trust and be a good father to your little ones."

That was Franny. Always thinking about babies. A baby, she'd told me once, was the only thing she truly wanted out of this world. A baby who would lie on her chest and coo and curl its little fists at her. But she never wondered whether a baby could kill—as I had killed my own mother.

"And I'll tell you this, Emma Rose Finnis, if you'll listen to me. When you get to Lighthouse Point, you forget all about Quint Lambry and his parents who'll never say yes to you any more than they would to me, and you look around and you see if you can't find a sweet lightkeeper with a snug little cottage to keep you in. And you get yourself married to him and you plant a sweet little garden out front, for all your little ones to crawl around in."

"How?" I laughed. "With the lightkeepers already married, and the first and second assistants already having families, and the head keeper old and away half the time because his wife's got tuberculosis?"

"But things *happen*, Emma." She nodded seriously at me, her eyes wide. "Accidents. And sickness. And men who get lonely. So you be nice to all of them, I'm telling you, and wait to see what time sees fit to bring you. Who's taking you out there?"

"The Lambrys' wagonmaster, at sunrise."

"Right. Because they want to be sure to see the back of you before another day is out. See what I mean?"

That evening a soft, needlepointed valise with rosewood handles appeared outside my door at Mrs. Strype's boardinghouse, along with a note in steep-slanted, boyish handwriting:

For Miss Emma Finnis. From Lambry House.

It wasn't Augustus and Eugenia Lambry who'd sent it, that was for sure. But I told Mrs. Strype it was. Then I packed my shirtwaists into it and my stockings and my two skirts, along with the hairbrush that had belonged to my mother, and a bottle of rose toilet water, and my second pair of boots.

The next morning, the long-faced wagonmaster helped me into the wagon. The sun was just up, and smoke hung over the cove and the idling schooners. I sat up tall, not looking back once, not up at Evergreen Hill, nor down to the docks, nor at anything else behind me that June morning. My only thought was of the path in front of me.

The horses nickered at each other and the driver turned them toward the north road. Yellow-red dust kicked up at our sides, and the stumps of cut trees rolled past us like stepping stones. Once we were clear of the village, the groves of redwood sprang up tall and the wildflowers craned their faces toward the sun, and the day went from slate gray to silver-backed blue. I found myself breathing in and counting my luck. I was young. I had new work. Better work. I owned a traveling valise, fine as a Turkish carpet, riding along next to me. And I had a chance, at last, to better myself, one way or another. I had nothing to do now but sit still and let myself be driven, like a queen. The day turned fine as a parade and the sun turned warm and rode on my shoulder.

I made small talk with the wagonmaster about how many automobiles there were on the road now and how careful a wagon had to be not to be shoved to one side. Before I knew it, the mills had vanished into dust behind us and the woods lost their height, and the land turned scruffy and naked, bending toward the bath of the sea. My driver pointed ahead to where the road twisted.

We topped a rise, and he said, "In a while you'll begin to see it."

We drove with the sun on our right cheeks.

And then there the Point was. A handle of land, thrusting out above the sea. At its end, like a spoon balanced over the edge of a cup, a circle of headland, and on top of it a cluster of white houses, each with a dark, red-shingled roof. And at the very edge of the Point, the lighthouse itself.

It looked lonely. Franny was right.

The wagonmaster dropped his wheels into a lane and moved us slowly under ragged cypress and over deep ruts. He explained supplies had no other road to come down but this steep one, in good weather and bad, to bring coal for the coal building, oil for the lamp, and metals for the blacksmith's shop. The lightkeepers had a great deal to do, he said, to keep the light going. But he supposed it kept them busy, having to do everything for themselves, all alone, and no one else to count on if things went bad in a storm.

We came out of the trees and onto the handle of land. My eyes went first to the biggest of the houses, shuttered in the distance.

"That one's for the head lightkeeper. And that one's for his first assistant." The wagonmaster pointed over the ears of the horses. "Now, the building attached to the light isn't one anybody lives in. It's called the signal house, and that's where they muster the horns and run the lamp. Here you see the coal house and the smithy, and the oil house and the pump house, and here"—he turned the wagon toward the first, smallest house—"is where you'll find Mrs. Folde."

The house and garden looked unready, with moving crates still tipped on their sides and straw slouching out. But white smoke curled from the chimney, and the picket fence was freshly painted, and sunlight bounced off an unshuttered window. I spotted a woman's face behind it.

I had high hopes Mrs. Folde would be a better employer than Mrs. Strype. I hoped she would let me do my work without complaints, and maybe even thank me, now and then, for doing it. I hoped that maybe being all alone, on a lonely spit of land, might make someone more grateful for help.

I looked again at the window, and the face was gone.

The wagonmaster waited for me as I went into my servant's cottage, behind the second assistant lightkeeper's house, and lit the kerosene lamp. I found a bed made with a quilt and a chest at the foot of it. Across, a washstand with a good mirror hanging over it. A coal stove in the corner. It was better than anything I was used to.

I set my new valise down on the quilt, then turned and came out again with coins in my hand.

"No! You don't have to pay me, Miss Emma." The wagonmaster shook his long chin. "Mr. Lambry takes care of everything."

"But this is from me. Take it for a thank you."

"Keep it in case you need a ride back into town. I can fetch you back, if you ever want me to. Just send word. If you get lonely. Good luck to you, now, Miss Emma."

He tipped his felt hat and clucked to his horses and swung in a wide circle across the short tufted grass and away.

When he was gone, I went back inside. I folded my clothes and my nightgown inside the chest. I put my shoes beside the bed. I put my mother's hairbrush on the washstand. The stove's cold chimney reached in a crooked black arm through the ceiling. There was no coal yet in the hod.

I pulled back a pair of thick gingham curtains from the one window, and the room felt warmer. I blew out the light. On the sill, someone had left the head of a tiny animal, a bird's skull, and a sprig of dried wildflowers.

I turned away to brush my hair in the mirror and pin it up again. My face was windblown from the drive, and the cleft in my chin had turned deep red, like a gash.

I straightened my shirtwaist, flung my shawl over my shoulders, and started for the Folde house.

The second assistant lightkeeper, the wagonmaster had explained to me, always had the smallest house, no matter what the size of his family. The second assistant was the "lowest" man at the Point. Well, never as low as a maid, I thought. Although now I could think of myself as a housekeeper, which was something, I remembered, as I walked toward the back stoop and saw at the screen door the face I took to be Mrs. Folde's. A moment later, the door was swung open with one arm, and then I saw a woman so big with the baby growing inside her she could hardly keep upright. Her narrow face was hot and her back tilted.

"Finnis?"

"Yes, ma'am. Emma Rose Finnis."

"Come up the steps, here, please, will you. I can't come down."

Her hand in mine was soft as butter. Her lips looked cracked and tired.

"I'm sorry I didn't come out before. It's hard for me to get around, these days. The doctor says I might have another set of twins on the way."

Another, did she say? "Then I'm glad I'm here to help, ma'am."

"The children have already had their breakfasts and are out. They should be having their baths, but it takes too much out of me."

"That's why I'm here, Mrs. Folde. To assist you," I said again, smiling at her, hoping she'd return the smile. She didn't.

"Come in then."

I followed her into the kitchen where she braced herself for balance against the white-washed walls.

"If you'd like, Mrs. Folde, I could give the children their baths as soon as they come back?"

"No. You've just gotten here. And I do like to tend to the children myself. Just not so early in the day. You don't know how things go on here yet. Your work," she said, letting go of the white wall and reaching for the pie cupboard, "will be mostly in the kitchen. And seeing to the rest of the house, of course. And the garden, if I can get one going." She opened the cupboard, showed me the tins. "When I'm over the worst."

"Yes, ma'am."

"But the *children*," she said, grimacing, "are my responsibility. Every mother knows that. Over here, this is our dining parlor." She opened a swinging door to a small, snug room crowded with a round table and six chairs. She stared at the bright lace curtains, batting her eyes like someone trying to stand and sleep at the same time.

"Mrs. Folde," I said quickly, "won't you please sit down? And let me get you some milk?"

"The children need the milk. There are five of them."

Five. A lucky family, then. "Where are they now, Mrs. Folde?"

"With their father. Out on the headland, checking the weather. They'll be dirty all over with grass and mud when they come back. He'll send them straight to me, because we have to keep everything neat for—" She seemed to wince. "And then they'll hate me for putting them straight in the tub. It's the same struggle every day. But we have to keep organized, the head keeper says. We never know when we'll have an inspection. This room is the front parlor."

She went in and leaned against an overstuffed chair with a knitting basket tucked against its cushions. The coal grate burned close by.

"A light station is like a ship. A ship," she repeated. "It has to be run tightly, my husband says. Although for some keepers' wives, it's easier than for others. The first assistant has a larger house and only one child. And don't you find it's always easier to keep a house if you have more room in it, and not less?"

I thought of the boardinghouse, all of the rooms to clean, all the linen to wash, and couldn't say so.

"Well. It *is*." She closed her eyes and opened them again. "Your job will be to help me keep things orderly. Because we never know when the head will come back or the state lighthouse commission will visit."

"Yes, Mrs. Folde."

"You'll cook and clean according to our schedule. We adhere to a strict timetable here. Around the clock." She nodded, and I thought how much her face looked like a china doll's, one that's been tipped back too many times so that its eyes close when they should be open and open when they should close. I didn't think she could be ten years older than me, but she looked so much older, burdened by her belly and her heavy skirt.

"We live by the clock here. With the head away so much, and only Mr. Folde and Mr. McHenry to see to the fueling and the winding, we . . . we get our fair share. Mr. Folde is often tired. Which is why we need privacy and rest in the afternoons. You'll be expected to leave the house then for an hour and a half. You can take your break after I've put the children down for their nap. Then you can go to your room, or go for a walk, or do as you please. That's your free time. Try to enjoy it."

"Yes, ma'am."

"Because for the rest you'll be doing the washing, ironing, mending, cooking, sweeping, coal-hauling and taking the ash out . . . But you *won't* mend Mr. Folde's shirts, because he's picky about that. I'll see to those. And the lampshades and curtains always need dusting, out here, with all the sand, and the dishes and silver need polishing, to keep the spots off, and the rugs need airing already, though we haven't been here two weeks.

"And—about tea time. Sometimes you'll serve tea but not with the good tea set, the one we inherited from Mr. Folde's family. It's very old," she said nervously, "and he'll fire you if you break even a saucer, as he did our last girl, at Eureka Point. And then"—she looked at me with her strained eyes—"where would I *be*?"

She led me into the front hall, holding her stomach with one hand and with the other lifting her netted hair, soggy as wet toast, from her neck. She moved her hands down to her back. "There's no room here in the house for you, though I wish there could be. You're in what used to be the grain cottage."

"It's fine, Mrs. Folde."

"You probably saw that the children put a few old things in there, on the sill. The twins, Roger and Timothy, are six. Theresa is five. Christina is four and Alva is three. Elizabeth was two when the croup took her. The children miss her and pretend she's still alive and living out there, in the grain room. Please don't indulge their morbid ways. And don't let them make a sister out of you, Emma. Your work is with me. We have no time for child's play. There are more ships sailing past, every day. And there are fogs and storms and nights that are worse for a moon, instead of better, although I don't see how, and the lamp mechanism has to be wound every two hours by Mr. McHenry or Mr. Folde, and the oil filled and kerosene put to the horns, to say nothing of all the repairing . . . And the weather report to make, and all of us answerable to both the head and the commission. It's—Oh. Here are the children." She backed away toward the staircase, away from the front door, as if to brace herself.

They poured into the house like weeds riding on a tide and stopped and stared at me—two identical boys, thin, their chests heaving; three little, pale girls with pigtails. The children were all blond and wan, like Mrs. Folde. The older ones introduced themselves politely, and then Mrs. Folde hurried them all upstairs, while the man I took to be Mr. Folde shut the door and checked the hour on his heavy steel pocket watch. He snapped it shut and then held out his hand to me.

"You're our new girl?"

"Yes, sir. Emma Rose Finnis."

"Wonderful! Thank you for coming all the way from town." He took a step backward, and I saw that he looked young, younger than his wife, with a downy mustache and lashes as soft as a girl's. But also with that strain around the eyes. Though he was dressed well, in the lightkeeper's coat, he smelled of oil and sweat.

"Mrs. Folde explained to you how things run here? Yes? Good. Then you know she's going to keep you busy until the afternoon. But then you'll have a rest. That's the hour when we observe what we call 'family peace.' Before the next shift begins. You might like to take a walk then." He smiled, and the smile almost reached his lashed eyes. "There's a little path that runs down to a small beach when the tide is out. I often go there myself. To take a constitutional." He reached up to stroke his stiff collar, and I thought his Adam's apple looked tight, as if it wanted to bolt from his neck. "Well, I hope you'll be happy here,

Emma. I think we all hope that. I need to get back to work, now. Have a good morning."

That afternoon I covered my neck with my shawl and followed the path that ran along the keepers' houses and away toward the lighthouse. The sun was sharp as tin. The first assistant's house was only a short walk from the Foldes'. With its many unshuttered windows it was much larger, it was true, than the house I'd just spent all day cleaning and dusting. It had a windswept garden and a cow tied in the side yard and a piece of stubborn lawn growing out front. The head lightkeeper's shut-tered house, farther along the path, was even bigger, though of course still nothing like the Lambry House, nothing grand, really, no more than a shop owner in town might manage. Beyond the head keeper's place was a space of long, flat, green turf, and then the block of the signal house and the towering light itself, its beacon swimming high up in its glassy cage. I stopped to look up but didn't come any closer, because Mr. Folde had warned me not to bother Mr. McHenry when he was on the watch. The light tower stood attached to the rectangular signal house by a slanted, red-tiled roof, but still somehow looked as though it were a thing apart, all on its own.

I swung around and walked the rough ledge of headland and looked down at the waves hammering one another. I stood there with my shawl tightly around me, and from time to time I craned my neck back at the lighthouse and saw what appeared to be a small man scuttling around its railed walk. When he went inside and I could see him no more, I walked away along the cliff, as far as I could along the edge. I sat down for a while with my back to a fallen cypress log, staring out at the open sea, wondering when Quint Lambry might come to see me. I sat till the bark gouged at my back. I had no timepiece, but the sun had moved over to the west and it was colder than before.

Time to go back, I told myself, *and tidy up and get ready to make the Foldes their dinners. Pretty soon I'll get used to all of this. Quint will come when he comes, if he comes, and if he doesn't, well, there's still seven dollars a week and a quiet room with its own stove and space to run around in, if I want to, and nothing to see me and frown or point at me, except a gull's beak above me in the wind.*

It was on my way back, while I was hurrying through the side yard of the Folde house between the empty crates, that I heard what sounded like a sharp cry. I froze, worrying that one of the children had fallen. But when I stopped to look through one of the lace-curtained windows I could see it was only poor Mrs. Folde, bent, holding onto the arms of her overstuffed knitting chair, while Mr. Folde stood behind her and tried to lift her heavy skirt. She turned and pushed him away, and he stepped back as though stung.

I hurried the rest of the way to my quarters and shut the door. It wasn't my business, I told myself, what married people wanted to do during their "family peace" time. But I hadn't liked the way Mrs. Folde's cry had sounded chipped, like a cup being bitten, or the way Mr. Folde had fallen away, stumbling, embarrassed, feeling for his balance in the air and finding nothing in all that tidied room to hang onto.

13

Why didn't you find out?" I hear Ellen ask through Pratt's telephone. "Go after it? Follow it down to the beach?"

"Because a hunter isn't the one who takes the bait. And the dead should never be in charge."

"So what now?"

"Will you stay home today?"

"Yes."

"Good. Keep away. I'll keep going."

Pratt's wearing sturdier clothes this morning. Boots, a black muffler, and a wool jacket with buttons. He's shaved and his skin is smooth now and younger-looking. He isn't in a hurry, finishing his breakfast in the hotel dining room again, where the waiters have covered all the mirrors.

But if he's so sure of himself, then why didn't he come to me last night, I wonder? Why should a hunter worry whether a ghost is in charge or not?

He leaves the restaurant. Early on a Sunday morning, Benito's streets are empty. The tourists who haven't run away are still clutching their pillows in their beds. The faithful and trusting haven't risen yet to walk to

St. Clements Church. The constable's deputies are still in their kitchens, drinking their coffees. The first of the shell-collectors have only begun their grave robbing on the beach. A visiting fisherman, curious, tries the door to Alice's hut but finds it locked.

Pratt's boots cross the dampness of Main Street and stop at the edge of the cliff. He looks down at the waves and then turns and looks back at his hotel window, then down again—as if measuring where my trail led. He sees the rail put at the top of the path to the surf so that the tourists can hold safely onto it on the way down. He grabs the wood, tests it.

The beach waits, skirted with foam and seaweed. I wait for him, too, in the cold sea, trailing my white skirt in the foam, like a piece of it. He's made it down to the tide line now. He hops over a strand of kelp and looks to his left and then to his right and sees, in the shadows he couldn't see from on top, the place where Alice's shack has been anchored, so far back against the cliff it's in a kind of cave.

The waves tumble and push at his side. The clouds, high and far away, chase at nothing. He trudges through the wet sand, in no hurry, neither slow nor fast, with his hands in his warm pockets. Pratt the patient. Pratt the calm. Well, two can play at that game.

At last he's a few feet from her door. The hut leans back, built by Manoel to take the wind. It sits on a wedge of rock safe above the tide but its metal shutters are beginning to rust.

I whisper, soft as a feather falling from a nest above:

Come inside, now.

No other sound but the clanging of the buoys.

So I say again, mimicking Alice, her words to Manoel:

Come, come to me now.

"Be patient," Pratt whispers back. "Everything in good time."

He's heard, at least.

He draws closer and sees I've unhooked the padlock from the door. He twists the band at his wrist. I know that preparation. I've seen it before. I stay safely back, outside, while he shoves the door inward, with a huff, and goes in, ducking as a trickle of sand falls on him from the roof. Now he can see her lonely easel and the skeleton of her chair left in the corner. But he can't see what I've hidden just behind the door. Not yet.

His breathing comes more quickly.

"So. What is it, now, you wanted to show me? I would have chased you last night but you looked so white and weak."

Pratt the trickster. But I won't be tricked or goaded. Not like that poor boy in the mine. I stay cold in the sun. He tries lifting his hand to his chest, in that gesture he makes that's purely his own. I've seen no other hunter trust his beating heart more than his weaponry. It's a brave touch, I'll give him that. But it's his heart I must somehow break, or trick. That buoy filled with blood and hope.

In a moment, now, he'll find it. The gift I've hidden, my fresh plan, waiting just by his side. The winking buoy my heart has dragged in for him, from the sea.

"Mr. Dane?" Pratt, my gift in his right arm, is hurrying up the steps from the beach and speaking urgently into his device. "Philip Pratt. Yes. How is Mrs. Dane? Good. Good. Glad to know it. A progress report for you: contact has been made . . . Yes. It's excellent news. No, it's better if you don't know too many details. For your own peace of mind. But you're going to need to pay me a while longer for my services, I'm afraid. This is a more complex case than we anticipated . . . Yes. A new development. Circumvention. I've just texted you an explanation . . . Circumvention, it means the ordinary rules don't hold. A getting around boundaries . . . Exactly. Just be patient. I know it's difficult, but you have to imagine we're being led through a kind of dance right now. What we don't know yet is if we're being led toward a conclusion or away from it. All I can tell you is that we've been given a kind of key. And now the trick will be to understand it . . ."

He's risen to the top of Main Street, and looks eagerly to his right and left.

"Yes. It could be a genuine effort to communicate with us. Or the whole point could be to confuse and mislead. Because—let me finish. Because some of them actually *want* to be found out. Others, no. And others might want to be found and laid to rest, but the part of them that wants that peace is hidden from them . . . Exactly. They don't know that they want to be found out. It's a delicate matter . . . Yes. I'll keep updating you on progress. I'm doing some research right now that should— Because that's—All right. Understood. Soon."

How easily he's taken my bait.

Pratt plants his feet and looks down and presses his device, sliding his thumb over it again and again, making its pictures flip like a deck of cards he's sorting through quickly. At last he seems to find the card he's looking for.

"Perfect. Here on Main."

He hoists my gift higher into his arms, the bright blue ball of glass I've brought in from the sea still wrapped in its criss-crossed pattern of rope, and makes his way carefully across the street toward old Hannan's shop. Of all the bright things that tourists like to buy when they come to Benito, it's our bits of glass and crystal hanging from twinkling strings they favor the most. Mr. Hannan likes to tell people it's like taking the sea home with you—and who wouldn't want to do that? He's behind his windows now, moving among his wares, getting ready to unlock the door to his shop, the Crystal Palace. He turns his sign around: Open For Business. It's a good business, like every other one on Main. Mr. Hannan inherited it from his father before him, who kept it full of not only chimes but hand-blown lighthouses and delicately masted glass schooners until he passed from old age, going without a whimper up to Evergreen.

Pratt sees the sign turn and walks even more excitedly, careful to balance what I've given him.

Inside, brightness, brightness everywhere. I go into the shop just after Pratt and blend in with the crystals and sea glass dangling from the ceiling. So early, we're the only customers, and so light and sparkling is Hannan's that I can move around easily. The flutter and sway of the chimes seems only a natural dance with the rush of air blown in from the street.

"Good morning, can I help you?" white-haired Hannan says from behind the glass counter he's cleaning with a soft cloth.

"Yes, good morning. Any chance you're the owner here?"

"Arnie Hannan. Welcome to the Crystal Palace. Wow. That is something you have there!"

"I was hoping you'd say so." Pratt nods, friendly. "It's why I came in. Your website says you appraise antique glass. And I think this is . . . old? I found it down on the beach."

He didn't find it down at the beach. I dredged it up, its glass scratched and gouged but still clear, and put it in Alice's shack, along with all her feathers and sand dollars and bits of dead reef.

"I hope you can take a look and help me, tell me exactly what it is." Pratt wrestles my trick onto the velvet mat on Hannan's counter. "It's some sort of float, right?"

"Yep. With the old hemp netting still wrapped around it. Very rare these days." Hannan wipes his hands on his cloth.

"I was guessing right then."

"This here is an antique glass fishing float, Mr. . . .?"

"I'm Phil."

"Lucky you, Phil! And a beauty, too. Well, why don't we get her a bit more centered on the . . . Now. There you go. Okay, so we'll want to be extra careful with something like this. We just don't see a lot of these around here, not anymore. This is a big one. A ten-incher." He turns it like a globe in his wrinkled hands. "We call this blue-green color aquamarine. See all the scratches all over it? That's how you know it's not a fake, that it was out there for a long, long time. No seal"—he murmurs as he tips it to one side, to look at its flattened bottom—"on this glass button, here, which would usually tell us where it was made. They call it the button where the glassblower cuts it loose and you get this sort of smooshed place where they stamp the mark of origin. Nothing here, but I'm guessing China. I can't get over there's still this wet hemp rope around it. That's awesome. There's water inside, too, a lot of it. That's what's making it so heavy. It must be cracked somewhere—although I don't see where. That's odd. Water inside's awfully dark. Did you find it near the mouth of the river, by any chance? Where it empties into our cove? That might account for the blood-red color."

"Just . . . on the beach."

"Imagine that." Hannan shakes his white head. "Intact right on the beach. Haven't had that happen since the days my father owned this shop. And never with netting still attached to it, like this. That should've rotted away a long time ago. But nature's a funny thing. It might've been buried, somehow, and just washed up." He strokes my gift lovingly, then pulls his hand away. "Um—you say you just found it this morning?"

"On the beach, near an old shack. How old would you say this float is?"

Hannan stares down, suddenly nervous. "If you found it down near that shack . . . that used to belong to an old woman around here by the name of Lambry. She used to collect things—or at least, people used to see her do it. She was a Lambry, so nobody got close to—or messed with . . . It's a name that used to mean something in this town. No buildings were even supposed to be allowed anymore down in the cove, not after the docks were torn down. But Alice got it done."

"The float?" Pratt says, pushing him. "Its approximate age?"

"Classic glass float from a long-line net. Would've been a ton of these, maybe even upwards of a hundred, threaded through the hemp to make a big fishing cast. Likely floated with the current from China. Or Japan. A hundred years old or more, I'd say. Before 1920, that's for sure. The nets used to break away from the fishermen, and then these balls, they'd float around with the current or get tangled up in propellers. It drove the captains wild. My father said sometimes a whole string of these would float into the cove—but usually only just broken pieces. It's not easy for something like this to last. You see how thick and heavy the glass is? It isn't the thickness. It's the circumference. And the quality of the glass itself. It's got be the right size and the right strength to keep enough air trapped inside it. But what's troubling me, is, this one must have a crack in it somewhere, but the water isn't trickling out anywhere . . . Maybe a seep-crack? Don't know. I do know people, collectors, who'd pay a good price for this. What I don't know is, is it me, or is there something else inside it?"

Pratt rests his palm on either side of the blue ball, steadying it. "Before 1920. Thank you. That's very helpful."

"I could swear something's inside the glass along with the mud. Am I going blind?" He crouches. "Do you see it? Something bobbing around in there? It looks like—like—a flower—" He straightens up. "Alice Lambry's shack, you said?"

"Yes."

"I guess that's all I have to say about this." The shopkeeper backs away.

"Mr. Hannan, are you all right?"

"No. It might be best if you take her—I mean it—away with you, now. Before it breaks, you know."

"Do you know something about Alice Lambry? I'm here to—"

"I think I know why you're here now. And I've done all I can for you. I don't want to do anymore. Okay?"

"Did you know Alice?"

"We all knew her, and some of us even tried to help her, like poor Manoel. But no good deed goes unpunished, seems like."

"At least let me pay you for your time." Pratt shoves his coat aside and digs for his wallet.

"No. I don't profit from the dead!" Hannan says loudly, as if he wants the street, the whole village—and the Lambry House—to hear. "My family never has!"

Pratt stops, uncertain, and takes his money back. "I understand, Mr. Hannan. But don't worry. You aren't implicated in my work. Only I am. Thank you very much for your time. You've been very, very helpful." He lifts my beautiful gift into his arms and presses it against his chest again.

"Be careful," the old man blurts. "It is a precious thing you have there. Rare. I didn't mean to suggest it isn't . . . worth . . ."

"Thank you," Pratt says. "I understand."

At the Lambry House, the gate is still tangled with yellow tape with the word CAUTION written on it again and again. It flutters in the breeze, and the flowers in the arbor weave, as if ducking all the trouble.

Pratt unwinds the tape and goes through the gate and strides back into the column of roses where he stood on that very first day he came to me, beside the yellow rose I called out to scratch his skin. Alice's thorned rose.

He holds the beautiful glass float with the rose inside it and studies the arbor. He smiles. There. I can tell. He's got it. Ellen, and Hannan, too, told him: Alice collected sea glass. He's seen for himself how she painted with colored water and framed her creations in glass. And Manoel told him how much Alice tended to the roses. It's plain to him, now, what rolls and bobs around in the red water.

When one of the yellow petals floats against the glass, it looks just like the flat of a hand, doesn't it, Mr. Pratt? Pressing, begging to be let out. So why don't you let it?

Pratt shakes the buoy like a toy and watches the cut rosebud swirl and whirl like a dancer.

Hannan's right: it's a precious thing I've made for you, Mr. Pratt, and very rare. Not just any ghost could do it . . .

"Talented," Pratt whispers. "But understand and hear me, my friend. Nothing dead, no matter how interesting or difficult, is worth keeping."

He lifts my gift high over his head, to the roof of the arbor, and before I can close my eyes he smashes it down on the flagstone path, crushing it. As I wanted him to.

I feel no anger. None. I don't let it come. Still, it hurts so much, year after year, keeping the pain inside, keeping it from breaking free. I don't know how I manage it. I feel lightheaded, watching this man do what I've asked him to do, because what I've asked him to do is learn from breaking a beautiful thing I made. Was this what Alice felt, I wonder, when she made her paintings and put them behind glass to protect them, so they wouldn't hurt or fade?

Pratt picks up the limp, dripping bud between his fingers, and steps around the puddle and shards he's made of my gift, which he now must believe was Alice's way of taunting him, and raises his hand. He holds the bud up to the vine that earlier cut him. He lifts it and sees where it's been sliced, sees how the angle of the cut on the stem matches the angle of the cut to the wet flower. So easy it is, to put two and two together, if you want to. So easy to give a man what he wants, as my Da said. As long as you don't care what gets mangled in the bargain.

Pratt reaches into his jacket pocket, pulls a clear bag out, drops my rose into it, and zips it shut, sealing it again, this time in his own way.

14

At the Point, I did my very best work for the Foldes. I scrubbed their china and polished their silver. I dusted and oiled and rubbed the mahogany sideboard in the dining room. I filled the lamps with kerosene, cleaned the grates, hauled out the trash. I cooked the meals while Mrs. Folde collapsed in her sewing chair, fanning herself with her knitting. When it got too warm, I was allowed to open the kitchen's screen door and then I could look out to see if Quint was coming toward me through the cypress grove, as he'd said he would. After a week, nothing. I turned back to kneading the bread.

I did everything Mrs. Folde asked of me. I stayed clear of the children, though they would come and ask me if I'd seen their sister in the grain room—I hadn't, she was never there—and stare at the cleft in my chin and run off again. Behind the house, I washed their soiled clothes, hanging up the ghosts of their tiny bodies to dry, then took the stiffened arms and legs down and brought them to the ironing board. Mrs. Folde couldn't manage an iron; her condition was too delicate. Yet she was nervous about Mr. Folde's shirts and would snatch them away from me if I offered even to sew on a button.

She gave the children their lessons in the morning after they came back from their walk with their father and, in the afternoon, knitted in the parlor until she fell asleep. Each day her stomach dropped lower on her body, like timber ready to unload, yet she still had two months to go. She was sure now it was twins. She felt two people kicking against each other, she said.

"I don't see how God could ask a woman to bear this twice," she moaned.

One day the ironing was finished, and I'd stepped out just for a breath of fresh air, and there was Quint, coming from the high road on a white-blazed black horse. I put up my hand to guide him toward the house. I tried to look peaceful and unsurprised. I'd thought he might come in one of the Lambrys' new automobiles and had imagined us riding around without a care in the world, showing off to all the wagons. Instead he was wearing his riding best, his hat wide-brimmed and his boots shining. I tried to keep my heart from surging, looking at him. It drew up anyway, like a wave.

Mrs. Folde and the children were already upstairs taking their naps. Mr. Folde was coming from the direction of the coal house and met Quint's horse before I could. I went inside and wiped my hands on my apron and hung it up and came back out.

Quint had already tied his mount to the fence and was busy making conversation with Mr. Folde. Mr. Folde turned around, his pale brows a little knitted under his lightkeeper's cap. I could tell he was seeing me in a new way.

"It seems you have a visitor, Emma."

"Yes. It's nearly my break-time. I thought we'd take a walk."

"Mr. McHenry is in the signal building. Have him show our guest— your guest—the lens."

"Thank you." That was a surprise. I hadn't even seen the lighthouse myself, yet. "I will."

"Well. Have a good afternoon. It's our family peace time, Emma, as you know." He tipped his cap.

As he turned toward the porch, he looked up, and I looked with him, to see Mrs. Folde's wan face at the second-story window, staring out longingly.

I went up to Quint's horse and carelessly stroked its neck.

"So. You've come," I said.

"Glad?"

His eyes smiled at me. Less shy each time we met. *He likes being with me*, I thought. *Or is it that he likes pushing his family to one side and cutting his own whip?*

"I asked Mr. Folde's permission to come once a week and walk with you."

"Mr. Folde's? Isn't it my permission you need to ask?"

"I thought I already did."

"It's lucky you did."

"I don't think Folde knew what to make of my asking him."

"A Lambry asking anyone's permission. What's the world coming to?"

"I think it's important people be treated equally." He looked down at his boots, flinching.

I said, "Let's walk, then."

We passed over the fits and starts of salt grass and strolled by the McHenrys' bright house. The McHenrys' garden was bigger than the Foldes', so much so they could grow standing crops. They were hardworking people—Mrs. McHenry digging daily in her herbs, and Mr. McHenry keeping mostly to the lighthouse—and they adored their little boy, who was rosy and fat.

"Nice bit of land." Quint nodded. "No timber, though."

We passed the head keeper's house, deserted except for the staked goat keeping the lawn short.

"I've hardly seen them at all," I said. "It's so quiet here."

"Do you like it, Emma?"

"It's all right."

"I was hoping you wouldn't."

I laughed. "That's not very nice."

"You know what I mean." He kicked at a clump of turf and stared off into the distance, to where the coast bent its way toward Fort Kane. "You see that strip of timber, over there? Uncut? That's the sort of land I'd like to have for my own mill one day. When I come into my own money. In three years. Unless my father agrees to help me sooner than that. In which case all kinds of things would be possible," he said, drawing closer.

"And how are Mr. and Mrs. Lambry?"

"Mother thinks everyone's becoming savages, dancing the foxtrot. Father is weighing where to put his investments next. I don't think he'll leave me hanging on much longer. There's no family pride in that."

"Ho there!" a man's voice shouted.

Mr. McHenry, coming out from the signal building ahead of us, holding his pudgy, gloved hand up.

"That's the second assistant," I explained.

"Hullo, hullo!" Mr. McHenry called. He must have seen, from the lighthouse, Quint's fine horse, his fine clothes. He'd never come running out that way for me. "We have a visitor!"

The men's hats were tipped.

"Come up, come up!" Mr. McHenry said excitedly. He was short and stout and didn't look as young as Mr. Folde. His eyes were thick with brown wrinkles from staring out to sea. I had planned on liking him, but he'd seen me walking on the cliffs for days now and never so much as a *you must see* had come from him, as he was saying now to Quint. Sometimes I'd pass him sitting with his wife and their boy, picking rosemary in the garden, and I thought Mrs. McHenry watched me with a wary eye and was happy when I kept on walking. The Point wasn't, after all, one *sweet little family*, as Mrs. Lambry had said it would be. It was more like a little island with two tiny wild tribes, each guarding against the other.

But now that I had a Lambry with me, I was taken right in.

"How many steps is it to the top, Mr. McHenry?" Quint asked.

"One hundred and three. But you won't feel them, not at your age," he joked, though he seemed a little nervous. He opened a low, black door and we passed into an all-white room filled with what looked to me like oil casks resting on their sides. Mr. McHenry explained these were the siren compressors.

"I see." Quint nodded. "And how do you keep the lamp running?"

"Vapor oil. We have the signal flash set at ten-second intervals. That's the Point's own signature, Mr. Lambry, so ships won't confuse us with any of the other light stations hereabouts. Now, the spinning action itself, see here, we keep turning by means of a clockwork." Mr. McHenry bustled around like a proud housewife. "See this chain going down? All the way through the hole in the foundation of this building, you see that?" He made us lean over the hole that yawned into the blackness below us. A chain disappeared inside it, oozing with grease.

"It has to be so long to keep the turns going. There's a weight on the end. We crank the chain onto this drum, see, every two hours. We go in shifts. That keeps the lamp spinning."

"But isn't that"—Quint wrinkled his nose—"awfully primitive and . . . dull?"

Mr. McHenry's pudgy eyes widened, shocked. "If you were a light-keeper, Mr. Lambry, you'd know that we *like* that sort of constancy. A lightkeeper wants everything to be predictable. Every day, every hour, the same. That's the key. And there's plenty of other interesting work for us to do, to keep us busy. Here, for instance, is the kerosene we use to keep the engines and compressors primed. And there are always import-ant repairs to make—here's where we keep our tools. It's work enough, I can tell you, for the two of us, me and Mr. Folde, with the head keeper away on his travels. Mind your step now, and we'll take the spiral stair for the top."

Like a daisy wheel, up we went. Round and round, clanging on the steps. I'd never climbed so high, turned so tightly. It made the heart pound. Mr. McHenry led the way, and I followed, Quint going last, like a gentleman. We ducked through a small hatch at the top and . . . bright-ness, brightness everywhere! We were standing inside a circle made of glass. It was like floating in a miracle. All around us the sky stretched, and the flapping white wings of the sea carried the eye to the horizon. Below us, the land fell far away and looked broken, only chunks of stone, and the sun came from all directions as though it were standing still.

The lamp's lens, above us, it was so strange. It looked like an oys-ter made of crystal, whirling. Mr. McHenry was telling Quint its beam could be seen as far out as fifteen miles. He walked us all the way around the base of it inside the house, so we could marvel at its clearness and steadiness. He said it was made in England, a Fresnel, the best kind in the world.

"Now see here, this is actually a glass door, and you can step outside on the walkway and see what a time we have keeping her painted and fresh."

This time Quint went out first. I followed and the wind hit and filled my chest and skirt. My boots echoed on the slick metal walk, and I made straight for the cold rail. It was freshly painted. I looked down over it and saw, below us and to one side, the signal building surrounded by soft tufts of grass and to the other, the open cliffs and the spray spewing over rocks, far down, in cartwheels.

Mr. McHenry went back inside the lamp house, embarrassed, saying he had spotted a smudge he didn't like on one of the panes.

"It's so quaint." Quint shook his head. "Two men pulling on a chain to make a light go around. There must be a better model."

"I like it. It's simple." I liked how easy it was to understand.

"Simple, yes. Childish, even. Just wind it up. Like a dancing toy. Maybe we should dance?" He reached to put his arm around my waist.

"He'll see you!"

"Do you care? I don't."

He swung me around, foxtrotting me backward around the walkway, lightly.

"Are you afraid being up so high, Emma?"

"No. I'm not." I smiled up at him.

The walkway was slippery with the mist and new paint. But I wasn't afraid. The rail was high enough. The sun only blinded you because it was perfect. The perfect day.

"Me neither. I've got you," Quint said.

"And I've got you."

And then, suddenly, Quint's elbow dropped, and mine. I didn't understand it. Where were our feet? My heels tried to dig in and found nothing but air. My chin was falling forward and my chest hit wet metal—I saw my hands clawing, scraping in front of me, like an animal's paws I didn't recognize—and there was nothing to hold onto and my skirt went over the edge and I thought, *how can it be that I'm only eighteen. I'm only eighteen, and this is the end. So this is how it happens—so easily. A foot in the wrong place. That's all. You were holding tightly onto his arm. But it's nothing. All the longing that you feel inside you? It's nothing. We're nothing. The truth, right underneath, all the time.*

Mr. McHenry's arm reached over Quint's shoulder. "I have her! We have you! Pull yourself up, Miss Finnis! Pull yourself up! Holy Jesus!"

I heard another sound. It was the blood in my head. Pounding.

I kicked and fought and wriggled my waist onto the platform. Only then could I turn and pull in my knees.

Mr. McHenry collapsed to the metal walkway beside Quint. Their faces were both so white, they looked like marble.

"She's all right." Quint swallowed. "She's all right!"

"Holy Jesus. As good as gone." Mr. McHenry shook.

"No! She *wasn't*! It was—if this was only—A better handrail!" Quint barked. "If only this place were properly up to date and maintained—"

"You're not going to say"—the keeper grew even paler—"this was *my* fault?"

"I am saying—"

"Stop," I shouted. And felt the hair on my head, and the pulse in my scalp. "Stop."

Quint held me. Close.

"We should, we ought to," Mr. McHenry babbled, "get you downstairs?"

I said, "We were only dancing."

"I'm sorry." Quint held my hands. "We were. You're all right now."

"We should get the miss down."

"You *go*," Quint said, suddenly sounding like lord and master, ordering the lightkeeper, "and get her something hot to drink and have it waiting for us."

"Yes, yes, yes sir!" Mr. McHenry stood and scurried.

Quint fretted over my chin when we were alone. "What a stupid, stupid—accident."

"Yes."

"Can I give you a kiss on the cheek, to show you how sorry I am?"

I didn't answer him. I wanted to stand. How good it felt to stand. To be whole. Yes. Like I had been an empty shaker, for a moment, but now the salt was poured back in.

"Just let me know at least you're not angry with me. Look at me, Emma. Please, look at me?"

There was anger inside me. I knew it was there because I felt it, lurking, but it was mixed with something else, some wild wonder at living, some pumping, jerking aliveness. Quint stood near me. His soft whiskers so close. Each whisker as clear to me as a golden thread.

"I'm not angry now."

"But no kiss?"

"Why should I?"

"If I'm better behaved? No more dancing pranks, ever again?"

His blue eyes were so serious.

"Maybe. When you come to the Point again."

"Then I can come again?"

And of course he did. Many times. And when he came, we stood at the base of the lighthouse instead of in its eye, and his mouth tasted as soft as it looked, and his hands were more certain at my tingling back, and I let them go where I wanted.

15

My work for the Foldes grew dreary. Mrs. Folde complained bitterly and suffered during the last weeks of her time. Mr. Folde grew cool, distant as a light on another shore. The children turned listless and fretful. Still, whenever Quint left, I would be smiling from our walks around the Point, and sometimes I would have a new ribbon for my hair or a silk flower to set on my window sill, next to the tiny bird's skull. After I told Quint I'd done well at Benito's schoolhouse until my father's accident had forced me to go to work, he started bringing some of his library to read on the little beach below the cliffs, where we sat on the shelf and I heard:

> *Who dreamed that beauty passes like a dream?*
> *We and the laboring world are passing by;*
> *Amid men's souls, that waver and give place*
> *Like the pale waters in their wintry race,*
> *Under the passing stars, foam of the sky.*

He told me that his mother was wondering why he went out riding so much and he laughed and said she'd been trying to interest him in some of the local girls who had come back for the summer from their boarding schools, but that each of them was as dull as soap and made him want to beat his head with a stick.

When Mrs. Folde's pains finally came on, it was late on a gray day, and I took the five Folde children to sit quietly with Mrs. McHenry and her boy in her large parlor, while she braided herbs in her busy hands and talked about what a trial life-giving was and that it was a good thing that men (other than the doctor, who Mr. McHenry had fetched from town) knew to keep away at such a time, because they couldn't understand it.

It was eleven at night when we got word that the doctor had delivered two baby boys: one sturdy as a mushroom, who'd screamed as soon as his lungs hit the air; and the second blood-soaked and lifeless, who'd never opened an eye or drawn a single breath.

Mrs. McHenry had turned red and held her own baby close to her. Mr. McHenry came in and said it was a dreadful thing but that it had to be accepted, that there was nothing, when all was said, that could be done if God had decided one soul was meant to be stronger than another.

I watch as Pratt leaves the Lambry House with my rosebud in his pocket. I've been lucky; everything is now going according to my plan. He must be growing more certain now that it's Alice he's hunting. For who else but an artist would make such a fanciful thing, a baby rose drowned in red watercolor?

There's this to keep me safe, too: Pratt's way of hunting is to call out the name of a ghost, and so turn her name against her. But if he doesn't know the right name to call, how can he turn the ghost and make her light and betray her anger, the way he lit the boy in the mine? He can't. For no man can call a soul unless and until he gives it a name, the way Mr. and Mrs. Folde gave a name even to their stillborn son, *Infant Joseph*. And no hunter who favors Pratt's way of killing can rouse a ghost, stirring her to betray her heart, unless he knows rightly how to rouse her.

Yet he might be made to call out the wrong name. And when he does, he might point his fist at a false flash of light, at the fire from a dragon's mouth, and believe that he has done it in, leaving me be at last.

Patient, I flit down to the cove, the beach. I trail the young couples, the lovers who've come out of their honeymoon suites, watching them take off their shoes and drag their feet through the waves, holding hands, picking up shells, happy, as if there's no shadow underneath us all. I wonder that they can't see love is a kind of ghost, too: a light that can't be seen but is real, with just as much chance of being snuffed out. I wonder if the living understand how ghostly love is, truly, how hard it is to put your finger on it. Is love the moment when your eyes fly up the lane and you think, wildly, not of the gift of ribbon he's bringing you, but of the laughing way he'll give it? Is it love when your feet move faster and the lane seems suddenly twice as long, is it love when eye meets eye, and mouth meets soft mouth, and mouths suddenly become another set of eyes, searching—as if kissing were a kind of seeing? Is it love when you see the future stretching out in front of you, endless as the sea? Or when an hour feels as shallow as a thimble?

I float back toward the woods now. What might Pratt know about love? I wonder. Or the Danes? Or little Ellen? When I reach Ellen's peaked cabin, in the garden where the plants have all died, a little mound of earth has been built up and a cross erected above it, with a kitten's pink collar buckled to it. Which must mean Ellen's wandering pet has joined the night of the animals, the dark air that stirs the leaves and pads in tracks that go no farther than your doorway.

The cabin is dark, the curtains drawn. Ellen is by herself. She's been upset by everything that's happened, I can see. She must want some company. She sits in an easy chair with a blanket wrapped around her small shoulders. Her shining tablet rests on her lap, its light glowing against her stomach. Her bobbed hair hangs straight down over her forehead. She looks like she's not seeing anything at all. Like Mr. and Mrs. Folde when their baby was put into the ground.

She stretches her fingers out and begins tapping on the slate. I settle on the chair like a cat behind her ear. She reaches up, not knowing, to adjust the blanket.

Philip,

Received your message. Sorry I didn't respond sooner. My cat died today. But I'm feeling better. I really want to keep helping out.

This is what I've found out: The first roses were planted at the house by the first Mrs. Lambry—her name was Eugenia—soon after her son died. The yellow roses growing there now and in other places around town are descended from those bushes. I asked Mrs. Fanoli from the botanical garden about Alice and what the roses might have meant to her, and she said Alice took special care of them for most of her life because it was a kind of family responsibility passed down through the women, but that she had let things go in recent years and some of the vines have gone wild.

My sense is, Mrs. Fanoli really wants to say more, but she's angling for a visit from you. She likes to make people come to the garden. I think you ought to go see her there. It's not far, just south of town. Across the cove. Mrs. F. is almost always there, and she knows everything, not just about the flowers, but the village. Her memory apparently goes a long way back. She said she'd love to talk to you. If you want, I'll go with you. I explained the urgency to her, and how important this could be, not just for us but for the village.

I hope you're making progress. Everyone is upset and anxious. They want to have this done.

Ellen

She taps the screen and leans back, into the curl of her chair.

In just such a way would Quint and I curl against each other on the beach, with the fire that he'd started glowing. He'd tell me, excitedly, about how we should all try to make great successes out of our lives and not do things the way they've always been done before, but try new ideas, and make changes when we had to, and not be afraid of the unknown.

"I know you're here," Ellen whispers. "I can feel you."

The room is very still. Ellen is unafraid. I can feel it. This is something new, now.

It happens like this sometimes. The living feel the darkness and know they're not alone in it. In every house, there is some space, unfilled. In that corner. Under that chair. In the shadow of a shelf. In a closet. It's when the living are the loneliest that they feel our possibility the most.

"I feel you. Friend. I'm not going to cry anymore. Thank you. Thank you, for that."

She isn't afraid—though her breath is coming faster now and she's leaning a bit forward, away from me. Alice was like this, too, in the beginning. Wondering what sort of companion I was or might be. If I was going to stay for a long, long time—as I'd stayed with all the Lambrys.

Ellen isn't a Lambry. She isn't one of the family I haunt—but it's strange, I can't help myself. I've grown to like her. And I think, like Alice, she needs a friend. And she isn't like Pratt. She isn't the one who hired the hunter, brought him in; she's only trying to work and make her own way, just as I did.

Maybe it's time for all of us to make a change. To think about the future. After Pratt's gone, after he imagines he's cleaned the Lambry House. Maybe it's time I started thinking about putting the name Lambry and all Lambry things behind me. Maybe it's been long enough. A new century. A new millennium. Past new.

A good housekeeper knows when the house needs airing, when the sheets need wringing, when a room has gone sickly and stale. Mrs. Folde's room, after *Infant Joseph*'s funeral—she didn't want her pillows changed. She lay there in bed, day after day, giving milk for the living twin but nothing else. She wouldn't get up. She wouldn't move. Until I told her I'd been mending Mr. Folde's shirts myself, and darning his underclothes, and teaching the children to read poems and stories from *King Arthur and His Knights*. Then the blood had gushed back into her cheeks and she had me help her get up, holding onto my waist tightly, like a raft.

For a while we were friends, even close, with Frances gone away to the Russian River and expecting her own baby. I helped Mrs. Folde find the strength to go on. She let me draw closer to the children, and teach them the stories I knew, about Ireland and the *far darrig*. I even thought we might be able to share secrets one day, that I could tell her about Quint and our plans.

"I'm so glad you're still here," Ellen whispers now. "I didn't want you to go, ever. I'm sorry I wasn't a better friend. I'm sorry I didn't always know what you needed . . . I didn't know how bad things were. I truly didn't. I tried to help you. Remember? Remember how I called you and tried to catch you? But you didn't come, not until it was too late. It wasn't my fault. But I'm sorry, Kittums, really sorry. Will you forgive me?

Before you go on to that better kitty-place? Is that why you're here?" She puts her hand out from the blanket, stroking the air. "So I can tell you I'm sorry for being so distracted by everything, all this nasty, ugly ghost business . . . I'm so sorry. I hope it's all better now. For you. You sweet, silly kitty."

She thinks I'm an animal.

Or she thinks I'm nasty. Ugly.

She thinks I'm—

Eyes. Fur.

She thinks I'm a companion, with nails.

Anger.

Anger.

Anger.

If you think so, then I am.

It takes only a few minutes to be strangled. For sight to go black. For the windpipe to close, for you to feel your head bang against a door, a wall, a ceiling, and no way through. You claw, but there is no room left for you on earth. She screams, and no one comes to soothe her.

16

I can't do it, Philip."

"You can."

"I can't. I'm telling you."

"Please, Ellen. Try. Tell me what you remember."

"I can't."

Pratt gets up from his hotel bed and paces in front of her. She sits on the edge of the bed with his coat wrapped around her. I watch from outside the window. They look small again, as they did on the porch of the Lambry House. Like two bruised toys in a doll's house.

"Try again."

"I woke up. It was all over."

"Before that."

Ellen fits her hair behind her ears. Her hands are still shaking.

I'm sorry I wasn't a better friend. I tried to help you. Remember?

"Can you focus on a few details? Anything?"

"Anger. I felt it, all around me." Her eyes squeeze shut. "Like a wave."

"All right. What else?"

"The blanket."

It coiled around her. She couldn't move. When she tried to move, I held her even closer.

"Then it lifted me. Up into the roof. High, into the peak. And there was water, rising from underneath me. I was pinned against the roof of the house, and I couldn't move, and the water was rising and I was trapped and I couldn't breathe and I didn't know how to—to hold onto . . ."

. . . that last chestful of air, ready to burst inside you. That awful clawing at the back of your throat, that wants to pry your mouth open, suck in the water. But you don't want to give in, you don't, you don't . . .

Pratt stops his pacing. "I'm so sorry, Ellen. This is my fault."

Ellen opens her eyes. She says nothing.

"I broke something belonging to it today," Pratt goes on. "Trying to get it to focus its anger on me. Something that mattered to it. But now it looks like it chose you instead."

He's wrong. It was that Ellen *didn't* choose me.

"Why, when it's never hurt me before?"

He stares across the room, without seeing. "Something is shifting."

Yes. I think so too.

"Maybe because I've been helping you help the Danes?"

"You've been helping them all along."

"But now I'm helping you to kill it. I was sending you a message when it came. I thought the hissing was my cat."

"I should have seen this coming." He locks his hands behind his neck, gripping it. "Like Manoel."

They each turn away from the other. Locked in silence. I'm so close, just outside the window, yet I'm nothing to them, I'm nothing compared to the weight of what they're feeling. Sometimes, truly, it's hard to watch the living live, and to be left out of throbbing life, even when it's unhappy.

He turns. "I need to get to your place right now, Ellen, if you'll let me. To see what kind of residue is there. If you think . . . if you think you can be left alone here for a little while?"

She lets out a strange little laugh. "Do you think it really matters where I am? Won't it be able to—to get me wherever I am, now? If it's that angry with me?"

"Maybe. But it's made a mistake this time."

"How?"

"It's revealed something about itself. You made it manifest. You said you thought it was your cat. Twice you've said it—that was the first thing you said to me, when you burst in here tonight. You said you thought you were whispering to your dead cat. I think, maybe, this is a ghost who doesn't like to be reminded how dead it is. What a beast it is. It doesn't want to be reminded it's a *creature*. That might be our way in. Not smashing the globe it *makes*"—he turns around, gazing out the dark window—"but smashing its world, what it thinks it *is*. No special, privileged, indestructible thing. It isn't. Nothing but a lowly beast."

You can try as hard as you want, Mr. Pratt. You can call me names and throw out your cruel ideas, but I know you're more dangerous than Ellen. So I won't lose my temper, not this close to you.

"Give me your address, Ellen. And your key."

"I don't think I even locked the door. I just ran to my car."

"Can I bring you some clothes back? Anything important?"

"There isn't much of anything in the house. It's a rental. But I've got clothes upstairs."

Pratt tells her to keep her phone handy and to call if anything happens or starts to happen. Ellen stands up and suddenly throws her arms around him. He didn't expect that. Nor did I—but the living can do strange things when they're frightened. He gives her a short, stiff, hunched squeeze, like an embarrassed bear balancing on a tree limb too small for it.

"I'll be back as quick as I can."

"Please."

17

A half-moon rises over the woods. In the trees, animals crouch in the blue shade and wait. Pratt's car bumps its way over the ruts and fallen needles, in between the dark cabins. The living inside them are asleep, the fires in their stone hearths gone out. A hunting bird, a night owl, flies overhead. Below my skirt a snake coils, flicking its tongue over its back. It sees Pratt's lights and hurries, in a wave, away.

Pratt pushes the door to Ellen's house open. He goes straight in. He doesn't seem afraid at all. I stand outside the window, bathed by the moon. Inside, flashing pieces of broken glass lie everywhere. The lights are shattered. Broken plates litter the floor. Ellen's comfortable chair has been tossed over and rests on its shoulders. The baseboards are all mucked, streaked with long, gray smudges, as if by a muddy skirt.

But of course, it must be that the animals got in here, I tell myself. Soon after Ellen ran away. Or else some of the young pipe-smokers, who still like to come into the woods and find a hideaway and be forgetful. Not me. I would never make such a mess. Not me, always so proud of my work—who kept the Folde house so clean and bright that Mr. Folde started to praise my talents, even if he looked unhappy himself. I was glad that Mrs. Folde kept her promise to herself and kept him at bay, telling him she couldn't get and bury any more children.

Pratt picks through the wreckage, holding his hand to his chest. Near the armchair he finds Ellen's tumbled writing slate.

. . . really wants to say more . . . she's angling for a visit . . .

He picks it up, slides it inside his coat. Now he sees something else. The tall shelf next to the mantelpiece with the picture of the father and baby. When he comes close to the picture, one of the books leaning over beside it loses its balance and falls from the shelf. A stray piece of paper comes to rest at his feet, fluttering. He picks it up and stares at it for a long time. I can't see what it says from my hiding place in the moonlight. He folds it and puts it, too, in his pocket.

He looks around the room again. He coughs and wipes his mouth as if the muck he's breathing in is too much for him. He goes upstairs and studies Ellen's tumbled bedroom. He starts putting some of her clothes in a bag. He looks around the loft one last time and seems confused. Maybe he thought he'd find Alice's robe spread out on the bed for him? I could have done that, if I'd wanted to. But I won't be so obvious. He has to think he's solving a puzzle all by himself. I have to let him be the hunter he thinks he is. I won't smash what he thinks of himself, the way he wants to smash me. What a cruel thing to do. Why would a ghost be cruel? Instead, I'll use what he is against the man himself.

At the hotel again, he stands outside his numbered door. He waits, listening. Ellen is inside. He doesn't know, as I do, from sliding in and out of the keyhole, that she's lying down. But he must guess because he turns away. I follow him down again to the hotel's lobby, where he takes a chair close to the great stone fireplace outside the dining room and sets down the bag he's filled with Ellen's clothes. He orders a strong drink from the sleepy waiter. He sits for a long time, staring into the dying embers. He sits for so long without moving that I finally grow tired of waiting for him to stir, and abandon him. He can have his cushion. I'll have mine. I can't be thinking about why he looks so unhappy, lost, even though it should have made me happy to see him that way—staring into the fire, his graying whiskers growing in, time forcing itself through him, one needle after another.

I find them both in the breakfast room the next morning, Ellen just coming down.

"I was worried," she says, shivering. "I fell asleep in the room and then I woke up this morning and couldn't find you."

"I had my phone off."

"Is everything . . . What did you find at my house?"

"Sit down, why don't you, and I'll tell you."

He hands her a sweater from the bag of her clothes, and she wraps it around her shoulders.

"Thanks for bringing my things. Why didn't you wake me up when you got back?"

"It was late. I didn't want to disturb you. And I needed time to . . . think. Have some breakfast and coffee."

"I'm not hungry. Are you all right? You seem—"

"Slightly hung over. I've been sleeping in a chair."

"You didn't have to do that."

"Lying upsets my routine."

"What do you mean by that?"

"You've been lying to me."

What? What's that? I draw as close as I dare out of the velvet curtain. What has Ellen lied to Pratt about?

She sits up taller in her chair, calmly. "What do you mean?" she says again.

"Your place. It was like a storm had broken loose inside. Everything rifled through. You said when you left it that everything looked normal. That as soon as the hallucination was over, everything looked the same."

"Because it did."

He slides the bag with her things on the floor toward her. He nods to the waiter for more coffee. "A few more personal items for you. Your tablet. And some personal papers."

"When I left I just ran. I told you, I didn't look back to see what or who—"

"Which brings us to the lie. Can you tell me what, exactly, this is?"

He takes a folded piece of paper from the top of the bag and drops it on the white tablecloth between them. The name at the top of the paper reads *Ellen Lambry DeWight*. She looks down at it. And her little face turns to stone.

Ellen DeWight a Lambry! *Ellen. What have you done?*

"How did you get this?" she says stiffly.

"It fell from a shelf. In front of me. Almost as if someone—or something—wanted me to find it. Interesting, don't you think?"

The truth about Ellen. The truth. What a thing to keep quiet all along . . . so cleverly.

"You had no business looking at this," she says.

"I didn't have a choice. I told you. It was practically thrown in my face." He brings his napkin up from his lap and wipes his whiskers with it and tosses it on the table. "Someone clearly wanted me to see this. Fate can be so surprising. It can suddenly decide to be so direct. A death certificate. For one Ellen Lambry DeWight."

"That's not me. That's my mother."

"Yes. I know. I already chased that down. You didn't think this was an important little tidbit to share with me? That you're a blood relative of the family whose house is currently being assaulted? Did it ever occur to you that you might have been singled out, last night, in your own home, because of your name? But you didn't think that was a detail worth sharing with me before I went in. And I'm guessing no one in town knows about your background, either. Am I correct?"

A Lambry and a liar both! Well, the two go hand in hand, after all. I could have told Pratt that. Look at him. So still. He's almost as cold as I am. And just as wary, now.

"I didn't want anyone to know, Philip."

"And why not? Well, we'll get to that in a moment. What I'm more interested in, Ellen, right now, is why you didn't tell *me*."

She looks down. But she isn't sorry. It takes one to know one, Franny used to say.

"Because it wasn't important. It's just a name. A lot of people have it, up north here. There are plenty of branches of the Lambry family. It doesn't mean a thing."

"Let me try this again. Why didn't you feel the need to tell me you were related to Alice Lambry through your mother? It somehow, I don't know, slipped your mind?" Poor Pratt. He's trying so hard not to rage.

"Of course it didn't," she snaps. "How could it? But it doesn't mean *anything*. The connection's so distant. I'm not some heir, somebody close. I'm not entitled to any part of the estate—except what I can earn on commission. By my own effort. I never thought of that house being connected to me anymore than anyone whose last name is King feels entitled to sit on a throne. It's just a coincidence."

"Do you take me for a fool, Ellen?"

155

"No," she nearly shouts but sees the waiter looking at her and, blushing, calms down. "I'm telling you the truth. Please believe me. Please. There are plenty of Lambry cousins all up and down this coast. It's just my middle name, a name that gets handed down in my family, like a bad habit. It doesn't mean what it looks like. I didn't even know much about the Lambrys until I got here. My name is Ellen DeWight. My father's name. It's the only name I use. I don't even care about that shitty family. Believe me." She looks as if she wants to cry. But if I were Pratt, I wouldn't believe it.

"Why should I?"

"Because you have to. Because I'm telling the truth."

"Have some toast."

"I'm not hungry."

"I never see you eat anything." It's a curious thing to say, just now.

"I'm not hungry. Just ask me anything, and I'll tell you what you want to know. I promise. Just ask."

"Then I want to know everything. Starting with that past you told me you were trying to get away from. I want to know it all—why you came to this village, and rather amazingly became the real estate agent for a substantial property you are clearly connected to."

"I told you. The heirs came up and liked me. They wanted a go-getter. Someone young. My broker travels all the time."

"That's not what I'm talking about."

"Fine, then. I'll tell you. But you won't get much out of it." She shrugs. "I'm a lot less Lambry than you imagine."

I listen to Ellen's story. A sad story. But is it all a lie? I watch Pratt's face go hard, and then softer, as he listens. How foolish and forgiving the living can be, and at the wrong times! I know all about that. You want to punch, jab at something. But then you let yourself be knocked down, instead.

She was born in a small town on the other side of the coastal range, she tells him. Her father owned an insurance business, and her mother stayed at home, sickly. Ellen's earliest memories were of her mother pinned to a striped sofa, looking out the window onto a street lined with eucalyptus trees, waiting for her husband to come home. He was a respected man in town but a womanizer, and when Ellen was still a girl, he was caught at another man's house with his wife. The man came in on them, in the middle of things, and shot them both dead with a rifle.

She puts her chin up. "It sounds like a tragedy, doesn't it? But it wasn't. It was small and stupid and ugly and horrible."

"Hard luck, you mean," Pratt says.

She shrugs. "Harder on my mother. She blamed herself—if you can believe that. She said it was her sickness that made him leave her. She was mentally unhealthy. She didn't know how to think like a well person. After it was all over she sold my father's business, but instead of taking us away from the valley like she should have, she used the money to strap us in and down. Just the two of us. In our house. With that striped couch."

Ellen saw to her mother's meals. She drove her to the doctor. She gave her her medicines. She came straight home from school and sat with her and read. When she was old enough she told her mother she was going to leave for college but her mother howled in pain and said, *Don't you understand you're like a cork in my body, that you're the only thing holding my life in?*

"Jesus."

157

"Get the picture? So I was responsible. Because there wasn't anybody else."

"You couldn't have reached out to your relations?"

"The Lambrys? Is that what you're driving at?" She laughs. "That's just it. My mother would never let me. She was a proud woman. Even if she was ashamed of her life. She said she would no more go to her family than she would ask for prayers from a stone."

But every year, Ellen's mother sank a little lower on the couch, looking out the window at the eucalyptus trees, waiting for her dead husband who never came. Every year Ellen went out less and less.

"But I found out I could study for a real estate license from home. It's one of those things anyone can try for. I didn't tell her. I just studied. And waited. And I knew what I was waiting for. How do you admit to yourself that you're waiting for someone to just give up? You don't. You just wait. And then one morning I woke up and heard this awful, rasping sound coming from her room. They said later it was her heart that kept on going. That her mind had given up but her heart didn't know it. I could see it in her eyes, she was somewhere else already, but her chest kept going out and in, and her throat, that sound, it wasn't breathing. It was—escaping. And then it stopped. When she died she only had one eye open. I stayed with her until the funeral director came. I blocked out everything about that for a long time. I went through a period of . . . depression. But then I got better. And I sold the house and sold everything and left."

"And went looking for the family connected to her."

"No. All I heard was it was beautiful out here. And the agency had an ad out; they wanted someone who'd work for a small commission, almost nothing. That was me."

"And how long was this after your mother died, Ellen?"

"A year."

"And what were you doing during that year?"

"What do you mean? I told you. I was depressed. I felt . . . dead. I thought maybe I even really was. But then I got better. I decided to give myself a new life. And here I am. That's it. That's all of it."

Pratt sits back. Watching her closely.

"You thought you were dead."

"I had my moments."

"And now?"

"I'm fine. I have my life. Everything was looking up, until— Shit." She reaches for her telephone. "We should call the hospital. To see how Manoel's doing."

"He passed. At four this morning. I called before you came down."

Poor man. May he rest in peace. Poor, unlucky Manoel.

Ellen's face unfolds all at once. "He's . . . dead?"

"Yes." Pratt blinks up at the ceiling, as if he might find the Portuguese there, still high up on his ladder.

"I can't . . . feel anything. Philip. What's wrong with me?"

"You're overwhelmed, maybe. Or you feel gutted, like me. Or you've just gone all hollow." He pushes some cold toast and jelly toward her. "Eat something."

"No."

"You don't eat, Ellen."

"Because I can't."

"Then we should get out of here." He signals to the waiter.

"Where? Where are we going?"

"To shake the past off. And whatever nightmares, for now, we can. Go somewhere pleasant. Beautiful." He says this strangely.

"Thanks, but . . ." She looks at him, her turn to be uncertain.

"I want you to go with me to the Botanical Garden. Remember? To see Mrs. Fanoli." He lifts the death certificate from the tablecloth and drops it, deliberately, back into her bag.

"Oh." She blinks. "Mrs. Fanoli."

"We have someone now who needs the truth. His name is Manoel Cristo. He deserves it. And he deserves justice. And the very best of us, I think."

"Of course, of course."

"It's time for us to actually work together, agreed?"

"Yes. I'm sorry I didn't tell you the truth, earlier. I guess . . . all I can say is I didn't know how."

"Do you want to go upstairs and change your clothes?"

"No. It doesn't matter. What matters is we have to *stop* whatever this is, Philip, that's doing all of this to *us*! Monstrous, indecent things are happening to *decent* people."

I don't like this sudden, emotional, dramatic Ellen. Trying to make Pratt think she's decent, after all, is that it? Her voice seems false and forced.

"Yes, they are." Pratt watches her carefully as she stands. "Monsters all around us. All the time."

I watch them as they leave the hotel. They don't walk as closely together as they did before. Pratt, especially, seems to tuck his bulk into himself as Ellen walks a little behind him on their way to his car. Something's different, it's plain, between them. It's loneliness that's come to them, I see. Loneliness with its sudden cold feeling of deadness in your mouth and all around you, though you still breathe, and another breathes beside you. One moment you think you have a friend you can count on. The next you're in a world full of sea and sound, but one voice is missing, the one you trusted, and you can't have it back again.

It was Quint who told me my beloved Franny had died. He brought the news from town, and gave it to me as we sat on a blanket on the beach. She'd died in her cabin by the Russian River before the doctor could get to her. The baby half out of her. Franny. My good, good, loving Franny.

I dug my hands into the sand. He put his arm around me but nothing could warm the surf, the world.

"A week ago, I didn't know if I should tell you."

"Her—husband?"

"They say he's mad with grief." He stroked my cheek.

No. I turned away from his hand. It wasn't right, being touched in that way, not then. It didn't feel right. To feel my living skin coddled while my beloved friend lay cold, far from me. My beloved Franny. I pulled away. I made myself go still and cold, apart from Quint. I wanted to be alone, in my heart, with my friend. Is it love when you say no to what you love, even though you love it? Because you love—loved— someone else, too.

The New Year had just turned over, 1915. Time wasn't doing what Franny had said it would do for us. The future felt as though it were slipping like a seal into the fog. The war news had reached our strip of coast. The men and boys in the logging camps all wanted to join up, but Quint's mother and father wouldn't give him permission to go. I let him rave and sulk, the next time he came to me. He had his own troubles, he said. Nothing was going his way.

"I have my own war going on, I tell you, with my father."

It seemed a small and petty thing to say, with Tommy Allston and all the others going over, and Franny lying cold in her grave beside the river.

He stood and paced the shingle of the beach. It was a miserable month, a miserable day, but we had nowhere else private to be. I wouldn't let him into my cottage. I wouldn't risk being alone with him. I thought of Franny. *Be careful, or you'll get a fawn,* she'd said. I thought of my mother, and how a woman could die in the breech, or from losing too much blood, too fast.

"My parents can't stop me from seeing you, anyway." He stopped walking the sand and grabbed me. "Not that they ever could, short of knocking me down and tying me up."

I let him kiss me. "Are they going to try to stop you?"

"I think they know I'm coming here and . . . they think I'll just grow tired of you. Which I won't." He turned away, angrily. "I know their game. If only I had the right to all my funds. They'd see the backside of me—us—soon enough. That would teach them. It's a modern world we're living in now, and a man should be able to go and do whatever he pleases. Lord, you should see the flabby-faced girls they're throwing at me now."

He came back toward our fire and held me again. "Give me another kiss, Emma. I promise I'll keep you safe and warm, and we'll get away. You're such a fine girl, Emma. Truly. Kiss me, kiss me . . ." he said, as if one more touch from me would stop all the wars in the world, and make everything right again.

18

Mrs. Fanoli sits, her thin lips pressed together. She carries her life collected in cups of skin under her eyes. Her back is humped. Her shoulders are as sharp as the gray cornerstones of the Benito Botanical Garden Welcome Cottage, behind her. Her knuckles are bluish, shimmering, the color of abalone, and woven together over the knob of her wooden cane. She's waiting for Pratt's car to roar itself up through the garden's gates and arrive at her perch. From her bench, she looks down the hill. Stands of purple heather fall in waves on one side of Garden Drive, toward the cliffs. On the other, banks of white roses crowd like a hundred brides.

It's noon, warm and clear. From where I sit, beside the old woman, I can see the cove and cliffs and beyond them the steeples of Benito, rising high as stakes. Brightness, brightness . . . I smile at the view. It's still summer, after all, and a ghost shouldn't let herself get too dreary.

Pratt pulls into the empty lot ringed with hydrangeas.

"Is that Mrs. Fanoli?" he asks, getting out of the car.

"Yes, that's her," Ellen says. "She spends a lot of time outside, waiting for visitors. She's the main docent."

"She looks like she's used to waiting a long time."

"Not as many people care about the garden as they used to." Ellen seems to be recovering her nerves after being caught in all her Lambry lies. How strange to think that all the while I was so drawn to her, it must have been because she was one of them. "Mrs. Fanoli. Here we are!"

They come up the terraced walk toward us. The old woman shifts her hands on the cane between her knees. She doesn't move from the bench. She lets Pratt look down on the knot of silver hair on top of her head.

"Mrs. Fanoli," he says. "Thanks for seeing us on such short notice, ma'am."

"Call me Agnes. Short notice is no trouble here at all, sir." Her voice shakes a little. Her free hand quivers, too, like a hummingbird. "And how nice to see you too again, young Ellen. Come a little closer, please, both of you. It's not so easy for me to see anything that isn't brightly colored, nowadays. You both have to keep still a minute so I can gather you in."

They wait on either side of her.

"Well, Mr. Pratt. You have the chin of a prizefighter, but the rest of you is pretty. Ellen, you're a pixie, as always."

Pratt offers, "Should I tell you what I see?"

"Oh, I wish you would. I can hardly make myself out, anymore."

"A strong face and eyes to match."

"Ha! I don't hear you saying the word *beautiful*. But all beauty goes, just like the rose. So. You've come out today to learn about our flowers, have you?"

"I have. And Ellen tells me you're the expert. That you've worked here along the coast for years."

"Volunteered. At my age, nobody works, young man." She shrugs. "But you don't want to lie down all day, either. When you lie down at ninety-three, you fall asleep almost right away, and when you fall asleep, you dream, and the dreams of the old . . . they can be terrible. The past haunts us."

"It doesn't have to."

"You'll find out differently when you get here. But no need to worry about it now. Let's get up and walk while I'm still chipper, and you can tell me what it is you both want to know." She stabs her cane into the ground, and leans forward and pushes to stand over it.

"I know you've come because there's been trouble in the village again," she says, leading them. "I've heard all about it. But I tell you what: I'd be lying to you if I didn't say I feel some sympathy for the poor thing causing all the ruckus. You might start to feel that way, too, when you're getting as close to the end as I am. You might be more inclined to ask a few questions, first, before you squash a ghost. Like: 'So how can I *not die*, too?' I think it's a bit ungenerous, what you do, with your hunting." She leans toward him, smiling.

"But I'm required to do it, Agnes." Pratt takes her elbow to help her balance. "I'm no volunteer."

"Ah, well. I suppose if we didn't know we were going to get squashed in the end, life wouldn't be so very precious. And we do know it, and we do get squashed. So"—she turns to Ellen—"wear turtleneck sweaters when you're my age, dear. To hide where the squashing's already begun. It's this way to the Heritage Garden, children."

The three of them walk slowly, Mrs. Fanoli showing off her knowledge between the rows and rows of color.

"Russell's Cottage rose, there. Teplitz. Hermosa. This beauty, here, is an Overboard White Moss." She bends on her cane to smell it. "Not to be confused with the White Pet. Here we have Devoniensis. *Wichuraiana. Rosa mutabilis.* Lady Hillingdon. Louis Philippe. Mary Wallace. Van Fleet. I'd love to have a rose named after me, wouldn't you? It hasn't happened yet, though I keep hinting to the breeder-gardeners. They'd better hurry. American Pillar, here. And Veilchenblau."

"You're extraordinary, Agnes," Pratt marvels. "How long have you been docenting?"

"Sixty years. I was born in Benito. And I've never left it, except on trips with my husband, God rest his soul. He died in a car crash not far from here, when he fell asleep and veered off the road. Now I don't drive. A neighbor brings me here every day. But for many years, Walt and I drove up and down the coast together, happy as clams, collecting local plants.

"Now, Ellen tells me," she says, stopping to rest under a vine-laced gazebo, "that you have a special interest in our local blooms. When this garden was begun, you might want to know—when it was started, that is, by a group of us in the last century who still *cared* about such things— it was only roses, plain and simple. We collected all the varieties we could find from the local homesteads. And we ended up finding other things you might not imagine could survive in such a cold, northern climate. Camellias. Magnolias. Flowers that had blown up from the desert and found the water and the salt they remembered. Or else brought in by the Indians, staying on even after the last of them were chased or killed off. Plants are living things that can adjust themselves, so they can stay.

"But first, it was only roses here. And the first thing you have to understand, Mr. Pratt"—she shakes her finger at him—"if you want to understand roses in a place like this, is that they're not just flowers. They're human landmarks. They're signs you've *arrived*. People plant roses when they know they're going to stay, and when they want to *show* that they're going to stay. Roses are narratives. In the old days, people brought them to the village not only to make the village seem less rough and wild, more civilized, but to tell the story of who they were, and what happened to them, and what mattered to them. That's really the origin of all the beds and terraces you see here." She straightens and waves one hand shakily over the grounds. "All of these flowers arrived here as part of a story. And they're still telling it, talking in their way, about what someone, or certain people anyway, thought was beautiful or valuable or necessary or something to add to their consequence. Something to express emotions they somehow couldn't or something they wanted to remember or memorialize. That's what roses do. That's why people give them as gifts all the time. Not because they're flowers. But because they speak."

Yes. A flower can carry a message in every petal. As mine did to Pratt.

"You speak beautifully yourself, Agnes."

"Young man, thank you. I've had plenty of practice, as you can tell. And I don't mind talking. It's all I do, now."

"Then I'll ask you about this." Pratt pulls the plastic bag from his pocket, and holds my message up in front her. "I'm hoping you can tell me what this might be saying."

"Good lord." Mrs. Fanoli blinks. "What is it?"

Pratt brings it closer to her cloudy eyes. "It's a rose, actually."

"Is it? Oh, such a sad little thing. Why have you put it in a baggie?"

"Because you won't want to touch it, or have to. It comes from the dead." He seems excited to be sharing my gift with her, and confident. "I hope you can see for yourself, the rose isn't the color of the water it's been soaked in. It's a kind of yellow, isn't it? It came from the Lambry House, I believe, from a certain bush in the garden, from the arbor near the front gate. Do you think you can make out the variety?"

The old woman balances on her cane and squints, making a pouting face at my pretty wet bud until the water wells over in her eyes. She pulls away, nodding.

"Absolutely I can tell you this variety. This is the rose we call Lambry's Ache. You've got the yellow petals, and the tiny border of orange, and the

167

distinctive curl. That orange isn't from any water stain, Mr. Pratt. That's the natural color derived from a Sutter's Gold variety, but fiddled with to create a stronger contrast. Used to be, the tips of yellow roses had to be dipped in red dye to get that effect. Not anymore. Not many people remember those days, of course, or remember this rose anymore, but there used to be quite a few of them around the village. And of course they were first bred at the Lambry House. Near the front gate. In the arbor? Yes. That would be right. There used to be many more of them, all around the house. It's a climber. Alice wasn't quite the gardener some of her forebears were.

"Oh, my dear," she says, turning to Ellen, "can you tell me if there is any news about her old handyman, Manoel? I heard about the accident, the water tower. He used to ask me questions about what to do with that challenge of a garden. I heard he was in an awful way?"

"We're sorry to tell you he died, Mrs. Fanoli."

"No! Oh no." She feels for the bench inside the gazebo and sits. "His poor family. And Alice! What would Alice say."

"What do you think she would have said?" Pratt watches her closely.

"Well, I don't know, exactly. But she clung to him. It isn't many old women who are lucky enough to find such a companion, such a help-meet, late in life. Trust me. If you want my opinion, it wasn't that old water tower that did him in. It was probably poor Alice who pulled the man down. Just to keep her company. The Lambrys always were a bit on the selfish side, you know."

If I could, I would fly down from the top of the gazebo and kiss the top of Agnes's head, so nicely is she filling in the story I want Pratt to hear.

Pratt looks at Ellen.

"Now, young man, tell me, why have you brought me a Lambry's Ache in such terrible condition? Does it have anything to do with Manoel?"

"It's part of the overall . . . cleaning."

"Terrible! Well, I hope that at least knowing the variety can help in some way. Manoel! That's unforgivable. I take back everything I said about not squashing ghosts. It was stupid of me to say. The past haunts. But we shouldn't let it. I can only hope that Alice feels she's done enough now, taken enough with her, and will go off to her sleep with the rest of her played-out family. Although nothing a Lambry would do would surprise me. They were always the kind of people you wanted to shake and ask: what on earth were you *thinking*?"

Ellen turns to look at the hydrangeas.

"Agnes, would you mind walking a little further and sharing with me more of what you know about the family?" Pratt asks. "Or would you prefer to sit and rest here?"

"Let's stay here in the shade of the gazebo. It's one of our nicest spots. And anyway, if you're going to ask me about that family, the answer may take a while. You sit down and make yourself comfortable, too," she says to Ellen, patting the small bench beside her. "Let the gentleman stand up before the female of the species."

She looks at Pratt, but her cloudy eyes don't seem to see him. "If you want to know about the Lambrys in this village, you have to go back to the first of them to do really well here, Eugenia and Augustus Lambry. He was one of our leading lights, a lumber baron who got his money, let's be honest, from his father grabbing the best land when they chased the Indians out. And then he made his fortune out of trees he never grew, cut by men he didn't raise. Augustus and Eugenia had four children. Three of them did quite well for themselves, as I recall. One didn't. He was drowned and never seen again. Your Lambry's Ache, now, it was bred in memory of that lost son. Many plants in this region, Mr. Pratt, have rather sad associations to them. Take that one standing so tall right there beside you, next to the hydrangea. That's called the ghost flower. Relative of the snapdragon. A foreign plant that's hybridized and reinvented itself so it can survive our damp and cold. It's said to wilt when the hot breath of misery comes too near it. But unless my poor eyes deceive me, it's in fine fettle today. Upright and sturdy. Beautiful specimen. I've seen it wilt only once or twice. We've seen bad things happen around these cliffs. I've seen them myself. Sometimes the past seems so close . . ."

"Lambry's Ache?" Pratt prods her.

"So single-minded you are," she says, shaking her knotted head, "with all this profusion and complexity around you.

"Lambry's Ache," she explains as she digs her cane between her feet, "was bred to commemorate the loss of the boy who died at sea. It happened one year, early in the last century, when a doghole schooner foundered, and the poor young man was drowned along with several sailors. There had once been rumors that the son's death was a curse the mother had brought down on her own head, and the father brought down on his own ship, for a sin, a cruelty they'd committed. A bit of scandal attached to the drowning. Some vague guilt that the family wouldn't claim or name."

And why would they? *It was only their own name they ever grieved*, I think and keep still on the gazebo's sunlit side.

"In any case, those bodies were never found, though empty graves were prepared at Evergreen and left unmarked, as is our custom. It's said that if you mark the grave of a lost soul, it will return angry to you, because it's been named and tied to a place where it didn't rest. So that's why, at our cemetery, you'll see a few graves with no names on them.

"Well, since Eugenia Lambry could leave no flowers by a stone with her son's name on it, she did other things to ease her grief. She built the Lambry steeple and the widow's walk, so she could look far out to sea where her son died. She cultivated a rose in memory of him. They say she had a very skilled Chinese gardener who helped her. There's no record of his name—so many people came and went through this town whose names were never recorded anywhere, isn't that shameful—but he bred her something special. That took the place of the boy's grave. But if you'd like, you can still see the boy's marker, Mr. Pratt, over at the cemetery, in the section for the lost and unknown. It says only, 'Dedicated to God.'"

"Yes, I've been there, and seen it and felt something directly over that very stone."

I remember and see Pratt again, standing in Evergreen—how he'd clutched at his chest and hurried off. But it didn't mean he understood anything at all, guessed at anything real.

"How else can I help you now? Is that sufficient?"

"Do you remember, yourself, any of the Lambrys you just described?"

"A few. Some more than others." She tilts her head above her turtleneck and closes her eyes. "Old Mrs. Lambry, she was pretty far gone by the time I was old enough to care about anything around me other than myself. She wasn't very interesting to me as a little girl. Tall and gray, worn-out looking. My family ran the mercantile in those days. We had dealings with the Lambrys, just like anyone else. We had dealings with everyone in town, but we weren't close to that family. Not many people were. Over the years, we watched one set of Lambrys after another grow up in that house. Some haughty, some nice. Eventually they would all drift away—especially after the mills started to close, and the Lambry businesses started to shut down, mostly after the Second World War. A few of them eventually came back . . . Like Alice's parents, who were Beatniks. I remember them quite well. Dressing like Indians, high as kites on drugs and prancing around in the garden. Poor Alice. She was an only child, and I'm afraid she wasn't much wanted or attended to. A strange, lonely person she was, even then. She was a good twenty years younger than me, so we were never friends. Not that she had any friends of her own. She preferred her shells and flotsam and brushes and paints. She never let anyone in, so to speak, not until her parents were dead and then Manoel came along. And *that's* why I think it's Alice who brought Manoel low; it's her not wanting to be alone, not after knowing what it's like to have *had* someone." She nods at Ellen beside her and Pratt standing over her, as if to be sure they're still with her.

"I know that feeling, to be honest with you. You get to a certain point, the only company you have are pictures in your head. I sit here, and I picture, for instance, a man I saw thirty years ago, drowning right in front of me, down below the cliffs, here. He was an abalone hunter but a dumb tourist, we found out later, not from our coast, and he didn't really know what he was doing. He let himself get caught in a riptide and no one could reach him. I watched him get pounded to pieces on the rocks. Right below me. Right here. I wonder if he saw me . . . Well. I never talk about it. I hear talk can raise the dead.

"Maybe Manoel raised Alice, without meaning to. There were always rumors about the two of them, you know. Being more than employer and employee, as it were. And I'm not going to say she wasn't entitled to some company while she was still alive. I don't know about *after*, what any of us are entitled to . . . The closer you get to dying the more . . . the more you see how lonely it's going to be. Lonelier, I mean."

"Are you all right, Agnes?" Pratt asks.

She's sagging a little on the bench next to Ellen, one shoulder slumping, her thin lips pressing between the clamp of her teeth.

"Agnes? Mrs. Fanoli?" Ellen touches her.

She lets out a small breath. "Oh! So sorry. It was just a little spell. I get them sometimes. I get them at night, usually. When I see the pictures in my head of that dead tourist floating all torn up and can't talk with anyone about them. I forget to breathe, and I wake up. Apnea, the doctor calls it. I guess being around a ghost hunter has raised a ghost in me, Mr. Pratt. Do you smell something . . . decaying? It's black spot, sometimes. The roses. They're my responsibility. To guard this garden . . ." She tries to stand and wobbles on her cane, vaguely.

"Ellen, will you take Agnes back to the Welcome Cottage? Agnes, do you think you can walk?"

"Do you smell it, too?" the old woman asks feebly. "It's coming from over there."

"The ghost flower," Ellen whispers.

"Ellen. I'd like you to walk Agnes back."

I've moved away from them all. I rise and balance in the air, so high I can see where the poor abalone hunter was ripped to shreds, thirty years ago. I fear what's coming next. I've seen it before. The ghost flower, a white spear standing tall above the other snapdragons in the garden, has gone gray and black. The puckered mouths of its blooms are shriveling and falling to the ground at the feet of Ellen, Pratt, and the old woman. It's telling them a crawler is near. About to surface and find us.

A dream-crawler isn't a ghost. It's a pitiful creature trapped between body and spirit. It's a thing that can't find air or light or hope. It has nothing to do with me. It's a soul that was buried in a place where it didn't want to be buried, and so it tunnels through the dark, with the worms, until something speaks, beckons to it. Then it rises. Wailing.

Pratt stands in front of the women, protecting them. The carcass of the crawler has begun prying its rotting fingers out of the roots. Its neck and spine hump, showing. It strains to break its hips free from the tide of dark soil under the flowers. Deep gashes, the marks of the rocks, scar the dead man's bones.

Ellen is trying to move Mrs. Fanoli, who can neither speak nor move.

"Get her out of the way. *Now!*" Pratt says.

Ellen lifts her—I don't see how—as if she's suddenly much stronger than she's always looked.

Pratt takes a single step away from them, forward, and then another and another, coming closer to the crawler. It breaches and falls to the path, pleading.

I had hoped to be elsewhere, it groans.

And why is it hope, I want to cry back, that causes more pain in all this world than such a sweet thing should?

The corpse rubs its thick, clotted skull against the gravel, writhing. Ellen and Mrs. Fanoli are scrambling away. They don't see, as I do, from high above, that Pratt has bared his arm. The silver band with its black marks now gleams. Is that weapon, I wonder, a thing that came out of all the wars? Some button that can be touched, some gas launched, some sickening taint?

I remember Pratt's words: *Not a human being, but the mold of something that once held a human being . . . Yet the mold of a thing can only hold so much . . .* Is that what it does, then? Fills a spirit with so much, it can hold no more?

I will not lose heart.

It takes heart to stand and stay with a spirit when a hunter comes to turn it to ash. It takes will not to turn away, to look and see what a hunter does. And so: I stay. I stay as long as it takes to watch Pratt raise his arm and ball his fist and then extend his fingers in a reach that looks like it might be kind, answering the cry of the pleading spirit. But it isn't. I hear screaming through the red beam of light, and I smell the burning in the air and I back away, away and high, far up, as far as the Welcome Cottage—though I know there is no welcome, anywhere, for those of us who challenge such horrors. But I won't look away, and I won't lose heart. I watch as Pratt steps forward to make sure the crumbs of the man are cooling under his feet, crouching down to touch the pathway, patting it gently, and I know this much: we must never make peace with the thing that is trying to kill us.

The cottage is filled with bright postcards and packets of seeds and bulbs waiting to be planted. It seems a terrible, thoughtless, heedless place to me now. Mrs. Fanoli puts her hand to her throat, looking through the window.

"Come away," Ellen says, strangely calm.

"I can't help myself. I need to remember this. If only I could see better. I need to see, so I can remind myself, when my time comes, to lie myself down flat in my grave and not give any hunters a chance."

"Come sit down."

"I know what that was. I recognized it. It was the picture in my head, the man from my dream, my memory. He's killed the man from my dream. What is Mr. Pratt doing now?" The old woman squints, anxiously.

"He's coming back toward us. He's finished."

"What a shocking thing. We all choose our lines of work, don't we? But I don't know. Why choose that one?"

"He says he didn't choose it. Are you feeling better now, Mrs. Fanoli?"

"I'm not sure I should be. Mr. Pratt," she says as he comes through the door. "What on earth would you call that?"

"A shadow. A creeper. A crawler, we call it. It won't bother you anymore."

"Is it gone?"

"It's gone."

"For good?"

"Yes. For good. Are you feeling all right?"

"No. I'm not. But lighter, somehow . . . I suppose I have you to thank for that."

I stare at them all, amazed. This is what the thoughtless living do: they thank men like Pratt for making their hearts emptier.

"I'm sorry the matter wasn't tended to sooner," he says, wiping his hands.

"How could it have been? I never spoke of it. I thought the garden had been thoroughly cleaned."

"Yes, I've been hearing that a great deal around here. May I wash my hands at your tap?"

"Please go ahead. And sit here"—she points—"in my chair, please. You look a bit—"

"No, thank you. I'm fine."

The hunter finishes rinsing his hands of someone's life. All in a day's work, for him. He wipes his forehead with one palm. "I just have one more question for you. And then we can put some of this day to rest. It's a simple matter. Do the words on Alice's gravestone, 'The last to see me be the first to rejoice,' mean anything to you?"

"No." Mrs. Fanoli sets her cane aside, not needing it indoors. "Except it sounds like some lofty nonsense a Lambry would have on their tombstone. Have you seen their memorial in the cemetery?"

"I have."

"Then you know how full of themselves they were. Are you all right, young man?" she says bracingly. "You look like you could use a hot toddy."

"It's been a long few days, Agnes."

"I can imagine. But why does one spirit give you so much trouble and another one you crush, I see, like an aphid? What's the difference?"

"Some are weak. Some are strong."

"What would I be, in the end, I wonder?"

"You'd be yourself. Ghosts were once people, so they have the traits of people. Some weak, some strong."

He stands, leaning against the chair he wouldn't take, and seems tired. I hope he's tired. As tired as death. I hope he carries inside him all the ash he's made and left in all the gardens of this world.

"Some ghosts have a great deal of self-knowledge," he goes on, murderer that he is, "and others don't. Some are honest, some liars"—he looks at Ellen—"and liars tell lies in death just as much as they did in life. Some are confident and can walk as plainly in the open as you or I would and almost seem to inhabit living form. They're the sharpest, the trickiest to deal with. But even they go down, too, in the end."

So sure you are of yourself, Mr. Pratt. Yet I'm in this room, plain as day, and you haven't found me yet.

"Well, that sounds final." Mrs. Fanoli shakes her head. "But still," she says—and I see in her eyes the shadow of her end so close it crowds her—"I wonder what it takes to be strong enough to . . . *not* be that poor man you just put down by the ghost flower."

Ellen says, "Sounds like something everybody would want to know, doesn't it?"

"I can only tell you, Agnes, that there are ghosts who convince themselves they aren't ghosts. There's a kind—but it's not very common—who convinces itself it isn't dead. Who firmly believes, with every inch of its soul and being, that it hasn't died, that it never died; who can conjure itself into believing it never passed away. Suicides who change their minds on the way down. People who die accidentally. In rare cases, they take on a phantom form that's nearly complete. At the price, though, of not being able to do the things a normal ghost can do. Like disappear. They also don't eat, or rest, or sleep. The eating, especially, tends to give them away. Would you like that, Agnes? To be able to walk around but not be able to do the things that give life its flavor?"

"I'd have to think about that," she admits.

"It sounds impossible." Ellen looks out the window.

Don't listen to him. It's all tricks. As if dying were something anybody could choose not to do. As if all a soul had to do, while its lungs were filling with water and its breath was being choked away, was pretend that it wasn't happening.

"It's rare." Pratt sits, finally. "It's unusual. The usual is what we're dealing with in town. A ghost attaching itself to a place that has meaning to it, an empty space. Like a shack on a beach no one thought to tell me about." He turns again toward Ellen. "A space belonging to a person or a family that did it some harm or wrong—or who simply ignored it. Maybe a family that should have done more for the ghost, while it was still living. Some ghosts hide in plain sight. They have a face. They—"

"Oh my word!" The old woman reaches out to touch Pratt's shoulder. "Did you just say a ghost could attach itself to an *entire* family? Not just one person? But a *family*? That maybe did it some harm or just ignored it?"

"Yes?" Pratt looks up at her.

"Well then, you stay right there, young man. Because I think I may have been sending you down the wrong garden path."

19

It was only a rumor but it was the kind of rumor that stayed with you for eighty-seven years, Agnes told them. Because there was a whisper of scandal around it. Whispers at old Mrs. Lambry's funeral, when the whole village of Benito came out—her husband already unbending in his grave for ten years. The Depression was in full swing by then. Many of the millworkers had already left, trying to find some better place that needed their muscle. What remained of the village came to Eugenia Lambry's funeral.

In the back pews, behind the family, in St. Clements Church, the murmurs went round and round and round:

Well maybe that old woman will have some peace at last . . .

Blood on their hands, on both of them, I say . . .

And more than just their own son's . . . Unless it was all lies?

Then why did the girl disappear when the boy did . . .?

She might have gotten herself into trouble and skulked off to hide . . . probably in another town for good. How else could a poor girl keep a rich boy tied to her apron if she wasn't letting him have what was underneath it?

And even old Mr. Folde said she ran away out of shame.

But they do say she was at the hotel the night before. Asking about the ship . . .

What was that schooner's name . . .

The Lorna.

Well, the constable wouldn't look into it. Too squeamish.

Because they stopped him, Eugenia and Augustus . . .

And what was her name . . . so long ago . . . nobody . . . Something with a flower in it, a lily? A rose? They do say that's why the old woman put up her garden and the widow's walk to let her see over the cove . . . so she could keep vigil . . .

Or make amends?

Or just keep an eye out for that slattern girl hoping to come back and cheat her way into the family again . . .

It can all come out, though, now . . .

Not that there's anyone left to remember . . . Just a few of us old biddies, not long for the world ourselves.

That's right, I think, and keep to the sunlight warming the Welcome Cottage's windows. No one left to remember. No one living. But I'm still here, while all the rest of you lie moldering in your graves, and an old woman stammers on. And what can she do to me, what can she say, what can she give away, when she'll be joining you soon enough . . .

"I was only six years old," Agnes says excitedly, "but the whispers stayed with me, because they were things that had never been said out loud about the Lambrys, at least not that I'd heard, anyhow. Like it wasn't safe to talk about certain things until Eugenia and Augustus were both stuffed under that monument.

"And I don't know if any of this will help you, Mr. Pratt, but this whole time I've been walking around with you, thinking it should be Alice you're hunting, these little whispers in my head were sitting and gathering cobwebs. I never heard of the Lambry House being haunted by anyone, but then again, I've never heard of a Lambry turning into a ghost, either. Why should any one of them, comfortable as they all were—and proud!—stoop to become something as lowly as a ghost? It wouldn't suit them. And Alice kept so much to herself; why would she suddenly take to visiting the hotel and dropping in and out of mirrors? What I'm thinking, Mr. Pratt"—she reaches down to touch his shoulder "is what if the old rumors were right, after all? And Mrs. Lambry knew of a girl, whoever she was, who had drowned along with her boy, and *not* gone off to some other village . . . And what if it isn't *Alice* causing all this trouble, but someone else who's been keeping a leash on the Lambrys all these years, one after another after another after another . . . only now there are no more Lambrys to haunt, so it's out into the open, as it were?"

"But there *is* one Lambry left," Pratt says, before I leave them all in my dust.

I fly toward the village.

Afraid now.

But I can't be. I won't.

Because nobody can find out the name of a nobody. Can they?

The name of an orphan girl, dead for a hundred years.

And if they can't know my name, they can't rouse me.

I reach the house, and how safe, oh, how good it feels to pass smoothly through the doors and glide up the staircase and visit the rooms and galleries and then go through the smaller door and out onto the circle of the widow's walk, and pace around it, and see across the cove to the Botanical Garden, and how invisible, how small, how *nothing* those people are over there. At this distance, who are the nobodies? And how good it feels to go in and float down again along the carved banister and over the newel post, and go through the parlors, one by one, and visit each beloved room, until finally I stand in the shimmer of our beautiful Glass Room, with its perfect dome around me, its floating panes. Built on the very spot where Eugenia Lambry used to stand and look out at the waves and wonder if it was me brushing against her shoulder, making her hair stand on end and the skin on the back of her neck draw tight.

So long ago, that was. That first dawn. After my death. At first, I didn't even know what I could do. No one explains it. There's no help. No one says, *Here you are, you've died, but you aren't dead now, spilling and rolling and tangled like this, like a baby seal, bloody, washed up on the beach.*

I don't remember much from those first few moments. Afterward, I remember standing. Feeling the emptiness inside me. My heart no longer swinging in my chest. Stopped forever, like an ax on a stump. My mind full of questions. *What do I do, then? So it seems I can walk. I can move. I can climb, high, higher, crawling up the cliff. Can I have some revenge? I can. I can make the electric light flicker when I find her alone in a room, when she sits and tries to write another letter to her children.*

First to her children. Later to her grandchildren.

How slowly time moves, I thought in the beginning.

But still I was quick to catch at her sleeve when she tried to leave a room before I wanted her to. Or slam a door in her face when she was rude to a servant. What seemed to frighten her the most was when I fogged the mirrors as they both dressed for dinner and made it look as though the breath was coming from right behind them, over their shoulders, panting. But when Mr. and Mrs. Augustus Lambry turned, in their starched fronts, no one was there. And when they turned back and reached up to wipe the fog away, they'd see a mirrored arm that seemed to be their own—but stretching for their throats.

Are you sorry now? I asked Lambry after Lambry. *Can your blood ever be done apologizing to mine? Will you ever be truly sorry enough?* It's four generations of Lambrys, now, who have quietly tried to make their amends to me. Too ashamed to share with the town, and the timid constables, what was happening in their own house. In some ways, I should be grateful. Because it's thanks to their shame, their leaving me to do as I've wanted, year after year, that I've learned more and more about what I'm strong enough to do, and how much I can do—more than I ever imagined in the beginning. Yet I'll never say to any soul living or dead that being dead is a good thing, or that suffering is a good teacher. Drowning is agony. Sadness is slavery. No one dying should ever see a back turned away from them; no one should ever be left alone, in the end.

And so I gave Manoel's watch back to him, when he asked for it. And I've appeared, faithfully, to every soul who has died in this house, to tell them it would be over soon. And I shut the blinds to keep the sun from blinding poor Alice, and put the pillow over her face when she was afraid and nothing was left that could help her; for all we can ever do for one another is the best we know how.

And so must you, Emma Rose, I remind myself. *You must do your best, now. Don't lose your will. Don't abandon it.* There's no one living now, after all, who still knows the name of the girl who sank forgotten all those years ago. Why, I might even feel sorry for anyone trying to find out who she was, with so little to go on, no more than rumors, a whisper, gossip over a grave. I might even feel sorry for Mrs. Fanoli, Pratt, and Ellen. Except I won't.

Maybe it's everyone else who should be sorry for everything, everywhere.

20

It was a dry, clear spring afternoon when Mrs. Folde asked me to come with her to the cemetery above the Point to visit her baby boy's grave. I carried the basket for her with the pruning shears while she lifted the fattening twin of *Infant Joseph* up to her hip. We walked together, up the lane, across the high coast road that so many months before had brought me to my new home. We followed a smaller, narrower track to the raised meadow. From there the headstones of some of the Point's keepers and their families rose with a nice view of the cluster of red-shingled buildings, and the lighthouse, and the shifting ocean.

I trimmed away the clover from the plot, while Mrs. Folde bowed her head on her baby's head and said the prayer:

Oh God, you do not willingly grieve or afflict your children. Look with pity on the suffering of this family. Sustain us in our anguish and into the darkness of Grief, bring light.

"All right." She straightened her sun hat and adjusted the baby at her breast. "I think we've done the best we can. It looks better now. The weeds grow so fast, don't they? We should plant flowers. For next summer. Pansies. Children do like pansies."

She stuffed her nose into the twin's neck. "He smells like spring. There's a ripeness to everything right now. A freshness. Maybe that's a good omen."

Maybe. Quint came at least twice a week now, and each time he was more anxious to take me away with him. But each time he still couldn't say how he was going to do it with no money of his own.

"Emma, you're not paying attention to me."

"Sorry, Mrs. Folde."

"I was just saying—the future is bright today. Guess why?"

"I can't."

"Because we've received a letter from the commission, that's why! Good news at last. Mr. Edgars, the head keeper, won't be returning to the Point. Mrs. Edgars' consumption has gone to both lungs, so they'll have to go away and retire from the damp. Which means—isn't it something—Mr. Folde and Mr. McHenry will get promotions. The question is: *who* will be promoted to head lightkeeper?"

She frowned and set her chin down again on the baby's scalp. "I'm prejudiced, but I know in my heart it should go to Mr. Folde. He's the better manager. And we've got the larger family. And I think anyone would agree Mr. Folde's common sense is superior to Mr. McHenry's. Mr. Folde would never have let you take that nasty tumble on the tower, isn't that right? And Mr. McHenry could stay on as first assistant, which seems to suit him and Mrs. McHenry very well, and there would be a new second assistant hired, so the men wouldn't have to run all the shifts themselves, the way they've been doing, putting such strains on them. It's overwork that's been making Mr. Folde so quiet lately, I'm certain of it. No man can expect to keep himself fit running twelve hours a day, every day, six hours at a stretch, for month after month, when it's only eight hours he was hired on for."

I didn't say anything to that. Not about Mr. Folde's drooping whiskers, or his tired, blinking look, or the way he'd begun to stare at me for a long time, dazed, while I ironed his socks. I looked down and brushed the weed clippings from my skirt.

"Now this is important, Emma. Something you and I need to discuss in great detail. We're going to have a visit from the commission to decide about the new head keeper. Ours is going to be the luncheon interview. So, you and I have to go over every little thing. We have to be sure everything is *perfection*. Especially since Dora McHenry is going to have the advantage of the dinner interview." She fidgeted with the baby's collar. "But it's *first* impressions that really matter, thank goodness. And we get the commission first. So let's have salmon, and cucumber sandwiches, and those tarts you make so well, and of course tea. I'll hostess, and you'll serve."

"The tea?" I had to ask, because I knew I should never, ever handle the royal blue and gold Wedgewood china tea set. That was the Foldes' pride and joy.

"Well, I don't see why not. Just this once. I need to look like a head keeper's wife, after all, and not an ordinary—Anyhow, I'm sure you'll be very careful, Emma. All you'll have to do is bring in the tray, and I'll do the rest. And I'll see to it Mr. Folde understands. That we need to show the commission we're capable of entertaining fine guests at the Point, and . . . and so on."

I'd been at the Point for eight months and seen no one finer than Quint arrive, but I didn't say so. It would have been cruel.

"We'll show them we're an excellent, complete establishment. My management skills will impress them, and you'll show them in what good order we are, and it will say something about us all."

"When are they coming?"

"Next Tuesday. A week."

My birthday. I'd been hoping to have part of that day all to myself so I could go and stand at the edge of the cliffs and make a plea to the spirits, to the *far darrig*, that I would be beginning my last year as a housekeeper, my very last. For it was—Quint said and I knew it—no primitive world we lived in now. Servants weren't content to be servants anymore. We were all going and working at the wharves and warehouses, and into the factories, and making good money doing war-enterprise. Even Mrs. Strype, I'd heard, was having a hard time keeping help on. Because girls weren't keeping to their places anymore. We were trying our luck at bigger things.

"It doesn't give us much time to pull ourselves together," Mrs. Folde said as we walked back down the hill. "We'll have so much polishing and cleaning to do. I don't know how I'll manage it. I'm still not very strong. As I keep telling Mr. Folde."

I told all the news to Quint when he arrived. How Mrs. Folde wanted so much to look like a grand lady she planned for me to wear a white cap like the ones the hotel and parlor maids wore. "And she said I should call her madam instead of ma'am," I said, laughing.

"The commission is made up of people my family knows." Quint pulled on his whiskers, distracted. "I don't like the idea of you serving them at all."

"Well, I serve here every day, and that's the truth."

"It's always bothered me."

"Has it? Or does it bother you more now because your family's friends are coming?"

"Of course it does. I mean, always has."

"Then what do you think I should do? Go work in the canneries? I ought to. There's good money for people like me, down south."

"*No!* I mean, no," he said, with less of a bark. "I don't want you to go away!"

"But you don't want me to stay here, either," I pointed out. "So what exactly do you expect me to do?"

"Can't we go into your cottage to talk about it?" he said eagerly. "And sit like two grown up people in a room, instead of like tramps on a beach?"

"No. We can't." I didn't think it would be a good idea. I remembered again Franny's words: *Like a buck out of the woods . . . you'd better watch out.* And I knew what the gossips in the village were already saying about me.

"Emma, please. You don't have to worry. Folde knows enough to respect my character and family. And he's a decent man."

"But it's never the men who mind about girls being alone in a room with them. And it's never the men who pay for it."

"Do you mean Mrs. Folde might turn you out, if she knew?" He moved strangely, excitedly. "But maybe that's exactly what we *should* have her do! Maybe we should give her a reason to fire you! Then you wouldn't have to wait on my family's friends—you couldn't stay here at all. You'd be free."

"I don't call that freedom." Coming back to town no higher than I was now, no better off? Except for the money I'd saved.

"But haven't I proven myself to you, Emma Rose? Coming here every week? Haven't I been true to you?"

"Yes. You have." I leaned my head on his shoulder.

"But you still say no to everything I ask for."

"No. Not everything." There'd been more than one yes.

"Then just tell me when the commission is coming," he said, suddenly hot, "because I can tell you I'm not coming anywhere near here while you're serving cakes to my father's cronies. I won't face that."

"Quint, why so angry today?"

"Because everything's impossible!" he raged. "I can't get engaged until I'm twenty! I'm dependent on my father till I'm twenty-one. My father says the government is trying to punish the rich with this new income tax, and he's closing his fist as tight as a monkey's around what he's got and he says he's doing it for us children, for our futures. To protect us. But I can't see how . . . and I can't will myself to play the meek son anymore. My brother, he'll do anything Father and Mother tell him to. And my sisters are no better—they trot like wind-up donkeys to the parties at Fort Kane, and my mother expects me to chaperone them. It's so medieval. It's not what I want. My mother says I should try to see the world the way my father sees it, but . . ." He shook his head.

"Quint."

"Since you have so much work to do, I'll go. Unless you'll run away with me, right this minute?" He kissed my cheek, distracted.

Should a girl ever leave something safe for an unsure saddle? Especially if her heart leaps every time she sees the fine horse and its well-dressed rider? How I wished I had a mother to guide me! And how foolish that I'd once imagined, when I came to the Point, that Mrs. Folde might be the woman I could confide in, when more and more, these days, she saw me only as the girl who would wear a white cap on the day the commission came, while she wore me like a feather in hers.

No, there was only me on the grass, and when Quint had gone, only me in my cottage, sitting on the quilt, the cold kept out by a few pieces of coal in the stove, and by the live sound of a mallet ringing through the walls. Mr. Folde, at work nearby in the carpentry building. Making some repair. After a while, the hammering came less even, less steadily. It sounded like a heart losing its rhythm, speed.

I came out at dusk with my shawl over my shoulders, headed toward the house to make dinner. Mr. Folde was coming out from the shop, his work vest covered in sawdust, a piece of heavy lumber studded with bolts balanced on his shoulder.

He stopped in front of me, the weight of the wood rocking to one side. "Good evening, Emma."

"Good evening, Mr. Folde."

"Has young Lambry left early today?"

"Yes, sir."

"I guess it's busy out in the logging camps, now that spring has started."

"Yes."

"You look a little tired." He straightened the wood as it tried to swing away from him.

"I'm fine, thank you."

"If young Lambry is coming too often, I can—"

"No! Thank you."

He said nothing for a moment, balancing his load and staring off toward the eye of the lighthouse, its long throat starting to blush in the sunset.

"You need to take care of yourself, Emma. It's important to all of us."

"Yes."

I said nothing more. I felt strange. I'd been careful around Mr. Folde ever since he'd started noticing my hair, complimenting my ribbons. I heard Franny's words again. *But things happen, Emma. Accidents. And men who get lonely, after. So you be nice to all of them, I'm telling you. And see what time sees fit to bring you.* I kept my eyes fixed on the Folde house. But I couldn't move toward it. He and his lumber were in my way.

"Mrs. Folde is expecting me, sir."

"Of course." He leaned forward and began walking, head down, into the dying wind.

21

Pratt and Ellen have walked and driven all over Benito together. They've gone to the village newspaper. They've gone to the library. They've asked at the Chinese temple. They've visited the thin-columned house at the end of Main Street that keeps the files and photographs preserved by the historical commission. They've driven over to St. Clements Church, to check the parish records, trying to guess at her name—my name.

Emma, I could tell them. Sometimes, when I'm tired of being hunted, I almost want to. Just to hear my name spoken again. Emma Rose Finnis. That's who I was and always tried to be—a friend, a hard worker, honest.

They sit together in Pratt's car, going over their notes. There's a lingering stiffness between them, like the tightness over a healing cut.

"All right, Ellen?"

"I'm fine."

"Need to call it a day? Go home?"

"No. Where would I go?" She taps her slate. "Nothing's safe till we finish this. I want to finish. What do we do now? I don't see a sign of any missing girl who might have wanted to haunt the Lambry family."

"Unless we consider their housekeeper, Mrs. Broyle."

"She died an old woman. Her grave is in Evergreen. Where else can we look?"

"In the gaps. The empty spaces."

"Well, we've done that, haven't we?"

"A different kind of gap is where we are now. The gap in a story."

"So how do we fill it?"

"My answer might surprise you."

"Try me."

"If the head is getting you nowhere, go with the heart." He taps his chest.

Is that what he thought he was doing, whenever he stroked his shirtfront?

"The *Benito Gazette*," he says, looking out his windshield, "reported the Lambrys lost their son aboard the schooner *Lorna*."

"But the *Gazette* listed all travelers in their shipping news section, always." She checks her device again.

"And they had no female passenger listed on board, that voyage."

"The schooners were packed with cargo, the docent said at the historical commission."

"'Trains of the sea,' they were called." Pratt frowns. "And piled high with lumber, more than any other commodity. Wood was given precedence over human cargo. Tickets for passengers were expensive."

"Mrs. Fanoli stressed the girl we'd be looking for wouldn't have had very much money. She'd be working class."

"A 'slattern,' she said they called her."

"A slut?" Ellen says the word as though it means nothing.

"Or maybe only someone who sweated at her work. But a dirty name. Who did the dirty work in those days?"

"The washerwomen pounding the laundry." She flips through the black and white pictures. Of girls like me and Franny. "Cooking in the camps and in the boardinghouses. Tending to everything no one else would do, or wanted to."

"And how do you think they felt doing that?"

It felt unimportant, I think, sitting right behind them.

Ellen closes her eyes and leans her head back against Pratt's fine, stitched leather. "I know exactly how they felt. At least, I think I do. I had to tend to someone all the time. Do everything. Because nobody else would. It makes you feel like nothing." She opens her eyes. "It makes you feel, if no one notices you, small."

"And when you felt that way," Pratt asks, "what did you want to do?"

"Escape. Get away."

"But what if you couldn't?"

"I did as soon as I could . . . As soon as I . . . As soon as there was nothing left for me to do."

"You say you left when there was nothing more for you to do. And then you left for somewhere peaceful. You told me that."

"But," she says and sits up sharply, turning, "*that's* why I don't think whoever we're looking for was on the *Lorna*. Because the *Gazette* said it was only taking a special load of lumber north to the fort and then turning around and coming right back to the village. It was just going to another roughneck place. An army post. Not even as nice as Benito. You saw the pictures at the history museum. Half of Fort Kane was nothing but mud and canvas. I wouldn't go there. Much less only to come back."

"But would that have mattered to you, if you just wanted to get away?"

"Not if I had any idea my ship was going to founder at—" She stops herself, blinking.

"Go on, Ellen. It's all right. We have to use our instincts for other lives. It's all we have. That's what we're doing, right now."

They sit silently for a moment under the cover of Pratt's roof. I don't know what's coming next, but I need to stay close. I need to be ready.

"The boat never got any farther than Lighthouse Point," Ellen says.

"So what about the lighthouse, then?"

"Six miles to the north."

"Still functioning?"

"Abandoned, years ago. They've got lighted buoys out on the water now. Everything's automatic."

"Would we find anyone there?"

No. Not me. I'll make sure of it.

"I don't think so. It's turned into sort of a den for delinquents. The buildings are sad. It's all a mess. Though a cleaner did come and flush it out, at some point."

"But maybe missed something useful. As other things have been missed in this town." Pratt taps his fingers on the steering wheel. "I say we go there now."

"It's getting dark, though."

"We'll drive back to the hotel and pick up a few lights. Unless you'd rather stay there?"

"No, I want to go. I'm feeling something. Something about how it feels. To come back from the dead. And want to make a life for yourself again. I think I'm getting the hang of this. Did you see how that crawler at the Botanical Garden didn't even really upset me?"

Pratt studies her. "I did."

Brave little Ellen. I'll give her that.

"So," she says. "Let's go."

22

I need you. I need you. I need you, Mrs. Folde said.

For soaping and scrubbing the baseboards until the children's scuff-marks were all gone. That's how she needed me. For beating and airing the hooked rugs and laying them down again. For taking the chimneys from the lamps and polishing them. For oiling the banister and burnishing the brass. *I need you, Emma, right now. For this work. I need you.*

If only a person knew, if only you knew when you were going to die, you might spend your last hours in some other, more treasured way than spitting on dulled brass. On a beach. With a bright boy. Reading a poem. *Who dreamed that beauty passes like a dream?*

Mrs. Folde grew so nervous about the commission's visit she decided to send the children and the baby away with her sister, who came with her husband in a Packard.

"I'm torn, oh Emma, I'm so torn," she said as she waved them good-bye. "I do want those men to see we're a growing family—but not such a circus we can't handle the head keeper's responsibilities. If only I hadn't let myself be burdened with so many little ones."

The sun rose on the day of the commission's visit, my nineteenth birthday, and I did nothing more than put a fresh ribbon in my hair and begin making the tarts. I missed Quint, who hadn't come to see me since we'd argued about my waiting on people he knew. He didn't know it was my birthday. That was my doing. I hadn't told him. I should have, and if I had, I would have said all I wanted, truly, was to see the same moon he did at night and not count what that might be worth.

"I need to make clear we're a *good* family," Mrs. Folde said as the hour drew near, fidgeting with her hair, coiled high on her head. "Not like *some* keeper's wives, whom I won't mention, whose bloomers have no lace on them. All right. Let's keep to our schedule. The men's shifts have been altered today. Mr. Folde is going early to the lighthouse, and then will come back to us. We're on our own for now. Let us rise to the occasion."

It was a warmer day than it had been all spring. The starch in the napkins was already wilting. But God took the measure of a soul, Mrs. Folde said, and so did the commission, by how well that soul bore disaster.

I tried not to think about Quint as I pulled the curtains tight to keep the sun out. Still, I couldn't help peeking through them, hoping for a surprise, something sweet, unexpected.

At noon I saw the touring car carrying the commission down through the woven canopy of the cypress trees. Three large men, all wearing bright yellow straw hats, sitting tall in their seats, like suns all risen to the same height. Such steady-looking heads. I supposed they had to be, since they had the job of supplying so many light stations with men they could trust, up and down this stretch of coast.

I called out to Mrs. Folde. She flung her apron aside and told me to put my cap on. She took one last, beady look around the dining parlor and checked her face in the hall-tree mirror. "I don't look *bohemian*, do I?"

"No ma'am."

"Madam. Don't forget."

She told me to stand ready to take the men's hats. We watched through the glass of the front door as Mr. Folde came boldly toward the car—he must have seen them coming from the signal house—and met them at the picket fence. If he was anxious, shaking their hands, he didn't show it, or showed it only by the slightest rise in his shoulders under his keeper's jacket.

Mrs. Folde whispered, "He looks so well, doesn't he? So fit?"

"He does."

"Oh, there's really only *one* choice of man, here. Anyone can see that. All right. Here they come."

While I carried the first luncheon tray into the dining parlor, the largest, most thick-mustached of the men was saying with a raised glance that they would take this refreshment and then walk outdoors. Mrs. Folde swept around to show them to their seats. As I started back to the kitchen I heard her say, in a higher-pitched voice than I was used to, "Oh, but who would have ever thought it would be so hot in April! But they say 'warm warns before storm'—as my husband's wonderful weather observations always bear out."

The first soup course in, I was glad to sit and rest for a while beside the pie cupboard. I had everything for the next course ready, the sandwiches, then after that the royal blue tea set—though why anyone would want to serve both soup and hot tea on a day like this, I didn't ask Mrs. Folde.

I wiped the sweat from under my cap and pulled at the front of my shirtwaist and looked out the screen door toward the empty lane. Nearly a year now since Quint had first started coming down it. Three seasons. Summer, winter, and spring. Yes, he'd proven himself, I had to admit.

He was no Johnny-come-and-go. I felt my heart twinge a little, with a strange, hot nervousness.

Mrs. Folde's little silver dinner bell rang—my signal to bring in the sandwich tray. I saw that Mrs. Folde was nodding across to Mr. Folde at the crowded round table. The thickly mustached gentleman, the commission head, looked sweaty between them, and the two others had adjusted their collars to the warm room. Mrs. Folde made a sign to me, even though I knew already who to serve first. The head was saying it was a pity electricity hadn't come yet to the Point; it would require less manpower at the station, he said, and free the keepers to "do more scientific work."

"True," Mr. Folde said, "but in the end that would mean less work and so fewer keepers."

"Yes, the fat of progress does lead to the thinning of labor. But times are changing. What else can we do but change with them?"

"Perhaps"—Mr. Folde bowed in his seat—"we could remember that nothing can replace what a man can observe and do—especially in cases of surprise or emergency. If the electric supply were to fail, for example, as we know it has at some stations"—he took a cool cucumber sandwich from me—"it's better to have two men at the pump instead of one. And it might perhaps be held as a loss to the lightkeepers' service, and maybe even to humanity—if that's not too large a claim—to allow certain forms of progress to lessen the chances of men earning their living . . . or even to live meaningfully at all."

"There is that, yes. But there is also a decided loss to the service, Folde, when we devote the energies of a man—say, a man of your obvious qualities—to the menial tasks of conveying grease and oil. The service notes this loss and feels it."

"Oh!" Mrs. Folde interrupted brightly. "But surely we can all agree the *head* keeper *always* has a great deal more time to devote to scientific study, and therefore such a position should be given to a man of—of obvious qualities."

"True, madam," the head commissioner replied. "But the head must also be willing to embrace modern principles. Especially if these are more efficient at getting things done. And even if they run counter to his own, er, humanitarian principles."

Mrs. Folde looked a little confused.

She sent me away.

The bell rang again half an hour later, and I brought in the tarts and cream and went back for the tea. The set was clumsy and old-fashioned, and I was expected to bring it on the heavy tray all at once—the pot, the sugar caddy, the milk, the cream, the cups, the saucers, and all the silver spoons. A queer silence hung around the table as I pushed through the swinging door, as though they'd had to stop whatever they'd just been saying because of me.

After a moment, the thickly mustached leader said, "But changes are afoot in that corner, I hear. My dear friend, Augustus Lambry, feels his son has learned all that he can in the camps and the mills and is sending him off to a private university on the next ship, in advance of next year's term. So he can get some private tutoring in politics and economics over the summer. The boy is suddenly eager, by all accounts, to learn the latest forms of thinking. It's just as well. Many of us out here in the wilderness don't want to admit it, but we deprive our sons of proper company and the right sort of associates and connections if we keep them for too long in the country air."

I felt the tray lower in my hands. No. I didn't believe it. It couldn't be right, what this man was saying.

Mrs. Folde leapt in. "Oh *yes!* I feel that so much, *too!* That we shouldn't keep our dear ones from their proper spheres! Though of course I do *hate* it when my little ones leave my side—they're perfect little angels, you know, and you would have loved to meet them—but I can't help but feel it's good for them to get away from all this primitiveness sometimes and see more of the civilized parts of our state. Left to their own devices out here, young people are apt to lose some sense of propriety." She glanced primly at me. "Despite the *best* supervision, I promise you."

Mr. Folde said quietly, "Sarah."

I couldn't move. I waited. I was a tree listening for the coming jack.

"So what you're saying, then, Mrs. Folde," the head raised his eyebrows, "is that you're not really *fond* of the isolation at this station? Or of the lightkeeper's . . . *uncivilized* life, as you say?"

"Oh! No! Of course not! I didn't mean—Of course I would never say—"

"Perhaps you mean you're not likely to commit to its duties for very long? Or fulfill them with alacrity and gratitude?"

"No, I—"

"I do take your meaning I believe, madam. Thank you very much for your frankness. I'd say we're done here."

Mr. Folde's face, I thought, was a mirror of mine. Stunned. Understanding. Seeing how, in one moment, everything was ruined. I told him with my eyes, as plain as day, *I'm not weak, and neither are you. But something just broke here, and you know it, and I know it, and there's no going back, not for either one of us. It's all done, just like that.*

I stepped back and, with one jerking move, smashed the tea set to the floor under us. For both of us. I saw the hot water splash the shins of the head and I heard the cups roll and shatter against the feet of the dining chairs, and I saw Mrs. Folde's guests all lift their fine shoes up, forgetting everything but their own leathers, their own skins.

And then I took another step and clutched my sweaty cap and decided, dishonestly, willfully, to pretend to faint. So that I couldn't be blamed for the accident. I took one look at Mr. Folde. As I sank, his arms flailed toward me, though it was Quint's arms I imagined I saw, waving to me, from the speeding bow of a ship.

Mr. Folde was quickly on the floor beside me, his one hand scraping the broken pieces of china from my apron while making his apologies to the commission, his other so tight on my arm it hurt.

I heard him say to Mrs. Folde, "Dear wife, would you please take our guests into the front parlor, so Emma Rose can catch her breath and see to repairing this unfortunate incident?"

Mrs. Folde, shrunken, humiliated, led the men out of the room. I pulled my arm free from Mr. Folde's as soon as they were gone and stood and walked like a frozen thing to the kitchen and pulled the broom and the dust pan from the closet and came back. The room was empty and I stooped and began mopping up the pieces of the Folde heirloom. Feeling nothing. Not even sorry.

So. Quint was going to the east, then. Far away. Because I'd shamed him by being a servant. Because I hadn't let him come to my room when he asked. So that was why he hadn't come back to me. To a university he'd go, instead. He liked books. Greek and Latin. He'd read me some poems. Maybe he'd even cared for such things more than he ever let on to me. And now he'd get to study all the latest ideas, too. So that was all it took, then? To replace love? Steamships and trains. Was that how easily love was swept aside? Afternoons curled on each others' necks on the sand. *No, if I let myself take all this in right now,* I thought, keeping my head down, *I'll never stop smashing things. I'll smash the lamps and their chimneys, too, and I might even burn the house down, to cover up this burning inside me.*

Mr. Folde came back and stood over the ruin. "That was a mistake, Emma."

"I know."

"We'll need to talk about this later."

"Yes."

"I'll have to go and join the others. Can you finish this?"

"I'll see to it all."

"Well then." He stared at me like a Fresnel that couldn't, didn't want to turn. But he went.

After the men had gone outside, Mrs. Folde staggered up to her room and shut her door, without a word to me. I hung my apron and cap in the kitchen and went to my cottage and lay down on the bed and cried for a good ten minutes. And then I didn't cry anymore. There was no point. Weeping—it's for people who can pump their longing out through their eyes and be done with it. I can't and couldn't. I still wanted. I wanted so much. I felt no end to it, how the wanting kept growing, like my own hair. But I stayed where I was. And let the afternoon go by, hot, the sun dragging its claws over the window. At sunset I stood up and saw not the usual fireworks of golden and orange and blood-red streaks in the sky but clouds going purple, dark, like a bruise. *Warm warns before storm.* Mrs. Folde's words. I had been waiting for her to come from the house and fire me. Or Mr. Folde. But they didn't.

When it was pitch black and I could no longer see my hand fumbling and lighting the lamp, I changed out of my tea-stained skirt into a fresh one and combed my hair and cracked the cottage door. I saw one light burning high in the Folde house, up in Mrs. Folde's bedroom. All the other rooms were black-eyed. I thought about how eager I'd been to leave my dirty, dreary work at the Point. But now that Quint wasn't ever going to come back again I wanted, suddenly, to stay on. With the children. And get to know them better. Those little boys and girls who stared at me, awed, as if I held the key to mysteries. The twins, Roger and Timmy, with their identical shovel-noses. Theresa and Christina, locking hands when the grass was wet. Little Alva, rolling on her chubby, piped legs. Mrs. Folde, who leaned on me and needed me, as troubled as she was. I didn't want to leave her. And poor, exhausted Mr. Folde, who'd knelt down to me on the floor when the other men had curled their spines like sea urchins poked in the center. I had to give him that.

I stepped out into a wet, spreading mist. Over at the McHenrys' house, between the lace curtains, the lights burned brightly. The first assistant and his wife would be having dinner with the commission now, and Mr. Folde would be alone at the lighthouse seeing to the compressors and to the bottomless winding.

Seven dollars a week. I had to keep my wages and keep my nest-egg growing, so I could do something on my own, one day, maybe, with a little luck. *Hold fast, Emma Rose Finnis. You can't let yourself be beaten, not by men in golden straw hats, not by the Lambrys, not by hook or crook.* I hurried across the shadowy turf as fast as I could toward the signal house. I was going to tell Mr. Folde how sorry I was for losing my temper and ask him not to let me go, not just yet.

I opened the low, black door. He was leaning over one of the barrel-shaped engines that stored the air that fed the sirens. His lightkeeper's jacket was off and thrown to one side, over a stool; his shirt sleeves were rolled up, showing his long arms. His back was bent and rounded over the compressor. He held a claw-shaped tool, fixing something that seemed hard to reach. He must have heard my step because he gave up wrestling and dropped the wrench with a heavy clanging sound, and straightened.

"Oh," he said vaguely, as if he hadn't really seen me at first.

"I'm sorry, Mr. Folde. To disturb you."

"It's nothing. I'm making no progress. Are you better?"

"I'm better."

"You've been crying."

"It doesn't matter now."

"No. I guess it doesn't. It's all decided, by now." He gestured vaguely in the direction of the McHenrys' house.

"I'm so sorry, Mr. Folde."

"Yes. I am, too."

"I don't know what to—I—I think I let the Irish in me have its way."

"Is that your excuse?"

"It's my excuse. But I'm still sorry."

"Things could have gone better for the both of us today, couldn't they?"

"Mr. Folde. About the tea set—I can pay—I've been saving up money. It'll take me some time to pay it all back, but—"

"It belonged to my mother's family. It was with us for many years. The only fine thing my mother ever owned. I owned." He looked at me.

"I'll find a way to get it all replaced. I will."

"Some things don't get—replaced—as you say. It doesn't matter. Life goes on making its decisions, great and small, without us." His whiskers were damp, and the back of his hands were greased. He rubbed one against the other. With frustration, I thought. I knew.

He came away from the compressor, looking sad and tired. He seemed, just then, like a horse on an endless carousel, a man for whom the pulling never ended. His face made me forget my own pulling for a moment.

"Well. I have to go up to the light, now," he said.

He came toward me and his foot grazed my skirt. He reached for his jacket as if to put it on but then changed his mind and threw it aside again.

He said, "Oh Emma, it wasn't a good day!"

"No, sir."

"Not for those of us who hoped to climb higher than where we started."

"I came to ask if I can still—"

"We understand each other, Emma, don't we? We can console each other. We should. We birds of a feather. We two . . . gulled gulls." His voice sounded empty and hoarse.

I moved to one side but didn't have much room with the compressors all around us. I turned around, and he was standing between me and the heavy, closed door.

"Mr. Folde, I have to go back to the house and see if Mrs. Folde needs anything. She didn't look so well when she went upstairs."

"Not yet, Emma. Please. Please. Not yet."

He took another step toward me. I understood. I dodged between two engines.

"Careful," he whispered. "You'll slip on the oil."

I hadn't. Not so far.

"We could make each other feel clean again, Emma. Find a new path. Even if we go nowhere." His eyes lit with the spark of a sailor seeking a harbor. "When one way is blocked, shouldn't we try to find another way?"

He tried to put his arms around me. I ducked, with nowhere to turn, in between the two machines.

I warned him: "I'll holler. They'll hear me."

Up over me, I saw one of his arms rise to the wall behind my shoulder, to the shadow of something there. I heard him push the handle. The engines began to hum.

"The sirens," he said despairingly. "Always needing to be charged. In a minute no one will be able to hear anything. Not even you or me. We'll be nothing."

He looked dazed. For a minute I thought he would let me go.

"We have to keep to our places in the dark, Emma. We two. We have to keep to our stations and not rise. Don't you see we're cursed?

Can't you feel the weight bearing down on you, always, always—my weight—like this—"

He was pushing me to the mucky floor.

I'd worked in a boardinghouse. I'd been muscled since I was fifteen. I wasn't going to go without a fight. I reached into a pool of oil and flung it in his eyes.

Pratt gets out of the car with his flashlight.

The Point, the place where I fought, is nothing now. A ruin of bricks and chimneys.

"Keep close," Pratt says, beckoning to Ellen.

A hundred years ago, I struggled under Folde. A heavy, jagged-toothed thing, time is. Like a full-grown man on your chest, the shrieking of engines in your ears. I reached behind me and felt the tool he'd dropped and lifted it and brought it down hard. Something soft gave—his skull—with a muffled crack.

And then I got free and was racing, racing through the night. The light from the lighthouse spun, raking the mist over my head. The fog sucked like cold gas into my lungs, even as they pumped, pumped the air out, and the noises of the night animals blurred and the moon hung colorless as butcher's paper.

The Point is nothing but shadows and empty shells now, stones hidden in grass, white walls thrown down, paths filled in, branches touching the ground, roots in barren post-holes. The signal house still stands but is boarded and locked, and the light tower rises up with a head, but no eye.

Pratt and Ellen shine their little beams over the sagging shutters and the fallen roof of the Folde house. And they still think to find me here, as hard as I ran, as hard as I ran away that night.

Pratt climbs onto what's left of the porch. He shines his beam through the hole that was the front door.

"Philip," Ellen says over his shoulder. "Don't you leave me out here alone."

"I won't." He holds out his hand to her. "Watch your step."

Inside, the Folde staircase has given up all its steps and the spindles have fallen away. They lie in dusty, scattered bones on the floor. Pratt swings his light toward the rotten dining parlor dressed in a thousand cobwebs and onto what was the coal grate, the brick base littered with the tiny skeletons of mice, paws closed in tight fists.

Across the floor, where I pretended to faint after smashing the Foldes' china, Pratt shines his light across a garden of broken green bottles and then lifts it to the chunks of falling plaster on the walls. He moves it to the foulness written in between the curtainless windows, and holds it there.

"What is it?" Ellen comes closer.

"Graffiti." Pratt stares up at it. "Carved into the walls."

"Delinquents. I told you."

He steps on the broken glass, crushing it under his heels. Coming closer, he reads, "'We all fall. We all die.'"

"Nice." Ellen shivers.

He traces his light higher, until it shines through the splintered holes in the ceiling. "Can't go up there. We'd fall right through."

Ellen shines her light nervously around the room before following Pratt's footsteps into the hall and back outside. I've woven myself into a spider's nest hanging on the porch. So little do the living understand: when you brush past a web it may seem fragile, but it's a powerful lace-work; a thing made of pure will.

"Over there are the foundations of the other buildings," Ellen says, leading the way in the thick night. "They were moved, years ago. They were all assessed as more valuable properties."

"This was quite the station, once." Pratt scans the ruins.

"But sad, now."

They pick their way over the turf and stones.

"Outbuilding. Over there." Pratt points. "Listen. Do you hear something?"

Crying—ah, but there's often crying here, now. I try to hush and soothe it. *There, there. You should go now*, I whisper to the local girl and boy drugged and confused in the coal house. *Before they get to you. Hurry along, as I did. Hurry, hurry, while there's still time.*

"Hear it?"

Ellen nods, following now behind his raised wrist.

Pratt pushes open the softened, coal-dusted door. Squinting through the circle of his light, he sees the poor, opium-smoking creature I was trying to comfort, coiled and whimpering against a wall cut with more carved writing. Her hair is streaked black and pink, her bare shoulder covered in inked tattoos, the same as the sailors used to fancy, but angrier and with more color.

Pratt kneels down at her side. The sleeping boy, his hair also streaked, rests his head in her dirty lap and doesn't move at all.

Pratt pats the girl's wan cheeks. Then the boy's. "Wake up. Come on. Both of you."

"Don't!"

She flies at him, hurling her arms at his face.

"Stop it!" Pratt wrestles her till she's quiet. Then: "How long have you been here? Tell me your names."

"Don't let her touch me or talk to me!"

"Who?"

Ellen shines her light down, sees the pieces of burned tinfoil.

"The woman with no face!" the girl shrieks. "She came and she took him away this time!" She slumps toward the boy in her lap. "Took his breath away. Made him see."

"Ellen? Are you hearing this?"

"I'm right here."

"You better keep everything inside you!" the tattooed girl howls. "So she can't get to it!"

"Change of plans," Pratt says over his shoulder to Ellen. "We need to get these two up and walking. Let's go!" He looks down at the girl. "Up!"

They manage, with Pratt taking her limp shoulders and Ellen her bony knees, to carry the poor thing outside the door.

"We need to get them to the hospital," Ellen says lowering her. "If I can bring the car down here?"

"Right. Take the keys. Come as close as you can."

In the rising moon, running with her light below the cypress trees, Ellen looks like a faint, ghostly thing, skimming low and fast.

Alone, grunting, Pratt carries the limp boy out, too.

The girl lies moaning on the ground. "I want her to fucking die."

"Who is it you want to die?" Pratt says.

"The woman with no face. Sucks the life out of you. From the mist!" She points toward the lighthouse. "It comes from there," she shouts. "From there!"

"From the lighthouse. Yes. All right. Hold on. We'll get you help."

"Can't. Know why? The world's a *fucked-up place.*"

Ellen, behind the wheel, pulls onto the faint stamp of earth where my cottage used to be. She opens the car's doors. Together they lift the dead weight of the girl, stuffing her clumsily inside, and then the boy.

"You'll take them to Fort Kane," Pratt says.

"You're staying here?"

"Come back as soon as you can. You have your phone?"

"I'm fine."

"Go."

The half-moon rises higher, brightening everything. Its edge is a filling sail. *Hurry. Hurry.*

23

I ran along the road, the Point growing smaller behind me. My only thought, once I'd left Folde in his own blood in the signal house and flown away to my cottage and grabbed the valise and put everything I had in it, my clothes and my mother's hairbrush and my savings, the only thing I could think of was that I had to get to the village and find Quint while there was still time. He needed to know I was leaving, too, and on my own. That I wanted to be a part of the world as much as he did, a world full of electricity and telephones and that wasn't all kitchens and coal and ash bins, but beyond these things, somewhere . . .

The fog whipped my face and I thought, still frightened, of how much time I needed. The man I'd left bleeding on the signal house floor had been expected to work all night, so no one would find him until morning—I hoped. If I saw and faced Quint, and then got my ticket, there would be nothing more to do. I'd be gone to San Francisco before a wagon could come from the Point to tell the constable. I kept my head down and my feet steady. The way was long and rough. I tried to gauge how far along the winding track I'd come. How long would it be until

I reached Benito? How much more of night did I have left, how many more hurrying footsteps?

I thought I was imagining the sound, at first. The clicking, rolling echo. A motoring sound behind me, coming closer, closer. Then I turned and saw the bobbing lights of an automobile.

As though I'd had some special power, as though I'd been able to conjure him out of the fog and night with my will alone, I saw Quint. His face stretched white above a dark slicker and his long driving gloves.

I felt stupid for an instant. I could see the flickering shape of him, jerking and setting the brake, standing up in the brass of the car, in the moonlight, pushing aside the wind screen; but I thought it was a ghost.

Then I heard his voice call out, amazed. "Emma? What on earth?"

I heard myself say, queerly, "Hello there, Quint. I'm going to town."

"This time of night? What on earth?"

"I had to leave the Point."

"Now?"

Why was he being so stupid himself? "Yes. Right now."

He climbed down to the road.

I stepped back as he came toward me.

"Mr. Folde," I said, shaking suddenly. "He behaved—badly."

Quint pulled off his gloves. "Good God. Are you sure? Are you all right?"

"I hit him. With a wrench."

"Good God!"

"I left him in the signal house. I can't go back." I calmed myself. "I've left."

"Well—of—of course you have!"

We didn't move any closer to each other. We stood in the road, some heavy thing between us.

"I need to get to the village, Quint."

"You're coming with me." He took my case and my arm, quickly, looking around to see if anyone was coming out of the shadows toward us. "I'm not going to leave you. Not like this . . ."

And now, as he hoisted me up, I couldn't believe how safe I felt. How high the automobile put me. It was like riding in one of the chariots in the glass windows of St. Clements Church. Quint climbed in and sat high beside me and loosed the brake, and the car leapt forward. I closed my eyes and then opened them again. I couldn't believe where I was. I was so suddenly and strangely free. Floating. How well-sprung the Lambrys' car was.

"Are you cold, Emma? Take the blanket."

"Thank you."

After some silence, he said, "You're sure about what Folde—tried."

"Yes."

"You should have come away with me when I asked you to."

"I couldn't. You know why."

"But Folde? Laying his hands on you? How dare he. It's disgusting." His gloves made a stretching, tearing sound against the wheel. "And I always thought you'd be safe there."

"I thought so, too."

"It's going to be a scandal."

"It's not my fault."

We said nothing for a while, him staring moodily into the dark between his headlights, managing the bucking gears shooting us forward down the empty, rough road.

"Quint, where were you coming from, just now?"

"One of my sisters. She needed a ride to Fort Kane. Eudora's engaged to someone there."

The trees rolled in dark planks beside us.

"I'm so sorry this happened to you," he said after a moment.

"It's done now. Only I won't go back."

"I'm sorry for something else, too. I can't explain it—No, I won't go on like this. I have to tell you."

"I know, Quint. I heard. You're going away east."

"But you couldn't have heard it *all*." He twisted toward me and away again. "I wasn't set on going in the morning. I wasn't at all absolutely decided. I promise. I was still . . . wandering around tonight, do you see? Driving around. Thinking. And trying *not* to think. Of you."

I kept my cold hands under the blanket. But they tightened. Warmer.

"Right now," I said, "what you need to do is take me to the Main Street Hotel."

"Yes, good." He nodded. "That's an excellent plan. It's perfectly safe for me to leave you there. And I can give you some money. What my father gave me to travel on. I can give some of it to you. Right now."

"No, I have money of my own." I let that sink in, for a minute. I didn't say, *I'll bet this wasn't what your mother had in mind when she said I'd put my salary to good use.* But I knew now exactly what I was going to do. I was going to use my savings to show Quint I wasn't a girl to be called up to the big house anymore. That I could pay my way in the world just as well as anyone else could. Paying my own way at the Main Street Hotel would let everyone in the village know I was a good, proper, modern girl—if Folde dared to try and say I wasn't. If he wasn't already . . . And then all at once it hit me, in the next, breathing moment, that he couldn't accuse me of anything—because either he wasn't going to remember anything, because I'd hit him square on the head, or else he was going to wake—he was still breathing when I left him—and realize it would sacrifice his pride too much, after losing the lightkeeper's job to Mr. McHenry, to say he was beaten by his own housekeeper. He was going to have to say, if he was going to say anything at all, that he'd hurt himself while repairing the compressor. I was so struck by this, my head, giddy, began to spin.

"But I *want* to help," Quint said.

"No, thank you. I'm not going to let anyone say you bought me a room in the middle of the night. That won't look good. Just put me down outside of town, and I'll walk the rest of the way. I'll say I'm going to visit family in San Francisco. I'll say someone there is sick and needs me."

"But do you have family there? Really?"

"No. But only you and I need to know that."

"And will you go to San Francisco alone?" He looked at me, wonderingly. "You have that much money?"

"Maybe. There's work there. I haven't decided everything."

We'd reached the edge of town and he stopped to let the motor die and the lights of the car dim. We sat for a little while, under the pines, listening to the wind far off in the cove.

"I feel terrible it has to be like this, Emma," he said quietly, but with what seemed like a new calm in his voice. "I mean, that you'd think for a minute you'd have to go on by yourself."

"It's all right."

"I wish I could tuck you in your room, be sure you're safe." His hand squeezed my thigh. "I want you to know I hate the thought of leaving you."

"I'll be fine till morning."

"You could go to the constable. Call Folde out on charges."

"No. I don't want anyone but you to know what happened. And you'll never tell. Will you?"

"Not a soul."

"And then tomorrow. Well. We'll each have things to decide, won't we?"

"Tomorrow. Yes. I'll come and see you. It will all be clearer then. Can I have a kiss, for now—until tomorrow?"

I couldn't explain. I didn't want a kiss. Not with the memory of Folde's hot breath on my neck.

"Let's wait till tomorrow," I said. "When everything's been decided." When we would be together, if we wanted to be, if it was meant to be, not in the dark, but in the open sun.

24

Alone, in the dark, Pratt moves along the white foundations of the forgotten lightkeepers' houses. The signal building stands deserted in front of him, leaning like a dead weight against the neck of the lighthouse. Its door was sealed and bolted with boards across it long ago, but the weather's warped the barricade and it's clear where hunters thinner than Pratt have been able to squeeze through. He cuts himself, forcing himself in. Blood rises on his wrist again. The same as when we met.

The oil pans left in place when the compressors were lifted and carted away are filled now with dirt and ash. They look like the open lids of coffins. He walks with a soft, padding sound around them, past the floor where I struck Folde, to the place where the long, grease-coated chain once hung, its black hole, the one Quint and I and Mr. McHenry once stared into, now filled with lime. Pratt looks up. Will he try the rusted spiral staircase? *Be careful, be careful,* I warn him. *Remember Manoel. Remember the writing on the wall. We all fall.*

"I hear you," Pratt whispers, "and thank you. Tell me more. I'm so very interested in this place. Were you, by any chance, aboard a ship when it went down not far from here?"

I won't answer that. I want him to believe again it's Alice and her carved words he's been seeing everywhere. Alice with her hidden Lambry ways, leading him on.

He tests the first metal step. Then gambles. He runs his weight up, holding onto the ringing, fishtailing scaffold. With his flashlight he bangs through the overhead hatch. And now he stands where Quint and I once stood below the Fresnel and marveled. But the center is long gone, the great, high oyster of the lens. The door to the metal walkway hangs open, but the walk goes around nothing, and for no reason, in the dark.

He clutches the metal frame and climbs outside the housing and onto the ledge under the blister of the moon, and his eyes crinkle at its shine, breaking on the restless sea. He travels the rusty railing, rubbing it back and forth with the palm of his hand, listening to the surf far below. I understand why he grips the rail so tightly. It's good to feel there's something between you and the bottom.

He feels something under his right hand and holds his light in his left and shines it onto the metal where he's just rubbed the flake away.

"Emma Rose?"

What?

He says it again:

"Emma Rose. Emma Rose. Emma. Rose."

My name. No. It can't be.

But it is. Etched in jagged writing, before it was painted over. How had it gotten there? Had I forgotten? Had Quint and I done it, after he stood me on my feet and we'd kissed and made up after my fall? Had I done it after I'd bashed in Mr. Folde's skull and shoved him, bloody, away from me and struggled up, climbing away from him, needing to find some clean, fresh, free air? But—how could anyone forget such a thing?

218

"Poor girl." He touches his chest, softly. "I can feel your pain. I can. I'm so sorry. But I'm so happy you left this here. So I could find you, dear Emma Rose. Tell me. Tell me what happened to you. Did someone call you by a dirty name? And leave you? Is it lonely, in the dark? Can you bear it, the loneliness? Isn't it terrible? Don't you want to rest?"

A hiss that isn't mine—it can't be—fills the night.

"Show yourself." He spins around on the narrow walkway. "Let's say our names out loud, together."

He doesn't, can't see. The white funnel of mist behind his head. Forming into a hand. A long arm. Reaching out from the curling, mirrored night, behind his back, snaking around the iron rail. With one burst of anger the metal with my name on it might be broken and Pratt would fall, as I had. That's all it would take. One tug. Just one. From her.

Because of course it's *her* that's doing all these things. *Yes, the woman with no face,* I tell myself, certainly. Who must have pulled down the water tower while Manoel was still standing on it—yes, it had to be *her* then, too. Now sneaking up on Philip Pratt with the twist of her cold hand, and he doesn't know it yet—oh, he's a card she's ready to play, if I let her, if I let her loose her rage wherever she wants to, but I can't, even with the best will in the world, stop it, stop it, how do I stop—

Sometimes it takes a little while before the pieces come together. Until you see the ghost of the thing you were blind to before.

One minute there is Pratt, smiling softly to himself, leaning against the railing. The next his arms are wheeling and he's reaching out for nothing as I did, falling, scratching and scrambling to find some hold on the edge of life and finding it with one hand only, one hand clinging to the rim of the ruined platform, his feet dangling over the waves.

It's *she* who's at fault in all of this, I know that now! It's *she* who doesn't yet know how to control her rage, as a ghost should be able to, has to, no matter what terrible things may have happened to her in her life. And it must be *she* who's angry with me, too, angry enough to give me away by scratching my name into a rail. So that Pratt could find it there.

I study Pratt dangling from the side of the lighthouse. His body hangs by a thread over the rocks and spray. I see now exactly what *she* was trying to do. She was trying to trick him into mistaking one ghost for another. Just as my plan had been. But then Pratt said, *Did someone call you by a dirty name? And leave you? Is it lonely in the dark?* and it set her anger off, a storm, and she'd torn the railing away and Pratt's arms had windmilled, and now he is . . .

I see Pratt's fingernails, white as wax, the blood forced out of them like pressed flowers, holding on. I see him managing to bear his own weight with one arm as he reaches up to the walkway with his loose hand. With two hands now on the rusted ledge, he begins inching his fingers around the walkway, bit by bit, so that his feet are no longer kicking out over the foam and spray but swinging over the soft roof of the rotten signal house, its red shingles green and spongy with moss. I see him strain over his shoulder, trying to catch a glimpse of the distant lane, and Ellen, for help. *Where? Where is the one we are looking for?* But it's a long wait, isn't it, Mr. Pratt? Wondering if someone you care about will come back to you. It could be a long, long night.

But I am not what you think I am. I'm no torturer, no murderer. *She* is. That other one, whom I can't see, for some reason. She must have done this and then flown away. *I can help you.* I will. I'm not her.

Pratt shakes his head and takes a breath. He doesn't want any help. He lets go.

It's a strange sound a body makes as it falls through soft shingle. A dull crashing, like a wave pounding on wet sand.

I fly through the hole in the signal house roof to see what Pratt has done to himself.

He lies in a heap with a cushion of moss underneath him. But his right leg and arm are pinned, trapped under a sodden roof beam that has come down with his fall. His eyes are closed. His eyelids flutter.

I wait until his breathing steadies and his eyes have opened. Then I do what I must: I let him see me. Because I need to be seen, and not be mistaken, myself, in who I am. And I won't let *her* outdo me, do me harm in the way she seems to want to.

I let him see my skirt floating. The flesh melting away from my bones, the water dissolving me. My skin floating away in tattered sheets. My fingerbones reaching out, glued together only by slim, blue-gray strands. *Do you see me now? Do you?*

This is who I am. This is what happened to me. Me.

He struggles. He's trying to get free of the beam, his mouth opening in soundless surprise as the water pouring in from the hole in the roof begins to fill up the signal house. As his eyes grow wider, I let him watch me float above him.

Look at me. Look at me now.

He sees me, and yet he doesn't. Because he's drowning. This is what happens when you drown. Nothing matters to you but air. *Please. Air. Air.* He sees, wide-eyed, as I write on the cracked plaster of the wall fast sinking under the rising flood. But all he can hold onto, in his lungs and in his mind, is how to wrench free of the weight that's pinning him down, how to reach that hole in the roof, in the sky, opened by his fall. The same way, before I died, I looked up and saw a patch of stars. I finish my little sketch for him, the last thing, he thinks, he'll see before he dies.

I glide away like a mermaid, my long skirt a tail, up through the hole. I pick up Pratt's flashlight where it still lies on the roof, so that Ellen can spot it waving and come. She's already driving down the lane, slowly, her lights bobbing over the rough ground.

25

Constable Knightley is upset.

"The tourists are starting to leave!" He pounds his desk with his fist. "I'm holding you personally responsible for this, Pratt. The handyman, then the hotel, Ms. DeWight's house, the Point—"

"The intensity. I know." Pratt massages the bandage on his hand.

"What's next? This office? Right here, under my own nose?"

"Listen to me and stay calm," Pratt says smoothly, trying to win him over. "This is progress. We have a key now. We have a name—or part of a name. We haven't found any record yet of an Emma Rose, but we have the name and the story Mrs. Fanoli told. My gut and my experience tells me they're connected. And we have the writing. The image the manifestation left me. What happened to me after I fell, the drowning, the white body, that was all pure hallucination—but the writing on the wall wasn't. Here it is." Pratt hands the constable his device, so he can see the picture Ellen took with it. "It's clearly a sketch of the Lambry obelisk. And the words: 'Look to the coffins.'"

"Jesus." Knightley stares at my fresh artwork. "But why would a ghost try to *kill* you, then try to *communicate* with you?"

"Because it's torn, I'd say. And unaware of how torn it is. Or it might be because it's exacting a price from me. That's not unusual. Sometimes you're made to suffer a bit before you're given a glimpse of what's struggling to be shared, to be discovered. The same thing happened to Ellen, at her house. She experienced a hallucination. Then her house was torn to shreds. And something was revealed."

But that wasn't me; that was her *pretending* to be me.

"She's a riot, your Emma Rose."

"Just a soul needing peace."

"So you're saying this is normal. For a ghost to torture you while giving you useful information."

"I wouldn't call it normal. Distressed, would be closer to it. But again, revealing. Which brings me to why I'm here. I have a request."

The poor constable, uneasy, adjusts his belt. "What?"

"I need to look into the Lambry coffins. Obviously."

Even with all his weight, Knightley nearly jumps out of his chair. I have to stop myself from dancing a little waltz on the window sill. What a satisfying feeling it is, watching a Benito constable squirm.

"Are you insane? Are you saying that, at the suggestion of a ghost, you expect this county to exhume—"

"Yes. Which is exactly what you'll do, Knightley, if you really want this thing finished once and for all, and the tourists to come back. Yes, I can see you don't want to believe me. But here are the facts: it's sometimes wise to do as the spirit directs. Why? Not because we want to be a slave to it, but because, when a ghost tells you to do something, it's usually telling you more than it means to. It's telling you more about itself than it should—and about how to deal with it. It's telling you something about its organization or lack thereof. Understand that some ghosts have endured so much trauma in their lives, so much death, that, like some of us living, they aren't entirely stable, or whole. They don't

know what will ease their pain or even how to ask for it to be eased. So
they fight the ease they want."

Poor, confused Pratt. What a ridiculous thing to imagine. As if anyone wouldn't want pain eased, their suffering ended.

Knightley looks like he might burst. "So now you're saying we dig
graves up because a *traumatized ghost* tells us to?"

"Think of it differently. Think of this more as a matter of chronology.
Think how the severed arms of a starfish can live on and grow into separate entities, each unaware of its starting point but still attached to it, by
history. Where's the origin of this haunting? That's what we need to find
out. We need to do the exhumation. To try to put the pieces together.
We need to look underground."

"And who is it exactly you want to take a look at?"

"As I said, the Lambrys."

"But which ones?"

"All of them."

Knightley explodes. "Impossible! Make do with the scanning technology. The coroner has it; you can see straight through the ground.
That'll have to satisfy you."

"It doesn't," Pratt says and stands. "We'll need to dig them up the
old-fashioned way, I'm afraid. I need to get close to them. And as soon
as possible."

"But there are a dozen graves under that monument!"

"Contact the heirs right now. Explain. They want this done and over
with, too. They want their money. You'll want to have the coroner on
hand and a funeral director or two and some deputies. Tomorrow, let's
say. Unless you want the tourists to keep vanishing?"

Knightley stands, amazed. "But what is it we're going to look *for*?"

"Clarity."

"And what if I tell you my deputies are too afraid?"

"I won't ask them, or you, to cross the line. Just order the exhumations and provide a few people for perimeter security. Send the bill for everything to Charles Dane."

"And he's going to pay for all this?"

"He told me this morning no one living or dead is going to best the Danes. I've told him it takes money to separate the living from the dead. So that's settled."

It's a polite look Pratt gives to the clerk behind the hotel desk as he passes by it. The same look I gave at that very same burled desk at the Main Street Hotel a hundred years ago, the night I left Quint at his car and walked toward my freedom. And it's the same suspicious look I got back, as Pratt does now. The look from the innkeeper that says: *I know you, but I'm not sure I trust you anymore.*

That night, I put my money down for a small room on the first floor, at the back, facing the wash-yard. Not for me the fine suites on the second floor; I needed to save my silver. Inside, I shut the door and turned up the lamp to ward off the dark and set my valise down. I reached for the pitcher and basin, to wash my face and my neck where Folde had grabbed it. Then I took off all my clothes and lay down on the bed and slept.

But maybe it would be better not to think of all this, right now. . .

About how I lay for so many hours, with nightmares of Folde's weight thrashing on top of me, and of his bleeding head, and of Quint's face coming like a slick angel out of the darkness, both of us waiting for the bells of St. Clements so we could find out what was going to happen next, what our wills were going to decide.

No, let me not think of that long night or stay to keep watch over Pratt's rest. I've trailed him long enough, all day today. Let him be, for a while, alone. It's all he and I have in common.

I need my rest, too. I fly back to the Lambry House and glide inside, up the polished banister and into the welcoming arms of the crystal chandelier, and then through the plaster rose in the ceiling, the small opening at its center that carries its electric wires into the sealed, modern attic, stuffed with batten; here I hide myself. In this attic Ellen said had no room for even a hand to fit in. Unreachable. Suffocated. The same way I died. No room to breathe.

We must do the things we're afraid of, in the end; go, if we want to last, into the very places they think we're not strong enough to face. As I let my thoughts settle and drift away, I whisper to Alice: *You know that we'll never be able to share this house again. No more. Never, ever. This house is mine alone now. It was mine to haunt, long before you ever came and were left here; long before I told you my name, the way I tell all Lambrys, at the end, and then set the pillow to your face, only to help you across, because you were suffering, and not in the vengeful way you imagine that I suffocated you. You have no right to be angry with me. So you go now and keep company with your Manoel. Keep him close to you—since that must have been what you wanted all along. And if you think that from wherever it is you're hiding now you'll trick Pratt and write the rest of my name for him in iron and lead him on to kill me so you can come and take my place—well, you'll find you're wrong. As mistaken as I was, when I boarded the* Lorna *and thought I was free. For sometimes, though it hurts to say so, there can be no life together, for two people. One, or the other, must sink.*

It's only a matter of time and then I'll have Pratt find her. Truly, I couldn't have planned it any better. Because now he'll do, *really*, what I only wanted him to *believe* he was doing before. And when she's done and gone, this woman with no face who haunts me, I'll be free again. Maybe, if I decide to, I'll wrap myself quietly and without a whisper around small, waiting Ellen, the next of the Lambrys in line, and we'll grow old together.

26

Evergreen Hill swarms.

I sit on the Lambry monument, high as a crow's nest, and look down on the staking and digging. It's curious, isn't it, how much the living like to gape at buried things. I think it's because they so love uncovering mysteries. Or maybe it's because they want to feel their advantage. *No, that isn't* me *there, being hauled by a crane out of grubs and mud.*

Half of Benito has turned out to feel how much better off they are than a dead Lambry. The grass lies trampled. Even a few tourists are getting more than they bargained for, this trip, snapping photos of crumbling coffins. It's as big a crowd as we used to see on the Fourth of July. The headstones outside the circle of yellow tape are being used as benches. Mr. Hannan of the Crystal Palace watches, quietly, from one of them. Mrs. Fanoli pushes through on her cane, saying she wants to get close enough to see her future. The constable and his deputies guard the yellow line. The black-suited director from the Chang Funeral Home waits off to one side. Beside her is St. Clements' new priest and his leather-bound Bible. The workmen swing up the last coffin. The crane lowers it to the ground. The groundskeepers unhook it. A dozen boxes now, all in a pretty row. Not every Lambry chose to stay and be buried in the village. Knightley should be happy about that, at least.

Pratt stands beside him, ready.

"Knightley." He looks suddenly past the constable's shoulder. "Have you seen Ellen this morning?"

"Who wants to look at their family's corpses being paraded? Now that we know she's their kin?"

"She's a Lambry. I told her some family should be here."

"The heirs gave their permission, Pratt. What more do you want? Get those gawkers back over there." Knightley turns to his deputies. "And tell these people no more picture-taking, for God's sake."

The crowd complains as it's pushed to one side. A tourist gets his foot caught in one of the animal burrows and lets out a strong word. Mrs. Fanoli thanks him kindly to remember where he is.

The funeral director, Mrs. Chang, calm and even, makes her way toward Pratt and the constable. "As we expected, some of the older coffins are lead. It's the material the wealthy preferred a century ago. It's why they've been slow coming out."

"Scanning technology wouldn't have worked, you see," Pratt says to Knightley.

"That's correct." Mrs. Chang nods. "You'd never have seen inside. But they might take a moment to open. Lead is bolted. I expect you know all this, constable?"

"This isn't my first rodeo," Knightley mutters.

Mrs. Fanoli whispers to her neighbor. "Lead coffins. As in life, in death. The Lambrys always pretended to mingle with the rest of us, the salt of the earth, but they never really meant to, did they?"

Knightley wheels toward Mrs. Fanoli, irritated. "Back, please."

"Oh, keep your temper, George. I'm not the troublemaker here."

How forlorn the coffins look, baking in the midday sun, with the mud still married to them and their decorative corners all scratched where animals tried and failed.

"All right." Knightley motions to the coroner. "Let's get on with this."

The expert slips his gloves on and pulls a hospital mask over his shaven face. Pratt and the director come along, also taking gloves and masks.

"Anything you need before we open them, Mr. Pratt?" Mrs. Chang, her smooth hair held back in a tight clip, asks.

"No. Everything look intact according to your records?"

"Perfectly sealed. My men have the tools to open each receptacle as required by its design and condition. Any particular order?"

"The oldest first, please."

She checks her tablet and nods to the black-suited men at her side. "Grave 211. Augustus Lambry. There."

Her men step forward and lean on the curved crypt. They pound in pins. They twist and screw bolts. They slide keys into dusty fittings and turn them and nod all together and heave their shoulders into the moaning lid.

I've a nice view of dry bones and dust whirling away in the sun.

The coroner steps forward. Pratt goes with him.

"I'm not sure," the coroner says, "what you're looking to find, but I can tell you that at least on first impression, this skeleton is intact. No obvious marks to the bones. No obvious disturbance, no grave robbing. I'm surprised the pieces of his spectacles have lasted so long. And the laces of his shoes. That strikes me."

"And what do you make of that?"

"Desiccated clothing. Chemically, it—"

"No." Pratt reaches a gloved hand in. "I mean *this*."

The coroner takes something from his pocket and lowers his mask to speak into his device, leaning in. "On closer . . . inspection . . . what at first appeared to be frayed clothing is in fact woven rope of a sturdy material. Possibly left or tied around the deceased's extremities." He stops, and his glove grazes the dead man's ankles, carefully.

"It's hemp?" Pratt says.

"I think so."

"Mrs. Chang?"

"I'll check our records," the director says quietly, "to see if any items of this nature were buried with the interred."

"He was buried with his legs tied?" Knightley comes closer and stares. "I've never heard of such a thing."

Pratt pays no attention to him. "We need to go on to the next, please."

"So quickly?" Mrs. Chang looks up at him.

"Yes. Please."

Again the pounding and turning and lifting, and again the light flooding into the shaking basket of a Lambry ribcage. Ah, poor Eugenia! Your hair in thin curls all around you. Your lips pulled back from your teeth. So angry and untidy you look now, who were once so tall and fine in your lace, with your sweeping embroidered skirt behind you.

"Ordinary decay," the coroner says again. "But again—!"

"The hemp around the ankles," Pratt says.

"The lead has preserved the material beautifully," Mrs. Chang marvels. "But why?"

Pratt touches my work gently, almost tenderly. "There is, in fact, some precedent—in some places—and cultures—for this kind of practice. A tradition of tying the feet of the dead so they can't walk the earth again. Among the old Irish, for example."

"But," Mrs. Chang says, shaking her head, "that's never been a tradition here. I would know about it. My family would know. We've been burying people here for over fifty years, ever since we bought the Benito Funeral Home. I've never heard of anything like this."

"Then you probably also haven't heard about the slicing of the soles of the feet of the dead, so they can't walk. Or cutting the spine in half. So they can't sit up. Or smashing the body with cudgels. Or ripping out the organs and filling the torso with rocks to weigh it down."

"Actually, I have, Mr. Pratt."

"Then you know all these things have been done and are still being done, Mrs. Chang, around the world."

"Yes." She nods. "But not here."

"And by what sorts of *people*?" Knightley balks.

"Ordinary people," Pratt explains, "afraid of the dead. Or of what the dead have done. Or of what might have been done to the dead. Or just those who prefer . . . certainty. Let's go on."

Yes, let's go on. One after another, they meet and prod and poke at the poor skeletons, and find my doing, my gift to each one, to keep them from ever rising or troubling the living, or themselves, ever again. I never meant to let a Lambry rise from the grave. I'd had enough of them in life. You never know what might happen.

"All right. Grave 223. Alice Lambry."

"Keep the crowd back. This one isn't going to be pretty, you understand," the coroner says and turns to Pratt. "You're accustomed?"

"The fresh dead often speak the loudest."

"Quickly." Mrs. Chang gestures to her men, putting up her mask.

Poor Alice. No lead coffin for you. It's nasty black jam you've become, in the heat and closeness of the ground. Air is no kinder than water. Look at your face, and your poor painter's hands, swollen and bursting, with the knuckles peeping through, like dice.

Mrs. Chang tightens her mask and presses her mouth. "I think," she says muffled, "we can agree there's no rope here?"

"But observe the creasing at the talocrural joint." The coroner breathes out. "As if something *was* there. And then removed."

Because it was. I removed it. And tied it around a glass float.

"I think it may have been used for another purpose," Pratt says and looks down the long hill in the direction of the Lambry House. He doesn't mention where the hemp is now, still lying on the flagstone path where he broke my yellow rose, my Lambry's Ache set in glass, leaving the wreckage there. To taunt me, he thought. When it was *her* doing all the harm.

Knightley has drawn back to stand beside the priest. "He's not saying this means she could be walking around?"

"Please," the priest says. "Isn't this enough? We dishonor the dead."

"I've seen all I need to," Pratt says.

"So it's Alice?" Mrs. Chang asks.

"I've seen what I need," Pratt repeats. "The rest is my work. I very much appreciate yours. We're done here now."

"All right, get these units back into the ground," Mrs. Chang orders her sweating men. "The last first, please."

Pratt turns to her. "'The last to see me be the first to rejoice.'"

"Excuse me?"

"What if it's self-deception?" he asks her, but seems to be asking himself. "Someone telling themselves their death isn't a curse on others?"

"I wouldn't know about that, Mr. Pratt. We just honor what the deceased want written," she says, and turns away.

"God, I hate death and rubberneckers." Knightley swears. "Move those people *now*," he orders.

"Knightley." Pratt pulls the constable aside as the crane rolls back into place, and the crowd shifts. "Listen. This has been very productive.

I need you to do something for me. I need you to stay here and make sure these caskets get back into the ground as quickly as possible. And I need you to make sure all these people don't start wandering over to the Lambry House. Get your deputies to spread a rumor that it's Alice I'm after, and that she's going to be taken out at her shack on the beach. That should send people down there, where they'll be safer. I'm going"—he glances over the constable's shoulder, seeing Ellen's car—"back to the house, now that Ellen's arrived. She and I will need to be there alone for a while. Detour everyone else over to the beach, would you?"

"Where they might tear Alice's shack to shreds?"

"Have any problem with that?"

"Not necessarily. Been meaning to raze it anyway. It's illegal."

"So you tend to the illegal. I'll tend to the inhuman."

"And then we'll be out of this."

"We're getting there." Pratt slaps the constable's shoulder and keeps an eye on Ellen, climbing the hill in her smart business suit. "We're making good progress."

Yes, it's going even better than I'd planned. The village will never know I was the one who tied the feet of the Lambrys so they'd never come back to the house I wanted for my own, but they'll know, soon, it's *her*, it's *Alice* who's been all the trouble, breaking apart water towers and coming out of mirrors and ruining cabins and throwing men through roofs. I drift over the trees and hover over the spot where Pratt meets Ellen. Pratt's right: we're almost there now. We're almost free.

27

I slept deeply in my quiet hotel room the night I fled Folde and left Quint, and heard the church bells not once. Instead, I went on dreaming. I dreamed that Quint was standing beside me at St. Clements, ready to marry me, looking so fine and happy. I dreamed I stood in a white dress with a long ribbon down my back, and then the priest asked me to say my name. *I, Emma.* But every time I tried to say it, it came out the wrong way, somehow. Backward. Over and over again. *Am me. Am me. Am me.*

The church went suddenly dark. Only the stained windows floated in great blue waves over me, and the white doves glittered and told me it was light, somewhere . . . But when I turned to tell Quint we should run into the sun, he wasn't there, and when I turned back only the Chinese families stood on either side of the aisle, holding their lanterns up like red bloated fish.

And then I was running toward the beach with Mrs. Folde's dead baby in my arms, only it wasn't the *Infant Joseph.* It was a dead baby seal. And I remember thinking, if only I could make it to Quint's side, together we could bring this wet, dead thing back to life. And I ran with the limp seal in my arms and somewhere the fog siren blew and it meant a ship was foundering, and somewhere my father was calling to me to stay clear of the cove because it would only cut your head off and mix it with the sea.

These were the last dreams I ever dreamed on earth. No more, after this day. Ghosts don't dream. Only the living. And I'll say this: perhaps you living should pay more attention to your nightmares. If only I had. Maybe if I'd listened, if I hadn't brushed this dream off as fever and confusion, I'd have seen what was going to come next.

I woke up in my cold room. April 14, 1915. The date of my death. No coal in the empty grate. The pitcher and basin where I'd left them. The curtains were drawn and thin. It was late morning, still and quiet. I'd been so haunted by Mr. Folde and all that had happened I'd curled into my nakedness and slept for too long. I hurried to button my shirt and pull up my skirt and unlocked the door and went down the hall and around the corner into the parlor with the cold fireplace and asked the sleepy desk clerk who'd let me in the midnight before:

"What time is it, please?"

He looked down, blinking, at his watch. He didn't seem to see it. We knew each other, a little; he'd once been hired to do the accounts for Mrs. Strype, until he'd turned to drink, I remembered, then joined the Temperance League and showed his back to sin.

"Nine-thirty, Miss Finnis."

"Has anyone been by to ask for me?"

"Quint Lambry has."

"What?" And I'd missed him?

"I said we don't give out the room numbers of our women guests. That's a rule."

"Did—but did he leave any message? Did he—board a ship, do you know?"

"Carlo Fanoli came by at eight to deliver the coffee bags, and he said, 'Young Lambry's on the *Scandia*, looks like.' So I guess he's boarded. I guess, Miss, it left with the tide."

He said this nervously. Pityingly. As though mine was a soul that needed temperance, like his.

How dare he.

"I need some coffee," I said.

"It's brewed and waiting in the dining room."

I wouldn't act like a girl spurned. Because I wasn't that. I was still me, Emma Rose Finnis, with money in my pocket and my heart lurching. No. I must pay no attention to my heart. It's the pocket that matters. That's what the world teaches us, doesn't it? I had money, money to go where I—and then I looked out the dining room window and saw *them*, going by in a flash in a smart horse and buggy. Reflected in all the mirrors, Mr. and Mrs. Augustus Lambry. Wearing stiff looks on their gray faces, above their white collars. Blank. Unhappy. But why would they of all people have been unhappy that morning? Then I guessed. I knew it for certain. They must have hated it, forcing Quint to go to get away from me. That was it. There must have been a struggle. I saw it plain as day. Because Quint had come to see me at the hotel, hadn't he? It had to have been to tell me something. Maybe more of what he'd told me last night, squeezing me.

I'm not going to leave you, not like this.

It was the modern world. A girl didn't have to wait and ask permission for what she wanted. She could take things into her own swift hands. Go where she liked. Follow him if she decided to. Reach and climb. There was always work to do, somewhere, for those willing to do it. There must be a way I could learn more from the world, how it worked, and how to get what and who I wanted out of it.

I left the coffee and went back to the teetotaler at his desk and asked for his ship's timetables. I fluttered through them.

"When's the next ship to San Francisco?" I asked.

"In three days. The *Scandia* went today."

"I see a loaded steamship in the cove right now."

"That's the *Lorna*. They're getting her fitted up with a special cargo, wedding lumber for Eudora Lambry's new house at the fort. She's getting married, you know. The *Lorna*'s only headed there."

I handed the timetable to him. "Here. There are boats that go from Fort Kane down to San Francisco." I'd seen them, steaming past the Point. And Quint would have to wait for a train to take him east, wouldn't he? The same train any girl might take, going the same way. And if he had to wait for it, that would leave time for me—but not if I lollygagged here. No, it would have to be the *Lorna* now and then the *Beatrice*, according to the shipping news, from the fort tomorrow.

"Who do I see about getting passage on the *Lorna*?"

"I don't think you can, Miss Finnis. I've taken the pledge, you see, and I have to be truthful." His face was red; he looked embarrassed. "The Lambrys own that boat, along with Captain Alstad. It's only taking that special-carved wood, like I say, columns for the wedding-house. The lady is going to marry one of the officers."

"What does that have to do with anything?"

"It's not up for public passage."

"That doesn't mean I can't get a ticket."

"They wouldn't let you." He blushed. "Not you, miss. Sorry. I've pledged."

I flushed back, then thought quickly.

"I wonder, have you said anything to anyone about my being here?"

"No. We won't say who our women guests are. Like I say."

"Thank you for that. And I'm going to pay you for another night. And for some breakfast I want brought to my room. And here's a little something for you, to thank you for not saying anything more to anyone. All right?"

"You don't have to do that." He held both hands up. "I've taken the pledge. And we don't give out—"

"A boiled egg. And some toast. And more coffee."

"Got you."

For the rest of the long day I hid in my small room. I picked at the shell of my egg. It rained a bit, and then more heavily. I walked back and forth in front of the curtained window, which only looked out on the washtubs and the flooding chicken yard. I waited, a gull who needed to keep her head. I had my plan. Since the Lambrys would never give me a ticket to sail with their daughter's wedding lumber toward the *Beatrice*, I'd have to stow away aboard the *Lorna* and hide in the hold. I had only to wait for the men to be done winching the lumber into place and for the crew to go off to the boardinghouses and saloons for their suppers— and then I'd get my chance. There'd be no moon if this rain kept up. No one would see me as I ran.

I closed my eyes and thanked my Da for standing with me on the cliffs all those years ago and teaching me all the parts of the steamers he'd loaded with wood from the mills. Showing me where the great planks of lumber were balanced on the forward deck. Pointing out the pilothouse, and the cabins for the captain and first mate. *Amidships*, he called that. Dead center in the boat. He pointed to where the double doors of the hatches opened heavily, but not too heavy, starboard and port, and led down to storage for other cargo, below decks, in the hold that was lighted by good-sized glass portholes, high above the water-line. Shallow drafted, these dogholes, he'd said. Perfect for whenever you found yourself needing to turn a tight corner.

When it's dark, then, Emma Rose, I cheered myself. *You'll creep to the harbormaster's office, and then down to the docks, and across and under the winches and onto the gangway, then get aboard and slip down through the nearest hatch—so quick, you won't seem like more than a gust of wind.*

That was my plan. So simple.

28

"Sorry," Ellen is saying to Pratt as they walk under Evergreen's treeline away from the workers burying the coffins. "I was just trying to have a normal day. Get dressed, go into the office. See about a new listing. Our broker, my boss, is on her way back. I was trying to get us a new deal."

"Because you think our job here is almost done?"

"Isn't it? I hope?" She looks at his bandaged hand.

She walks a little distance ahead of him and reaches up to touch a low cypress branch. "In a way I did want to be there today. But I also wanted to . . . I wanted to get clear and have a peaceful hour. I thought maybe I had a feeling for all this, Philip. But I don't. I just can't face what you face, on and on. It's too ugly."

"So that's why you didn't come to see your family." He leads her past Evergreen's stone gate and into the street. I keep close behind them.

"Well, would you want to see your family like that? Your ex-wife in a coffin?" She looks up at him.

"If I thought it would do some good."

"I've had enough of doing good for a while, I think. I'm just ready to live life again. I don't want to keep picturing things like you screaming tangled in all that wood and shingle. Hearing you moan in the ER."

"I wasn't moaning," he objected.

"You were. And saying her name, over and over—Emma Rose, Emma Rose—and bleeding all over the place. I can't believe you didn't break anything. Are you made of steel?"

"No. Flesh." He pauses. "You?"

"I thought you were dead when I found you at the Point." She shakes her head.

"You saw what I saw. It was worth it. To get that message from her."

"But I'm not the one who—oh." She stops, seeing where they are, how far they've come. "Are we going to the house now?"

"We are."

"Why?"

"To do exactly what you want, Ellen. Get things back to normal. Find peace."

"That's wonderful! I was thinking today—let this be the last day, please. There are limits. There have to be limits. We're only human."

"Yes. There's always that excuse." He takes her by the arm and stops her. "Tell me truthfully. Are you in any way happy about all of this? About how it's turning out?"

She shifts and slips away from him. "No. Of course not. Just the opposite. Sometimes I imagine that because of my name, because of everything that's happened since I came here, I'm to blame, somehow. As if I brought it all on. In some way. But I don't see how I could have. It has nothing to do with me, I've decided. I'm not responsible. I don't care about any of them. I never have. I didn't even know this family. And I'm nothing to them. Just a means to an end. And they're nothing to me. Except that I want to sell their house. That's it."

"But I'm a little confused, Ellen. In practically one breath, you've told me it was too painful for you to see your blood relations dug up and now that you don't care about them at all, feel no real connection to them. So which is it?"

"Can't it be both? Don't you ever feel torn?"

He takes something from his breast pocket. A drinking flask. "I do. All the time."

"What's that?"

"Agnes Fanoli was right. Sometimes the soul needs a hot toddy. Or a whiskey, at any rate. Good for the pain. I bought this at a nice shop near the hotel." He holds it up in the air to her. "Care for a swallow?"

"No. I don't really drink."

"I've noticed that. You don't drink. I don't see you eat. You're very . . . strict with yourself. You work hard at being you, don't you? And you're committed to that work. Your work."

"My job is to always be available to my clients." She looks down, embarrassed. She must hear how stiff and false it sounds.

"Which is why you'll come to the house with me now?"

"If I have to, yes."

"I just need to test something."

"Well if we're going back in, I've changed my mind." She takes the flask from him all at once and drinks. A good, long swallow, like a sailor's. "Ouch. I wish we didn't have to, though. I wish it was all done and over with already, and Dane could come and just do whatever he's going to do to the place, gut it and tear it to pieces for all I care. That's what I really feel. That's me." She hands the whiskey back to him.

"Yes." Pratt smiles and drinks and exhales and seems, although I don't know why, relieved. He puts the flask away. "I believe you now. I know you're exactly who you say you are."

"You seem happy all of a sudden." She smiles back. "What happened at the cemetery? Did you—did you get—?"

"We're getting close. But I need you. We're in this together. For just a little longer, what do you say?"

"Is that why we're going to the house now? Because you know something? You know how to call it out, how to make it—manifest?"

"We were always going back to the house, Ellen."

29

I waited until the sailors were singing noisily in the saloons. I hurried through the mist and rain to the lee of the harbormaster's hut. I saw the *Lorna,* lying quietly at anchor. I clutched the post at the head of the cliff steps and saw no one stirring outside the ship's lighted cabins. The gangway took my feet without a sound. The hatch was exactly where my father said it ought to be. I had to set my wet case down to pull one of the hinged doors open. Then I was shivering and pulling my valise in and closing the door behind me and creeping toward the round windows still glowing with a little light, even in the mist and the lingering gale. A yellow haze from the electricity burning all around the cove fell into the hold. From time to time I heard voices, shouting. I backed deep in, soaked to my skin, and found a berth for myself by sitting on a coil of rope beside three tied barrels of fish oil. I hadn't thought about what they would do if they found me. I had to make sure they didn't. Slip out again at the fort, when it was safe.

After a while, the rain stopped and I heard footsteps coming out of a cabin. A low voice spoke, and then a higher one, and as they grew louder near the hatch I could begin to hear them both.

". . . a special shipment from my father to my sister . . . our best redwood . . ."

"Duty . . . this is over-diligence . . ."

"But . . . I'm happy here."

"You don't want . . . ashore?"

"Captain, my father insists. I'm to keep an eye on this shipment until it reaches the fort. He's testing me, in his way."

"Well I'm sure you'll rise to the test, son."

Their voices funneled down from above me.

"Is this rain finished, do you think, Captain Alstad? Will the wind shift now?"

"All is well, Albert. I'm less concerned about the weather than whether you'll be bored keeping company with an old man."

My breath caught. It was Albert, the younger Lambry son. The eager one, Quint always said. The one who'd do anything his father asked. I remembered how his face looked in the glow of the July fireworks over the harbor. Excited. Round as a cherry. Not a hair on his chin.

"I'm not bored at all. And I like doing what my father asks me to do."

"You're a good son. You and your brother both. Were you sad to see him leave for Eastern climes?"

"Not at all. I was happy for him. And my parents, too. My brother was starting to feel restless and tied down here, Captain. He wanted to leave."

"Wanderlust."

"I'm a much more steady type. Easy-going."

"Would you like to go in and play some cards? No harm?"

I couldn't hear what Quint's brother answered. And I didn't care to. It didn't matter to me. He couldn't know what was in his brother's heart, could he? I'd seen his parents' faces. He didn't know what had happened. Only Quint and I did.

The hull of the *Lorna* rose and fell so sharply that I had to reach for one of the barrels beside me. This was no time for losing my balance. I was glad I wasn't one of those squeamish girls who get sick just looking at a skiff rising and falling on a crest. I'd never been on a big boat but I'd watched them long enough, and the *Lorna* seemed sturdy and weatherly. She rolled without much groaning, the hold smelled fresh and rich and live with oils and new wood, and I heard mice scurrying around on the beams. She was a good, new boat. Only a little rainwater had trickled through the hatch when I came in, sliding around my feet.

After more time passed I heard some men shouting, as if from the dock, sounding a bit drunken, and then coming closer and lowering their voices and seeming more sober and serious. It was late now. The captain walked about and gave an order, and someone sounded a bell. Now hurried footsteps, and the checking of the ties, and the sound of the hatch lock sliding and shooting into its bolt-hold over me. A sharp voice over my head shouted the wind had turned sou'sou'east.

"It's a little surprise we have tonight, boys! All hands on deck! We cut and run. Not what we'd planned. But we have to keep Mr. Lambry's lumber safe."

"But Captain," I heard young Albert shout into the rising wind, "why do we have to—I thought it wasn't till morning that we would—?"

"We don't want to fall under this wind, son, and get smashed on our own rocks. We cut, we run. Now!"

It was exactly what the dogholes were meant for, and why they worked the coves. Because they were trim and fast and could turn on nothing but a prayer. I heard the *Lorna*'s deep engines roar to life, and the fireman clanging and bringing up her head of steam. I felt her backing and turning just as flashes of lightning started to break across the night sky at the porthole glass. One. Two. Three. And then light and a clap at the same time, so close it nearly shook me from my hiding place. A strange, long shudder followed, as if the ship were letting go of something she couldn't keep. A terrible crash jolted it.

"Clear that mast, please. Now!"

My Da said that when the winds shifted sou'sou'east with no warning, a schooner must clear the cove in five minutes, or face a crushing wall of air. I balanced myself and clung tight to the ropes. The wind had felled a mast, as I'd seen happen to other ships, but she could use her steam to drive herself out before the squall came and pushed her back in again. You see it often enough, my Da had said. But I'd never been so close to it as this, rattling inside the hull, holding tight as it rose and pitched and a terrible grating noise sang all through the beams, sounding like shrieking horses trapped between two walls. I hung onto the barrels and to my travel case and felt water splashing at my heels; it was so cold it burned me, the same burning I'd felt when I'd gone swimming up to my waist, with Quint at the beach, both of us without our stockings, our hands holding onto each other and bobbing in the waves as we laughed and tried to keep straight and true.

Then came the crack of window-glass breaking, letting in wind and rain. I could see by quick bursts of lightning that the clouds were scudding low and fast, and so were we. I held tight to my beam. Voices shouted and swore and grew louder, almost panicked. Someone called for the fireman. Another that the engines were dying.

"We'll be carried too far! Lively now, boys! See to the timber! I'll be damned if Lambry sinks us by loading on too much of his—"

I strained to find some break in the wind, a space without some shouting in it. A keening sound, from deep inside the ship, came through my boots. For an instant, I had a sickening feeling of being launched—then I was rolling on one side of the hold, and falling, as if into a pit.

"The captain's let her loose! The captain, he's trying to run ahead of—"

What did that mean? I found another beam with mice running across it and used it to steady myself and pull myself out of the rising water. Where were we? Was the *Lorna* doing what I had seen other ships do—flying past the lighthouse in a gale, dim and gray, bow streaming ahead on a white sea—*running out the storm?*

Cold water above my ankles now. My skirt was beginning to float.

"You! Albert! Go with the lifeboat, son! Make for the lighthouse! Hold fast! Tell your father—"

Were we near the Point, so fast? I had come back to the very place I'd run away from.

The captain's calls were drowned. The *Lorna* went on pitching and heaving. There was too much silence, all at once. *I can't hear them shouting*, I thought. And I could no longer hear the ringing of the fireman's warning bell.

I let go of the beam at my head and, as best I could by the flashing light, pushed against water up to my shins now and found the stairs that led to the leaking hatch. I called out, "I'm here! I'm here!" Because there would be someone to hear me soon, surely, and the hatch would be unlocked and I'd be hoisted up, grabbed, steadied, and freed. In the next crash of lightning I saw my valise floating by and wanted suddenly to be rid of everything, everything in my past, Quint and the Lambrys and all that had happened to me, everything I'd ever fretted and worried over. What did any of it matter, now? I shoved the case aside, shouting, and the hull shrieked and I was pitched back into it again, into cold, cold water, and I felt the ship slowly turning on her side, water pouring in from one direction now as I turned with it, rolling in my skirt, like a body into a shroud. I felt my foot wedge under a piece of metal of some kind, and then I knew that I was going to die in this darkness with the black water hurling down on me.

But why poor me, who only ever lived her life as best she could? I thought, queerly calm, as the lightning ripped and the hold turned into a bright, watery mirror, as if it wanted me to see for myself the sinking of the ship around me, and only one eye, one broken window, shining above the black sea. One way out. *But if I'm so little, so nothing,* I thought, again strangely calm, *shouldn't that be of some use to me?* I jerked at my leg with both arms, with all my might, and got my foot free and with a mighty push clawed and swam toward the broken porthole and felt myself cut and sucked through it, kicking and kicking until I was flailing by the ship's frozen rudder. But no, I had to get away, because that was sinking, too. I kicked in my heavy skirt out into the open sea and the backing wind, and I could just make out the whirl of the lighthouse at the Point, the only light I could see as the waves cut my face. The great smoking flash that was the *Lorna* went down beside me, her load of wood still strapped to her, all that wood that might have carried me, going down. Below me, my legs were already tiring, and my skirt was too heavy, and my long wet braid was uncoiled and pulling.

It'll be over soon, I told myself.

The skipping beam of the lighthouse, instead of drawing closer, grew small, smaller. I was drifting away.

The tide was too strong for me to kick against, even if my feet hadn't already turned to lead and my eyes grown heavy. How strange that you might, at the very end, be glad if you could go back to the place you'd just escaped from. Go back and tell Mrs. Folde what Mr. Folde had done and hold him accountable. Go back and say goodbye to the children, each one. How beautiful the light looked, as it dotted and drifted away. The sirens were only now sounding, someone seeing a struggling lifeboat, maybe, and knowing something was terribly wrong. Mr. McHenry, maybe. Too late.

I thought I should open my eyes for one last time, very wide, to see the swelling night before it took me down. And I did, in time to see a great, reaching fork of lightning stretch soundlessly across the sky, reflecting something close to me—a bright, bright and glassy something, somehow more than one thing, bobbing just a few inches from my opening and closing and spitting mouth.

30

The Lambry House rises before Ellen and Pratt. The points of its wrought iron fence. The sweeping curve of its porch. The parlor windows I used to look into and dream of. The white steeple and the weathervane spearing the air.

Ellen is looking up and so she doesn't yet see what lies under the rosebush, the pieces of broken glass and torn hemp where Pratt left them, to hurt me. *Her.*

"Wouldn't you want to buy this, if you could?" Ellen sweeps her hand around. "I mean, look at it. It really should just sell itself. Look at how the sun's hitting the widow's walk."

Inside the arbor she notices the shards. "What's that?"

"Some glass I broke." Pratt kicks the pieces away.

A glinting necklace over a patch of dark sea. A great, wide net of glass. That's what saved me. A fishing net, ringed with floats. I grabbed each one with my hands, one after the other, round and perfect, woven into the knotted ropes between them. I splashed and coughed and knew, somehow, something as big as this would be strong enough to cradle me.

With all my will, I pulled a piece of hemp underneath me until my chest and stomach were over and I could feel my skirt being buoyed up, and my hair, and my feet, and then with a reach and a twist I turned on my back and could feel the web of strong line holding me and the embrace of blue glass all around me, I crawled on my back to what I thought must be its center and looked up at the clouds just beginning to part and the stars just beginning to glisten. And I laughed, for pure joy. Because it wasn't over. The storm hadn't taken me. The deep hadn't done me in. Maybe, after all, I wasn't meant to die here. Not yet. Not me, Emma Rose Finnis. I was meant to live and breathe and float, in spite of everything. As if the spirits of the night, the *far darrig*, had saved me for some better plan, as no one else in my family had ever been saved. Maybe the spirits had seen in me something they'd never seen in another Finnis. They'd seen I wasn't finished.

I rode the water lightly, like a cork. The rain had ridden out to sea and the wind had shifted and was pushing me right along the coast. The full moon came out and showed me how fast the current was taking me along. Before long, I saw pinpricks—the first lights of Benito, darting up from the headland. The wind was still rough and the cold split my lip and my shoulder was cut, but I was riding on a good course, and if I could make it to the cove, why then the turning tide might still pull me in the rest of the way. I wound my fingers and boots through the net and hung on. My heart beat fast. Look, look how easy it was not to die! Oh, if only my Da, and my mother, and my siblings could have known. That you had to show the darkness you had will, and you had to keep yourself up as long as you could, and fight.

I could make out the black reaching limbs of the cypress trees around the cove now. The wind was pulling me one way, and the tide another.

But it's all right, I told myself, *you're almost home. Just keep your heart calm and your eyes steady, and watch for the first rocks. The back-current, the undertow, that'll be strong nearer the cliffs. You don't want to be washed out to sea again. Fight for that first bit of land. Reach it on the first try.*

Ellen is taking the key from her satchel and unlocking the door.

Pratt stops her hand. He takes the key from her, so he can lead the way into the house. He closes the door behind them and then turns toward the dead Lambry photographs.

"Portrait of a family that had all the good fortune it could have ever wanted. And then lost it. Piece by piece. Once upon a time, this was a house that nothing had happened to. Nothing had really happened to the people in it. But then a beloved son died. Businesses started to falter. Times changed. It's all recorded here. In the garden. In the steeple. In the very bones of this house. But there's always an original sorrow. Albert Lambry. Only sixteen years old. Remembered by a flower, Lambry's Ache. Why not Albert's name on a headstone, Ellen? Why wasn't his name remembered?"

"Because of the old superstitions, Mrs. Fanoli said. Or maybe because some things are too awful to remember."

Yes. Like a father who lost his head to the sea. Whose head was later pulled out, with a fishing hook, by a Lambry dinghy.

"Possibly. Or maybe it's because we never name the thing that really is the culprit. The real demon in the house. I need us to test that idea, Ellen, and see. I'm going to say aloud that there is something in this house that is a curse. And I want you to say the same thing with me, please. You're a Lambry. You have the power."

He draws Ellen gently closer to the stairway. But I don't care what he's doing or saying. Soon everything is going to be clean. Clear.

"Something in this house is a curse. Say it, Ellen Lambry."

"Something in this house is a curse . . ."

"Some creatures are cursed and are a curse."

"Some creatures are cursed and are a curse . . ."

"And never bring real happiness to anyone. They're selfish and self-centered. They bring darkness and chaos to everything they touch. They leave ruin and injury in their wake. Unless you manage to escape them. They're purely a thing to escape. Nothing more."

"Who are you talking to?" Ellen says, nervously.

Pratt presses a finger to his lips and pulls her deeper into the hall.

I've never cursed anyone I touched or was close to. There's no proof of it. My poor mother? Because she died giving birth to me? No. My father, because he died where he once stood with me and taught me to read the sea and its ships? No. Not Franny, my only friend, who I wasn't with when she died, nor Mrs. Folde's baby boy, and not Albert, and not all the men aboard the lifeboats, because I set foot on their ship, no. I wasn't a curse on them, surely, not me.

"Something that wants to take and take. To drag your soul down, and own it. For revenge. Lonely and hungry. Can't you feel it?" He turns to Ellen, taking her arm at the bottom of the stairs. "Empty and cold and terrible. Starved. A ruin of flesh and hair. An angel of death. A bringer of ruin. That's what she is. It is. And yet nothing. Nothing. Just a beast."

He thinks I wanted my Ma to leave this world bringing me into it?

And bury my father's severed head?

And leave Frances to die with her baby between her legs?

And let all the men on the *Lorna* drown?

And let the tower fall on Manoel?

And let the railing give way under Pratt, because I'd once fallen out of Quint's arms?

How could I be the one cursed when, so long ago, out on that tossing, moonlit night, seeing the outline of the cove and the little curve of our village that never looked so beautiful as it did to me then, hovering near it as I kicked and fought and gasped and gripped the salt-and-earth-smelling hemp and tried to steer myself and my net of glass toward its beach—how could it be *me*, when all I'd wanted was to live and be at peace with the world, and hold always, always, to the skimming thing life is? What a precious thing, this life, for as long as you can hold onto it, if you can. But oh, how hard the wind will fight against you, and how hard you'll have to fight for life, kicking and struggling with your glass and rope, crying out toward the beach, shouting for anyone at all to hear.

The stars stayed hushed. The moon kept shining. The next swell brought me closer to the rocks. The seals had all abandoned the harbor. Just one lucky push, I told myself, and then I'll swim free and paddle toward land, and if I have to hit there on the rocks, I will. I'll land on them and cling till dawn comes and one of the fishing skiffs launches and sees me. And then I'll cry out, proudly, "I am here, I am here, I am me, I am Emma Rose Finnis. I'm still alive. Me."

"Come into the hallway now," Pratt says.

Ellen stares at the broken picture frames, amazed. "Everything's been shattered!" She reaches up. "The watercolors. Alice's paintings!"

"It's begun. The thing that haunts this house is getting angry. Very angry."

I've done the damage, true enough. I've broken the pictures. Smashed them with my fists. But to anger *her*. Only to bring *her*.

"But why hurt the house?" Ellen touches the glass. "If the ghost wants to live here?"

"Because it's only a beast now. Angry it's died. A beast doesn't live anywhere. It—"

"Because it's always hated this house, though it seemed to love it."

Pratt turns to her.

She's closed her eyes. She's a Lambry. Yes. She can see. At the end. As they all can.

"Ellen!"

"Finish it, please. Please finish it."

"Say why. This is your test. You're a Lambry. Say why it must be finished."

"Because I hate this beautiful house. I hate it. All this was here, while I sat alone, while my mother died. I hate that I didn't matter to it. I hate it. I hate it."

"And it's why you've been helping me, all along."

"Let the Danes have this miserable place, all of it. I want them to tear it to pieces, I want them to gut it and rip it to shreds."

"Good, Ellen. Thank you. Now we'll see. We're almost finished. Come upstairs with me. We're almost there."

"Her sea glass. Her easels. Her shells. Everything's crushed."

"Yes. Hold on."

She will have to come, leave her grave, and Manoel's cold bed. She'll come, because she hates me, I know now. The spirit who was with her at the end, who put a pillow over her suffering face, her lost, sad face. She'll come because she has to stop me from taking what's hers and breaking what's hers and from living in a house she thinks belongs to her blood but hasn't since that morning I rose dead from the beach, dragging my broken net behind me. She'll come. I know it, it's not me. It isn't me. It can't be. Please.

"Listen." Pratt holds still. "It's happening all over the house now. The windows. The chandelier."

"She's breaking things."

"She's breaking everything." They've reached the upstairs gallery, ducking and hunching as they come nearer the flying glass.

I fly around the house. Where is she? Where is she? She *must* be here. She must have come. The windows are bursting; she must be very angry now. More anger than I've ever thought could live inside one body. To be abandoned by your parents. To be alone though you tried not to be. To have died, smothered. Look, how she's turning every shrieking room gray and dark. But outside, the sun shines . . .

"Can you stop her?" Ellen pleads.

"Say it. How were you attacked in your house? What did she do to you? Close your eyes. Try to remember. Remember. How did she do it? Say it now. What did she do?"

"She—she shoved me into the roof of my house. No light. No air. No room. I couldn't breathe. Stop!"

"*Where* did she put you? *Where*? Name it."

"In the attic. She put me in the attic. Only there was no attic. Not in that house. She shoved me where there was no air—"

"The attic here?"

"It's stuffed. No room. It's sealed—I told you—"

"Where can I get closest to it?"

She opens her eyes.

"There." She points. "By the balcony. Over the Glass Room. There's an access grill right over it."

"Stay close now to me, very close."

"Please, will you finish it now?"

"I will."

"This is the door to the balcony here!" Ellen pulls Pratt forward.

"Stay behind me!"

Wait. Wait. You must wait for the right moment, or be smashed on the rocks. A wave. Another wave. But not the right one. Not yet. Not yet. Wait. Now.

31

But the wave I rode was too strong. It battered me on the rocks. I heard a sound, like a shot, a pistol crack, and then another and another, and didn't understand what was happening. *Why am I cut again? Why am I bleeding? Why am I still*—I was being flung against the reef and my hand flailed toward the gash in my thigh where it oozed from the barnacles' kiss—*please, wait,* I wanted to shout, *let me try again, I can do this*—

What was it that pulled me down, so heavy now? Why was I being dragged out and under, why were all the lights failing? What was this cutting, tugging underneath me?

All the glass. All broken. Sinking me.

I have to keep above it. Keep above it.

Alice has to come now. Please. Pratt and Ellen balance above the Glass Room on the balcony floating like a raft above the dome. She has to come. I've shattered all her pretty paintings, her veiled fogs and cold clouds. She's coming now. I feel it. Yes. We're almost done. Pratt pushes back his sleeve, raises his bandaged hand.

"There!" Ellen shouts.

"Where?"

"On the roof!"

"Say her name, the ghost you see. Now! She heard what you said about destroying the house. She's coming for you."

"Alice Marie Lambry. Alice Marie Lambry!"

"Stay behind me."

"She's coming!"

As I knew she would. From over the top of the roof she comes, in slithering pieces, first the sleeves of her robe with its dragons curled, then the wild, streaked hair, then the rotten, missing face and beside it the ruined hands with their hungry knuckles bared. Reaching out toward little Ellen.

No. I reach too, answering. *Not her!*

Pratt raises his fist. He doesn't see Ellen, terrified, struggling to get away, leaning over the balcony's edge. His eyes, selfish, hunt only for Alice. The prize he wants. And now I'm angry at last. He can't see Ellen climbing over the ledge, crying, trying to escape. I have to let him see my white charge and shape and my stretching howling jaw, and I've only an instant to scream and point—*Ellen!*—before Alice unmoors the balcony and Ellen is falling. I can't see her with the terrible red light from his hand shooting between us. Alice screams like an animal wounded and swings toward me where I fly above the roof, to face our darkness together, our loss.

But true darkness—I look into her rotting eyes—*true darkness can't save us, Alice.* No, nor bitterness for what might have been, for the love that would never return or satisfy us, buried somewhere in the east. I know it in my heart now, and I knew it then, my heels tangled in the netting, my body going down, down, my eyes still flickering toward the stars and the hope of the sky, reaching and trying to fight for it, feeling the pain ebbing from my leg. Feeling the fish already nibbling around me, while I still felt life and light in me as I choked and drowned and my arms went loose over my head and my hair swung away from me. I thought of how my mother's brush had stroked it, with absent love. Me, Emma Rose, still able to feel and see, even then, and even then not wanting to turn into the depths below me, no, not even then letting the bleakness claim me. Even then still not dead. Still thinking, when my lungs had no more life left to feed me, *Oh, but I have to live past this, somehow, because this isn't just, it isn't fair, when all I ever did was strive and love and look for my future. This is not justice*, I thought, and kept my eyes open as the sea waved me back and forth, dragging me down to the bottom.

And this is not justice, I think now, as Ellen smashes through the dome of glass below and Pratt, falling, reaches foolishly after her, too late, as if he could cradle her before she's hurt. *This is not justice*, I think as I see them both lying there—Ellen, eyes wide open and fixed, a piece of glass piercing her throat, Pratt curled at her side, his bandaged hand pulled tightly into his stomach, like a child, breathing heavily. *This is not justice*, I think, and let my anger spread far, and I throw my arms wide to show Alice how strong a tide my will can be as she creeps, half blasted, arm over arm toward me, black ooze gurgling out of her side.

And now—look at that—that strong-willed Pratt. He's twitching. He's still moving. He's rolled onto his back, lifting his broken arm, and even now, I see, he still hopes to kill us both, with one shot. He still can't see what blind part he plays in the blind business of this world.

What is it you want to kill, Mr. Pratt? Are we anything more than our hurt, our love? Why not let our pain, and our joys, too, haunt the earth forever? Why should I be sorry for having lived and risked and tried?

Pratt braces his right arm with his left and a shadow—pain, confusion—crosses his face. I think he's seen me with my arms thrown out to stop Alice, seen what kind of will I have, how good I was, how much I still have, or could have done, if I'd had a chance. But what was it he said in Agnes Fanoli's rose garden across the cove? That if a ghost believed and had will enough, she didn't have to die. That if she could only believe with all her heart and soul she wasn't dead, she might even walk the earth again, almost like the living do—if only I believed with my whole heart. That I didn't die—as Alice crawls toward me and Pratt opens his fist.

That I didn't die—but grabbed onto that sharp black rock, crusted with pain for me though it was, I grabbed onto it that night and I held to it with all my hope and spirit and held and held while the waves surged away, carrying the net and the jagged broken glass along with them. That I scrambled up high, my legs wet and free, and clung all that starry night long, till my hands were sore and my body bloodied but still fending off the ocean, and my lungs still pumping and full of air, and in this way I didn't die, no, I didn't, but believed and lived long enough to see the first fisherman come out at dawn—and here is his skiff, even now—and here is the light of the morning sun washing over me, and here now is the long beam of light, this brilliant light from a cold hunter's hand that flings the last Lambry in this village into a thousand tiny pieces.

And here is me, passing my will, my heart, my faith, into the future, into *her*—as the bright red light flashes once more. Here I am, standing up now in a clean little business suit and turning my bobbed hair toward the cove, and the speeding fisherman's skiff, and waving to him, and saying:

You think I'm a stranger to you, but I'm not. Don't you recognize me? Rejoice.

I'm not finished. Lifting her hand, *my hand*, to the sun.

I lasted.

Epilogue

From: G. H. Knightley

To: Charles Dane

Subject: Case Number: 392857

Dear Sir,

I will do my best to answer your questions but understand there is only so much I am able to relay to you now while your employee is unavailable for further questioning. It is my understanding Philip Pratt's condition has been upgraded from critical to serious. You will need to reach his doctors at Fort Kane for updates. I advise that you do so immediately, as well as his licensing board.

Regarding the condition of the property: the damage is to the interior as well as exterior portions of the house. You will need to discuss with the current owners any arrangements for allowances or halt of sale. At the moment, however, the property is being assessed to determine if it is a crime scene. It can't be entered.

Post-human remains have been removed from the property. Your employee, as well as subsequent testing, was able to confirm for us that that these belong to Alice Marie Lambry, late occupant of the property. The whereabouts of the property's representative, Ellen Lambry DeWight, or of her remains, are unknown. I'm afraid I can't assist you in that regard. It is however my understanding that your employee, from his hospital bed, has listed her as deceased and asked for an alert to be issued statewide.

I would like to offer an opinion as to whether you should continue to consider your purchase of the estate in question. My understanding from your communication is that you may no longer wish to be a resident of our community. That is unfortunate. We pride ourselves on the serenity, beauty, and rich history of our region. Recent events are not taken as the norm here. We do not anticipate further disturbances, and we will continue to provide our visitors and residents with both the protection and the recreation that have always been the hallmarks of our unique and spectacular peninsula.

In future communications regarding this incident, please refer to the case number provided.

Sincerely,
GHK

31901060873330